Catatopia
BY

J. L.
ADDICOAT

CONTENTS

ACKNOWLEDGMENTS

Where does a writer get the names from for the Characters? Many places is the answer. Baby books, magazines, friends, as so on.

Family members rarely escape. Within this novel are the names of most of my grandchildren and my pets.

The main feline character is based on a much loved, and much missed Norwegian Forest Cat cross-breed called Purdy, who was too smart for his own good.

So, for you, Purdy, and the many other felines who have graced and now grace our lives, this novel is dedicated to you, our feline furry friends.

R.I.P Purdy 08.2005 – 10.2008

PROLOGUE

In the early twenty-first century, two important events occurred. One, the most noticed, experienced and talked about, was the Last War. Called the Last War after a trio of thermonuclear explosions destroyed entire continents and spread radiation worldwide, delegates of the remaining countries came together across an invisible table, making a peace pact, bringing all under the one world banner. Never again would any religion or country be allowed to hold the world to ransom.

It was a dirty war in so many ways. Bombs and bullets were only a fragment. The bio-engineered viruses, made to attack a person's DNA, played the larger part of the arsenal. As all viral illnesses except the common cold had been eradicated by vaccinations, the CCV (Common Cold Virus) became a carrier of the mutations. Designed to cause sterility among the male youth, and to cause cancerous tumours in others. Sprayed into the air over unsuspecting countries, no one stood a chance. One inward breath and anyone could be afflicted.

Dirty bombs, made cheaply with radioactive waste, dealt the world its largest blow. Placed around the planet in buildings, schools and kindergartens by operatives, ransom demands were made. If the relevant governments wouldn't pay, the bombs were detonated, spewing radioactivity into the atmosphere and rendering vast areas uninhabitable for hundreds of years.

The end of the war came when agents infiltrated and sabotaged three thermonuclear bombs simultaneously in separate continents, wiping out the enemy and their countries instantly, destroying any chance of survival.

The second interesting event, only known to a select few, was the colonisation of an extraterrestrial earth-like planet.

CHAPTER ONE

Hope's heart-rending sobs played over and over in Conrad's head as he walked through the dim corridors of the government research building.

He was a failure as a man. That was the way he felt. He was the broken, infertile one. His swimmers couldn't make it out of the starting block.

Balling his hand into a fist as he approached the end of the corridor, Conrad drew back his arm and punched the wall in front of him … hard. Pain shot up his arm, spreading from his assaulted knuckles and fingers. The sobs cleared from his mind. Nursing his injured hand, he loosed a roar, giving voice to his inner frustration.

Once he'd calmed down, Conrad returned to the security office having finished his patrol of the building. It wasn't much, but it was a job, and better than others had.

Conrad waved to Bill, his offsider, as he entered. Fluffy, the resident cat, received a rough pat on the head.

No one knew where Fluffy had come from. He'd appeared about a year before and appeared to like hanging around the security room. Who wouldn't want an affectionate long-haired brown tabby cat around who loved being stroked?

'Nothing to report, all seems to be okay. At least with the building, that is. My life is in the toilet.'

Fluffy jumped into Conrad's lap. He grimaced when the cat butted his head against a painful, and now swollen, hand.

'What's the problem?'

'Oh, just the usual, Hope isn't pregnant. I tried to calm her, but the thing is it's my fault. She's fine. She's healthy. I'm the one that's broken.'

Conrad found himself close to tears.

'I meant what's the problem with your hand?'

Conrad shrugged his shoulders. 'I hit the wall. I had to let it out somehow.' Warmth crept over his face, ashamed of what he'd done.

Bill flicked the paper he was reading, and looked over the top. 'You talk all you want. It's better to get it out than let it fester inside you. Also, talking doesn't hurt as much as your hand will. I'd get some ice on that if I were you.'

Conrad looked at the purple and black bruising creeping across his hand. He'd be lucky to not have broken something. He rose, dislodging the cat who gave him an annoyed look, crossed the floor to the first-aid cabinet, picked a cold pack, cracked it and placed it on his hand. The cooling gel calmed the pain throbbing through his bruised flesh. He returned to his seat, and Fluffy retook his position on his lap.

'You know they are working on the infertility thing here, don't you?'

'Yeah, not having much luck, are they?'

Bill grinned, folded his paper, and leaned forward. 'That's not what I heard a few hours ago. One of the scientists has made a breakthrough, but they've been keeping it quiet until they're sure of everything. I heard some scientists discussing it on the third floor where they do the testing,' he paused. 'They said they have some shots ready to be tested and are looking for people to try it on.'

Conrad's mood changed from maudlin to hopeful. He leaped to his feet, unsettling Fluffy again, who yowled in complaint and sat in the corner of the room, giving him dirty looks.

'Are you serious?' This could be the answer to his prayers. A fertility injection. One that could possibly work.

Bill nodded. 'Never been more serious. I hear they're bringing in some test subjects tomorrow. Why don't you see if you can get yourself on the list?' Conrad felt the adrenaline course through his veins. Thought's rushed through his mind. Why wait until tomorrow? Go see them now. There may still be someone on the floor. I can see about getting on the list.

'Thanks, Bill. I'm going to try. I have to. Hope needs me to.' He grabbed the ring of master keys, opened the door and sprinted out into the hallway.

****

Bill mentally kicked himself. Why had he told the boy the treatment was ready for testing? Watching Conrad and Hope trying for a family had been painful. They'd both tried so many ways and the heartbreak that came after each trial failed broke his heart.

He'd never had children and looked on the boy like a son.

Conrad's father, Richard, had been a soldier/medic in the same unit as him. They'd been the best of friends, and Bill had sworn he would look after Richard's son and wife if anything happened to his friend. Richard didn't survive the war. His tour of duty had been in the East when the bombs dropped. There was no chance of coming back from a thermonuclear blast.

Bill had grieved deeply for his friend, resulting in a medical discharge after a nervous breakdown. He'd recovered, but the days had passed in a blur. Conrad's mother, Chloe, had nursed him back to health, and along the way he'd become a surrogate father to young Conrad.

He knew how much the infertility had been affecting Conrad and Hope's dreams and had wanted to help. He hoped Conrad wouldn't do anything stupid like injecting himself with the hoped-for cure.

****

He was young and fit. The room was only five flights up. Two sets of stairs separated the second basement from the ground floor. He'd have to change stairwells to get to the third floor. Damn the security regulations in government buildings not allowing access from the bottom of the building to the very top. He'd probably beat the elevator anyway. He opened the secured stairwell with his keys and ran. Concrete stairs were hard on the feet, especially in the safety boots he wore. After the first two flights, his calves burnt with the rising lactic acid. Reaching the ground floor, he paused for a few seconds to control his breathing, before opening the next door to get to the third floor. He took the stairs two at a time.

Arriving at the third-floor stairwell door, he bent over, forcing the breath in and out of his lungs. With his heart racing, he used his keys to open the inner stairwell door.

Test tubes and microscopes lay on every stainless steel table. Refrigerators stood in lines. Petri dishes, bottles, and glasses, all labelled with different names and symbols, sat on the shelves. Conrad called out, but no one answered him. He was alone on the floor. His heart sank. There wasn't any way of getting himself on the list.

But was there? If the tests were to be conducted the next day, then the scientists would have everything prepared, ready to go.

He peered into each refrigerator, finding what he was looking for in the fifth one he checked. The receptacle only held a couple of boxes of vaccine. 'Come on, which ones are you?' The print was so small, and with only torchlight in the darkened room, the labels weren't easy to read.

'Aha, there you are.' The tubes labelled 'Fertility Treatment—FELMC—Sample A–1–0–1' sat in a lined case. *I wonder what FELMC means?*

'Doesn't matter, if a shot will make it possible for me to give Hope a baby, it's worth it.'

He opened the door, removed one of the syringes, found a rubber cord and tied it on. Rolling up his sleeve, he slapped the skin on his arm, and injected the solution straight into a vein. Those medical security workshops he'd attended had come in handy. He untied the cord and placed it back on the tray. Holding the empty syringe in his hand, he refilled the tube with tap water to the same level it had been before. Not until he rolled the test tube in his fingers when replacing it, making sure the tube sat label up, did he notice the warning. Do not administer if body is under exertion.

Was it safe for him? Pulling his sleeve back down, he shrugged. Any problems could be dealt with at a later time.

****

The door opened, Conrad walked in, throwing the keys on the desk. His face was bright red, as though he had been running.

'Was someone there? Were you able to get your name on the list?'

Conrad avoided his gaze. 'No, no one was there.'

'Damn, I'm sorry to hear that. Maybe there will be a second trial.'

Conrad didn't answer, becoming engrossed with something on the security sheets.

Bill noticed the telltale pin prick of blood on Conrad's sleeve. He reached over and grabbed him. 'Please tell me you didn't do it.'

Conrad pulled his arm out of Bill's grip.

'What have you done? You don't know of any side effects. You don't know what this stuff will do to you.'

Conrad shook him off. 'Bill, it's okay. They wouldn't decide to trial something on humans unless they were really sure of it, would they?'

Bill stepped back. 'Are you going to tell them what you've done? You know they'll find a vial missing, and they'll start asking questions.'

Conrad shook his head. 'No, they won't, because there's no empty vial. I filled it up with water and put it back with the others. They always do a control anyway, and they use purified water for that.'

Bill was still concerned. 'What about your own health and Hope's health? What if something goes wrong?'

'If I start feeling bad, I'll go to a doctor. If it gets really bad, I'll tell them what I did, okay.'

He cautiously accepted what Conrad said. 'Okay,' and checked his watch. 'It's the end of the shift. The day shift guys have just arrived. Let's lock up and go home. Four days off. I've been looking forward to this.' He'd let Conrad off for the moment but would keep a close eye on him. Bill let Fluffy and Conrad exit first. He checked the room one last time and walked out, closing the door behind him. They walked to the car park, got into their car, and drove out.

****

Fluffy sat beside the slightly open stairwell door to the third basement. As they left, he turned and slipped through the door. It closed with a soft click behind him.

CHAPTER TWO

Conrad opened his front door. He peeked into the bedroom. Hope wasn't awake yet. He stood in the doorway, admiring her sleeping form. Her blonde hair lay strewn untidily across the pillow, one of her hands under cheek, and that little purse to her lips. Often he wondered how he'd been so lucky to marry her. Lord knows he wasn't an oil painting by any stretch of the imagination.

Conrad had a quick shower and slipped into bed beside her.

Hope mewed annoyance softly in her sleep; he smoothed her hair to calm her, before laying his head down on the pillow and drifting off to sleep.

****

Hope woke and automatically felt the bed next to her. Though she hadn't woken when Conrad slid into bed, she knew he was there. She felt his warm body and turned to face him. He worked so hard, long hours and extra days, just to give her the things he thought she wanted. What he didn't realise was the only thing she wanted and needed was him. Raising her hand, she gently stroked his handsome face. They had a good life going now. A baby would make it complete, but she'd come to accept that wouldn't be happening. She'd enquired about adoption, but Conrad wanted a child made by him and her, not someone else's. She felt the same way, but with Conrad's infertility problem, it didn't look like it would be possible.

Taking a good look at her man, she noticed a slightly raised red lump on his arm. Insects were always a problem, especially in the summer. She hoped it wouldn't get infected. With bacterial and viral mutations continuing to occur, even a wound as tiny as his could prove problematic.

Hope rose from the bed and tiptoed from the bedroom, closing the door behind her. She grabbed her uniform from the walk-in wardrobe and headed to the bathroom to start her day. A shower was what she needed to wake her up and brush the webs from her mind. Nightmares plagued her sleep too often lately. Memories of a troubled childhood, the worst times being out her control.

Losing her mother when hardly more than a baby affected her father badly. He mourned his wife and had no idea how to cope with a young child's inability to understand why her mother was no longer around.

When she became a teenager, she rebelled; running away, living rough on the streets, until her worried father found her and took her home. Her time of having nothing, and scrounging for food, showed her that while her father may not have had much, he'd given her everything she could have needed.

Hope had learnt a valuable lesson. To accept what you had and not want for something you may not be able to get. As long as she had Conrad, she was happy.

She did cry when each monthly cycle arrived, telling her she wasn't pregnant. She tried desperately to get her crying under control. There were a lot of people who didn't have babies. The same micro-engineered cold virus that had affected Conrad when he was a child, rendering him infertile, affected a great majority of men. She would have to learn to live with it.

Slowly soaping her body, she let the hot water cascade over her, soothing both muscles and her mind.

Having stayed in the shower until she was slightly wrinkled, she turned off the water and stepped out to towel herself dry. She caught sight of her reflection. Blonde shoulder-length hair, messy and wet at the moment, bright blue eyes and a slim, shapely body with narrow hips. Others had called them boyish, but as Conrad told her repeatedly, there was nothing boyish about her. She wondered if being pregnant would have changed her shape much?

Breaking away from her musings, she towelled off, dressed, and headed to the kitchen.

She and Conrad had done their best with the house. The furniture wasn't new, but what they had was functional and comfortable. The old brown leather couch with the mismatched chairs they'd found at an abandoned house. They'd had to carry them at least two kilometres because they were too big to fit in the car.

She laughed quietly to herself, remembering the time. They'd made the house a home. It was a bit rough around the edges, and the paint might need a bit of retouching here and there, but it was their home.

Hope made herself a fast breakfast. She was due to start work at the hospital within the hour. A professional nurse, she enjoyed looking after the patients. Many didn't have much and thought it a luxury to have a comfortable bed for the night, and a meal they didn't need to steal or scrounge for. It saddened her thinking of some of the poor wretches she had seen come through the hospital doors, knowing if times had been different, one of those wretches may have been her.

Breakfast finished, she tidied up and collected her bag. Before walking out the front door, she checked on Conrad. His face had reddened, and wet sheen covered his skin. She walked over, putting her cool hand against his brow. He felt warmer than usual. She hoped he wasn't coming down with something. She frowned, worried. The best she could do was to let him sleep. He had the next four days off, so if he did have something, hopefully it would be over before he had to return to work. She would check on him later when she returned home.

Hope closed the bedroom door so any noise wouldn't disturb him while he slept.

The walk to work only took a few minutes. The hospital was the next block over. It was one of the reasons they had picked the house.

As she walked along the cracked concrete path, she noticed tiny sprigs of green grass poking through the ruined brown lawns. Tiny leaves peeked out from bare tree branches. Spring had finally arrived. Nature could recover from virtually anything, even a war fought twenty years ago, it seemed.

Arriving at the hospital, Hope waved to her working companions as she entered the sterile building. She walked to her locker, removed her outside coat and scarf, and donned the sterile overcoat worn by all doctors and nurses.

The war may have caused destruction and death, but it also brought technological advances. Medical-surgical coats were one of them. It didn't matter what was spilled on it; blood, mucus, vomit, everything was neutralised by tiny little nannites woven into the cloth. The same nannites were in the paint on the walls, and the linoleum on the floor.

Hospitals no longer had the problem with Staphylococcus infections they used to. They were now as sterile as they were supposed to be.

Hope looked at the admissions sheets, sighed when she saw the workload and began her day.

CHAPTER THREE

Dr Helga Ell and Dr Herbert Mann were discussing the upcoming infertility trials when they were interrupted by a loud crashing sound.

They looked in the direction of the noise, in time to see a refrigerator, the fifth in the row, topple and crash into the bench in front. Giving each other a panicked look, both ran to the now silent and diagonal refrigerator.

With the help of others, they pushed the refrigerator upright and examined the contents. Luckily, all but one of the special vials was intact. One had broken. They both breathed a sigh of relief. One breakage was okay, many breakages would have caused a problem. A laboratory assistant poked his head out from around the corner.

'Sorry. I accidently bumped it with the motorised trolley. It got away from me.'

'If any more vials had broken, you would have been "accidently" fired. Be more careful in the future,' growled Herbert.

The assistant nodded, his head hung low. Herbert watched as he made his way out of the room without hitting anything else.

He carefully swept up the broken pieces of glass and put them in the hazardous contents bin.

Helga carefully carried the remaining vials to another refrigerator. They needed to be kept cold until they were injected into the willing subjects recently interviewed. These men were willing to try anything to have a child. All other experiments had failed, but the researchers held great hope for this serum. Only men with proven infertility would be injected. The serum rebuilt their reproductive glands so their sperm would have the ability to impregnate.

'That was close, Herbert.'

'Too close. Can you imagine what would have happened if we'd lost the whole lot? All that work down the drain.'

'I don't think the donor would have been too happy to give his sample again.' Helga's wry smile gave her away.

'Yes, he wasn't exactly happy the first time, was he?' said Herbert, mimicking the smile.

Helga looked at the stack of files in front of her. 'Do we have all the necessary forms and releases ready so we can start the tests?'

Herbert grunted an affirmation while rifling through a stack of papers.

'Okay then. Do we also have the control group's syringes?'

'Yes.' Herbert tapped the small cooler box next to him on the desk.

'Then let's get started. We have some subjects who wish to start making babies as soon as they can.'

Both of them walked over to a secured room, opened the door and went inside. The room held twenty men. Ten men would be given the control, which was a saline solution. The other ten would be given the Serum Fertility Treatment—FELMC—Sample A–1–0–1.

The only people who knew which man received which injection would be Helga and Herbert. They had already worked out which men would receive the true serum. These men were young, fit and had a clean history of health, as did their parents. The other men, while equally deserving, had a few problems in their own, and their families', medical histories. In any research, it's best to find out the effects, both good and bad, with healthy specimens. Helga and Herbert passed out the forms for their subjects to fill out and left the room.

One by one, as the men finished filling out their forms, they were shown into another room. Their blood pressure was taken before they were injected. For the serum to work, the men needed to be calm, not nervous or stressed.

All test subjects received a light sedative if they felt they needed it. They were then given the injection of serum, or the placebo, thirty minutes later.

Helga felt sorry for the control group. All of them wanted children, but for the sake of their health, it was better if they didn't receive the true batch.

After the treatment, all participants were given a cup of tea and something to eat, before being given a sheet with symptoms to watch out for. The sheet marked out fever-like symptoms, headaches, aching muscles and joints, nausea and blurred vision. If they experienced any of these symptoms, they were to contact either Helga or

Herbert immediately. They would then be brought back and monitored around the clock. No hard physical work of any type was to be attempted for a week after the injections.

After fielding all questions, the men were free to go home to their families and were escorted from the research building by security.

After the men had departed, Helga and Herbert sat down and went over the results so far. Only two of the men who had been given the real serum had needed sedatives, whereas seven out of the ten in the control group had needed it.

The result justified Helga and Herbert's first thoughts. Healthy, fit men were able to control their fears and stress, better than those who had a few medical issues. Now they had to sit back and wait.

****

Conrad woke to steel hammers hitting anvils inside his skull. This was worse than any hangover he'd ever had. Holding his head in his hands, he eased his way out of the bed and stumbled into the kitchen.

Opening the drawer containing the headache tablets, he took two with a glass of water before stumbling back to bed. His body ached everywhere. Every muscle. Every joint. Even his hair hurt. Groaning, he hoped the pills would stay in his stomach long enough to work. He had planned to paint a few rooms in the house on his days off. If he couldn't kick this bug, or whatever it was, he wouldn't be picking anything up, even something as light as a brush. As his headache eased slightly, he drifted off into an uncomfortable sleep.

****

Hope finished her shift and signed out. Twilight beckoned. Flocks of birds wheeled above in the sky. She took a few minutes sitting on a nearby wall to watch them circle and swoop, catching the night insects as they emerged from their daytime hiding places. She watched as a starling swooped, catching a moth on the wing, then settled gracefully in a nearby leafless tree to eat his evening meal. The sun slowly set behind the houses painting the sky as only nature could. Oranges and reds dominated the skyline, painting the clouds with vivid hues. Hope thought how nice it would be one of the birds, flying and swooping through the air. The freedom would be exhilarating. She wasn't too sure about eating the moths though. Smiling at the thought, she continued on her way home.

Hope called out to Conrad as she entered the house through the front door, to let him know she was home. No answer. It was unusual he wasn't awake. Usually when she arrived home he had a cup of tea waiting for her.

A soft groan sounded from the bedroom. Hope dropped her bag and hurried into the bedroom. Conrad lay on the bed sweating heavily, bright red and groaning. His eyes squinted at her as she entered the room and he raised his arms to shield his eyes.

Hope rushed to his side in time to hear him whisper, 'The light hurts, turn out the lights.' There was hardly any light in the room, but she rushed to the window and drew the curtains together as tightly as she could. Hurrying back to his side, Hope felt his forehead. He was burning up. She raced into the bathroom, threw a towel in the sink and drenched it with water. Running back to the bedroom, she threw the dripping soaked towel onto his burning body.

He gasped loudly when the cold, wet material hit him. Hope grabbed the top part of the towel and bathed his face with it. A loud sigh escaped his lips. The coolness seemed to be appreciated.

Leaving him on the bed, Hope returned to the bathroom and found the thermometer. She grabbed another towel, soaked it and returned. She removed the now warm towel and replaced it with the one she had just soaked. She removed the t-shirt and shorts he usually wore to bed and tossed them to the side. They were so drenched in sweat she could have wrung them out.

Hope wondered how long he'd been like this as she placed the thermometer under his tongue.

Conrad reached toward her, trying to find her hand without opening his eyes. Catching hers, he grasped it tightly before gasping hoarsely. 'Get Bill.'

Hope grabbed the telephone beside the bed and dialled Bill's number. It was all she could do to not scream down the telephone when Bill answered. 'Bill, Conrad's in a bad way, and he's asking for you. He's burning up, he's bright red all over and … oh hell, he's just thrown up all over me. Can you come now, please, I need your help.'

The phone went dead in her hand.

CHAPTER FOUR

Bill couldn't get Conrad, and what he'd done, off his mind. While the boy may not mean to hurt himself or Hope intentionally, people often did the wrong thing for the perceived right reasons. Hoping it wouldn't affect his sleep, Bill had something to eat, then went to bed.

He'd been up and about for a couple of hours when the telephone rang, bringing Hope's impassioned plea.

Finding the front door ajar, he headed straight for the main bedroom. He found Hope caressing Conrad's fevered brow with a wet towel. The boy didn't look good at all.

'Hope, what have you done so far? What is his temperature?'

She looked at him, helplessness in her eyes.

'Come on girl, pull yourself together. You're a nurse. You're used to this type of thing. You deal with it every day.'

He watched as she quickly pulled herself together.

'His temperature is 41° C, and I've been trying to bring it down with a wet towel.'

'Good. Go run a bath—tepid water, not too cold. We don't want to send him into shock. Hopefully, it'll bring his temperature down.'

Hope left the room to run the bath.

She'd pulled herself together, that was good. He didn't need a hysterical woman around. Crossing the room to where Conrad lay, he sat on the edge of the bed. 'Okay lad, what's wrong with you. Trying to get out of doing the painting? Let's sit you up and have a bit of a better look.' Bill slipped his hands under Conrad's head and shoulders to manoeuvre him into a sitting position.

Conrad groaned as he moved him. 'Sorry lad, I know this must hurt, but we have to move you into the bath to cool you down before you start fitting. You're burning up. You'll feel better in a short time, I promise.'

Hope appeared in the doorway. 'The bath is ready.'

He motioned her over, and she put her shoulder under Conrad's arm. 'Closer into his body, Hope, you need to take some of his weight on you.'

Hope did as asked. Between the two of them, they half-carried, half-dragged Conrad into the bathroom.

Bill tested the water, finding it just right. Conrad gasped as coolness engulfed his body, then sighed as his burning body off-loaded its heat. Bill stuck the thermometer in Conrad's mouth.

'Hope, could you change the bedclothes to clean ones?'

Hope left the bathroom silently to take care of the bedclothes. Bill shook Conrad a little to get his attention. 'Conrad. Do you think this is a reaction to whatever you injected yourself with?'

Conrad didn't answer, just groaned. Bill figured the fever was still too high for him to understand anything. He may as well keep quiet and hope the temperature dropped. The thermometer indicated he wasn't as hot as before. The number was down to 40.5° C. Still high, but he wouldn't be fitting.

He continued bathing Conrad's head and shoulders. After about ten minutes, the boy appeared to regain consciousness. A low moan sounded. Hope rushed into the bathroom, concerned. 'He's okay, Hope, his temperature's coming down. We might get him out before he starts shivering.' Bill looked around. 'Can you get me a chair we can sit him on? He's still too weak to stand on his own.'

As Hope re-entered the room with the chair, Bill motioned to a place to his right. 'We'll bring him out, sit him down there and lightly dry him off. I'm sure he would prefer you to do that instead of me.'

Hope smiled at him.

Good, she's calming down. Between the two of them, they managed to get him out of the bath and propped on the chair.

'Call me when you've finished and I'll help you get him back into bed.'

Hope looked at him. 'Thanks so much, Bill, I really appreciate you coming over and doing this. I'm sorry I kind of lost it before.'

Bill gave her a hug and looked her in the eyes. 'Never apologise for caring about someone, sweetheart. I'll be in the lounge room. Give me a call when you're done.'

Bill left the room while Hope dried Conrad. He wondered how long the fever would last. A regime of cool baths in the next couple of days should make him heal faster. The fever was a side effect of the infertility treatment Conrad had taken, he was sure, but it could have also been something he'd picked up. With any luck, this was just a stray flu bug that had been passing, and the boy had been unlucky to come down with it.

Here he was, acting like a father again. Chloe, Conrad's mother, had often told him Conrad looked on him as a father. He'd have been proud to have Conrad as a son. The boy was hardworking and driven, loved Hope with all his heart, but occasionally did do some crazy things. Today was a good example.

Bill heard Hope calling him, and returned to the bathroom. Conrad looked less red and sweaty than he had an hour ago.

'Okay, let's get you back to bed. One arm over Hope and the other over me.' Bill looked at Hope, 'On three, okay.'

Hope nodded.

'One, two, three—and lift.' Both of them stood together, easily lifting Conrad off the seat.

Bill heard Conrad whisper something. 'What was that? Speak up boy.'

'I want to sit in the lounge room. I don't want to go back to bed.'

Bill looked at Hope.

'I can't see why he can't, Bill, at least for a little while.'

'Okay, off to the lounge then.'

Once they had Conrad seated, Hope left to make them all a cup of tea.

Bill sat beside Conrad. 'Are you going to tell Hope what you did?'

Conrad shook his head. 'Let's see what happens and how long this lasts. Who knows, maybe this is supposed to happen. Remember all those injections when I was a kid? I got sick with them too.'

Bill nodded. It was Conrad's decision to make. If he didn't want to tell Hope yet, he didn't have to. 'If you don't get any better within the next couple of days, you're going to have to see the scientists. You told me you'd do that.'

'I will, Bill. I don't want Hope to know what I did, not just yet.'

'Well, she's your wife, but I think she deserves an explanation soon before the stuff starts working and she gets pregnant.'

'I will tell her, Bill … eventually.'

Hope came back in with three cups of tea, some headache tablets, and a glass of water for Conrad.

'Good thinking, Hope. Here lad, take these, and try to keep the water down.'

He watched as Conrad swallowed the tablets along with some water. No gagging or retching followed. No longer needed, Bill left him in Hope's capable hands.

CHAPTER FIVE

Fluffy indeed, thought Rufus, as he padded down the stairs and into the car park with the two-legs who walked beside him.

A regal feline like him shouldn't have to put up with being called Fluffy.

Yes, he had lots of black and brown striped silky fur. He was extremely proud of his coat, but Fluffy? Really? His ears were beautifully marked, with a tuft of fur on the top. He groomed as often as he could. The air circulators in this huge cave dried out his fur, and he had to lick hard to keep it in shape.

He didn't mind the two-legs. They fed him tasty morsels of food every day, and he didn't have to run after the little rodents they called mice. There wasn't a real meal in them, but they were fun to chase. The two-legs seemed happy when he caught one. Not so happy when he dropped it at their feet, or on top of the bits of paper they used.

He pushed the door closed with his tail and continued on down the stairs. The Great Siam expected his latest report, and he didn't want to be late. Under no circumstances did you make the Siam wait.

Rufus's mind wandered as he made his way down the stairs. He knew the two-legs inhabited this planet, having been informed by the old ones back home, but he wasn't aware of how dull they were. They couldn't speak the language, for Bast's sake, and telepathy didn't touch their thick brains. They made incoherent noises to each other. Rufus couldn't understand them at all. How backward could they be? Back home, even the youngest kitten could speak a little after they opened their eyes.

The Siam had sent him here. His mission: to find a solution to their breeding problem. The task was to find and return with new blood lines.

He'd arrived and escaped the confines of the cave. After travelling a fair distance, he caught the smell of a queen. The scent intoxicated him, and she was close. He may have been a male, too young to be able to sire kittens, but instincts kicked in, and he went in search of her. What he found appalled him.

A queen of mixed breed being serviced by a male of a similar parentage, which meant no proper breeding at all. As much as his instinct was saying it didn't matter, he was a purebred warrior. He wouldn't stoop that low. Breed to breed only. That was the rule.

This world appeared populated with indiscriminate breeds. Mustering his courage, Rufus approached a few toms to ask directions. They instantly arched, puffed and challenged him. He halted. The information he needed may have to be fought for. Diplomacy was needed.

Rufus called out, 'I come in peace. I only need directions'.

The other cats looked at each other, then back at him. They made a snarling, wailing noise and advanced on him. Rufus knew they hadn't understood him. He tried basic language, one all felines should be able to hear and understand.

The two toms paused, confused. The messages Rufus received from them were unreadable. *Oh, Bast, I'm amongst savages.*

Rufus tried sending his telepathic messages slowly.

'Come on, even a kitten could understand what I'm saying'.

Both males stopped. They appeared to try to understand what Rufus sent. One of them seemed to catch on. Rufus noticed his stance change. Both males stopped their assault and answered Rufus in a broken fashion.

'You … asking where our pure females are? Why? Why you talk in language we not know?' The question came from the smoky-blue tom.

'I come from far away. I am looking for pure females and their kittens. Our world and kittens are dying. We need new blood for our lines, but we need pure blood, not breedless blood.'

'Are you saying our queen's breedless blood is not good enough for you? Can you not smell the queen? Is she not good enough for you?'

Rufus considered his answer carefully. He didn't want to get in a fight. Only Bast knew what diseases they carried on their claws.

'Your female smells wonderful. Where I come from, we are not allowed to mate outside our breed. I need to find females of pure breed to take back.'

The explanation placated the two males. They conferred for a few seconds. Rufus was able to pick up a few words. They sounded derogatory to him.

'We understand some felines are not like us. We will show you where the pure females are, but we warn you, they think themselves better than us.'

Rufus trilled his acceptance at the news.

The journey to find the pure bloods was uneventful, but long. They arrived at what looked like a very comfortable cave. Even better, a surrounding forest provided cover. To top the day off, Rufus's nose picked up the overwhelming allure of pure queens.

This is what he had travelled the vast distance for.

'How do we get in?'

One of his companions gestured with his head and ears. 'Over the fence. Don't let the two-legs see you or you'll get splashed with water.'

Rufus wasn't sure what a "fence" was but was sure he'd work it out. 'I don't mind water, so I'll be fine. If you wait here, I'll be back soon.' Making himself as flat as he could, he approached a mat of tangled vines he couldn't chew through, then realised this must be the "fence". He leapt up, scaled the vines to the top, jumped down, and landed with barely a sound. Keeping low, Rufus belly-crawled over to the females. As he got closer, he could hear them talking to each other. Thank Bast. I can understand them.

Rufus drew himself to full height and marched out of the bushes, keeping a keen eye on his surroundings. These females were the same breed as the Siam. He would be mightily pleased if he could manage to get at least one to come back with him.

'Hello to you, lovely queens,' purred Rufus. 'I am looking for a fine queen to accompany me on a journey.

My king has need of your services, if you know what I mean.'

The females looked back at Rufus. The lead queen sidled up to the fence, checking out Rufus as she wandered over. 'What could your king offer us that we don't have here? We are fed twice a day, groomed twice a week, and have these lovely homes to live in.' she gushed sarcastically, indicating the wire enclosure with her tail.

'My king could offer you many things. Open air in which to run and hunt, food available to you whenever you wished, silken beds upon which to lie. For such lovely queens as you, my king would offer everything. All you have to do is join me. You are welcome to bring your kittens as well.'

There was a bit of a racket as all the queens began talking at once. It seemed none of them liked being cooped up. They wanted to be out, they wanted to roam, they wanted to chase those horrible feathered things that flew down and taunted them. At least, those were the points he could hear the others talking about.

After a short time, the lead queen approached him. 'Can you take all of us … and our kittens?'

Rufus couldn't believe his luck. He thought it'd be hard to get one to come back with him. Now they all wanted to come back with him. What a fantastic outcome. The Siam would be pleased. Rufus then paused, realising he had a problem.

'How many of you are there?'

'Oh, only five of us, but we do have thirteen kittens. Only three kittens need to be carried. The others can walk.'

Rufus breathed a trill of relief. They still made a large group, but Rufus believed he and his new friends could do it. 'How do I release you from your prison?'

The queen pointed with her paw. 'The latch is up there, but there is a trick to opening it. You must push up the rounded part then draw out the bar that goes into the other side.' Rufus looked at the latch and gave a mighty leap. He examined the latch and put his paws to work. He lifted the rounded part as the queen had directed, but his own weight stopped him from pulling the rest of the bar out. He leaped down, then leaped back onto the other side of the fence, and easily pushed open the bolt with his hind leg.

The queens gasped in amazement as the gate swung open. It took them seconds to corral their kittens, pick up the smaller ones who had to be carried, and leave the nasty wire prison they all hated.

Rufus moved them to the cover of the bushes. A hole in the fence he hadn't noticed before led to his two waiting friends. They stared in shocked amazement as the queens came out, closely followed by their kittens. Rufus brought up the rear, hoping and checking their escape hadn't been noticed.

He marshalled them all around the corner. Getting the group back to the safety of the basement seemed easy enough, but he would need the help of his two new friends.

Rufus called them over. 'I need to get these queens and kittens back to my cave. Can you help me?'

The two turned away to converse. He waited. They turned back to face him. 'Yes, we'll help you, but we want to go where these queens are going. Life on the streets is no good. We want to go where it's good to live.

If you take us, we will help you get more females of other breeds as well.'

Looking into their eyes, he couldn't smash the glimmer of hope he saw. 'Okay, but as you say, you have to help me get more pure breeds.'

The two toms agreed without a moment's hesitation.

'Well, if we are going to be together more, what are you known as? What are your names?'

The smoky blue looked at him. 'Call me Smoky, and him, Ginger. As you have noticed, he doesn't talk much, if at all. What is your name?'

'My name is Rufus, although the two-legs call me … actually, don't worry about what they call me.' They didn't need to know. He could imagine the snickering behind his back if he'd let that name loose.

With names learnt, and daylight growing dimmer, it was time to move. 'Okay, free felines, let's go to a better place.' Off they trooped, Smoky and Ginger leading, five pure queens and their kittens in the middle, with Rufus bringing up the rear. It took longer to return to the area where Rufus had picked up Smoky and Ginger because the kittens couldn't travel fast. Eventually, they made it back to the alley. Rufus took over, leading them into the grey stone cave.

Rufus revealed a hole large enough for any feline to get through, but not large enough to gain the attention of any two-legs. This was the only way in and out of the lowest cave.

Once they were all in, Rufus led them to a huge metal box. Buttons glowed on the side. The queens were reluctant to enter, but Rufus talked them in. He joined them and pressed the green glowing button.

Rufus asked them all to place their paws over their ears. A high-pitched whine cut the air, followed by a flash of light. Rufus, Smoky, Ginger, five queens and thirteen kittens disappeared.

****

Rufus, Smoky, Ginger, all the queen cats and kittens, walked out of the transporter. He'd checked them all over, one by one. Good, all whiskers and paws in the right place.

Marshalling them together, he walked them out of the temple. He noticed them gazing around them at the buildings, red grass, pink sky and the yellow trees blowing and swaying in the breeze. Noses sniffed the air. He knew the feeling of amazement at the difference. Rufus had been amazed when he saw the blue sky, green trees and green grass on the two-legs' planet. Things just looked so wrong compared to what he knew. He heard the queens whispering together and saw the looks directed at him. He stopped the group to talk to them before they walked in to see The Siam.

'Gather round, my furry beauties,' he trilled.

'This is Catatopia. As you can tell, colours are a little different. The wind smells different too. The odour that makes us who we are. No two-legs can come here and live for long. You are free from the two-legs captivity. I am taking you to see The Siam, our ruler. He is the same breed as you, and will be pleased.'

Rufus paused at the front gate to The Siam's residence and bowed his head to his paws.

'Great Siam, it is I, Rufus, your messenger to the two-legs world. I have returned from the first of my missions and have brought you some new visitors. They welcome the freedom of Catatopia.'

'Welcome back, Rufus. Come closer. Bring our new visitors, so that I may lay my eyes upon them. It is a brave thing you have done, and one that will bring happiness to Catatopia.'

The little group moved closer. Rufus heard one of the queen's gasp in amazement. In front of them sat The Great Siam, a huge Seal Point Siamese Cat. He was easily twice as large as what they would know as a normal Siamese male. A true beauty to behold.

****

The Great Siam let his gaze fall over the approaching queens.

Very nice indeed. They will make wonderful mothers for my kittens. Bast knew they needed new blood lines. Inbreeding had become a huge problem.

The two-legs hadn't brought enough pairs to keep the lines pure. Mutations increased. The queens gave birth to stillborn kittens. The rules still applied though. Only breed to breed. The Siam knew about the 'loose' queens who would accept any tom. The kittens from those matings were handy as underlings and soldiers, but they couldn't breed back into the pure gene pool. That would be a disgrace. Rufus had just turned up with the answer to their breeding problems.

'Hello, my new gracious ladies. Welcome to Catatopia, where you no longer have to worry about the enslavement or captivity the two-legs subjected you to. There are many caves here, where you can raise your kittens, but you first need to be educated on the rules of this colony. I will hand you over to my knowledgeable instructors. They will let you know where and how to get food, who you can breed with, and other rules you must follow while you live here. Thank you for agreeing to be the first additional colonists to Catatopia. You and others who Rufus will bring us, will save our race. Please follow the educators who are standing to the side of you. Your freedom on Catatopia has begun.'

The Siam watched as the queens and kittens left the room. He then turned his attention to Rufus, Smokey, and Ginger.

'Rufus, you have done well. Who are these strangers with you?'

Rufus raised his shaggy head. 'Thank you, Great Siam. These two helped me in the world of the two-legs. I have explained our predicament to them, and they are willing to help us in exchange for being allowed to live amongst us. They are not of noble breeding, Great Siam, but come as willing soldiers to our cause. I have learnt enough of their language to be able to speak to them, but they would be what we call—slow, Great Siam. They aren't brainless, only breedless. They have grown up in a different type of world to our own Catatopia.' Rufus finished his speech and dropped his head to his paws again.

'Hmm, I can see they would be helpful to you. I have tried to communicate with them, but I am getting no response. I was wondering if they were rude, but as you have explained, they are slow. Very well, I leave them in your care. If they can help bring the new blood to Catatopia, they will have earned their place here. Do you think they should be neutered or left whole? We do not want them breeding with the breedless ones here.

Unfortunately, the breedless ones seem to be thriving, where the rest of us are failing. Bring us more pure breeders and their kittens, Rufus. We depend on you.'

'I don't think you need to neuter them.' Rufus shuddered at the thought. 'I will let them know the rules. We will not let you down, Great Siam.' He, Smoky and Ginger backed out of the room, with their heads down.

****

A year had passed since he'd started his mission. Smoky and Ginger still accompanied him. Together, they had succeeded in placing many new breeders on Catatopia.

Now the Siam needed to know about the experiments, and what the two-legs in white coats had done to him. This could prove embarrassing.

Rufus approached the Siam's residence and requested entry from the stocky soldier guarding the doorway. The soldier's ancestors had been British Shorthairs. Even though the soldier was larger, he still resembled them, despite his muddied lineage.

The soldier allowed him entry and audience with The Great Siam.

Rufus approached and bowed his head to paws.

Lifting his head, he began his report. 'Great Siam, I bring you news from the two-legs world. It is disturbing.

The Siam leaned forward. 'Yes, go on.'

'In my time on the two-legs world, I have been used for experimentation. It is not bad. I was not injected with anything, but they have used my ... umm ... seed, in their experiments. It wasn't a pleasant experience.'

Rufus looked up and saw The Siam attempting to hide a smirk. Rufus became acutely embarrassed.

'How did they accomplish that, my little soldier?'

'They ... manipulated ... me.' Having to explain, especially to the Siam, was a blow to his ego.

The Siam roared with laughter. 'I am sorry my little soldier, but I couldn't help myself. I didn't think the two-legs could do that, but it has been a while since I saw one. Do you know what they have done with your ... umm ... seed?'

'Great Siam, I do. The two-legs breed has had problems in breeding their young ones. We felines tend to have a larger birth rate, and they have combined certain parts of my seed with a two-legs serum. They hope it will repair the breeding system of the two-legs toms. I scratched and howled to tell them to stop, but they took it anyway.'

Rufus dropped his head in embarrassment.

'Rufus, my little soldier. I have no doubt they did not get your seed easily. You have nothing to be embarrassed about. The two-legs breed will greatly benefit from having feline genes. They obviously thought you were a feline from their world, even though you are larger than their normal feline. Do you know of any result as yet?'

'Not yet, Great Siam, but my two-legs pet has taken the serum. I will monitor him for changes.'

'Excellent idea. Go now and see your family. I understand kittens were born to your queen a couple of weeks ago. Maybe one of your kittens would make a nice present for your two-legs pet? When it's old enough to leave its mother, of course. Farewell, for now, my little soldier.'

Rufus bowed his head to his paws and left.

CHAPTER SIX

Conrad opened his eyes on a new day. His temperature had dropped, but his head felt as if it were made of lead.

Thank God he didn't need to go to work today. Yesterday was a virtual blur.

He had a vague recollection of having cool, wet towels draped over him by Hope, and Bill sitting beside the bathtub. He would have to ask about that.

Conrad heard the door to the bedroom open. Hope walked in.

'How are we feeling this morning?'

'A bit rough around the edges, love. What happened yesterday; and why was Bill sitting next to the bathtub with me?'

'You seem to have come down with something. You were burning up, and I panicked. You asked me to call Bill, so I did. He rushed over, and we got your temperature down. It was really high, and I was worried. Bill was worried too, but he calmed me down. We got you into a cool bath, and let you sit up for a while before I helped you back to bed.'

'I'm sorry love. It must be something I picked up at work. I'm sure I'll be okay soon, but I don't know about doing the painting today.'

Hope accepted the explanation, so Conrad didn't push it any further. Something he'd picked up at work. Most definitely. He'd picked it up, and stabbed it into his arm. But he wasn't inclined to tell her the whole story, not yet anyway.

Conrad pushed himself up on his elbows, manoeuvring himself into a sitting position.

'I am a bit hungry. Is there any toast on the go? I thought I could smell some being made.'

'You can't smell the rubbish when it needs to go out, but you can smell the toast I have just made. I can't smell it, maybe being ill has increased your olfactory abilities.'

'Maybe it has. I feel fit enough to get up and sit in the lounge room anyway. I don't want to spend any more time in bed. Gee, I must have sweated a bit, the bed reeks of it.'

He wrinkled his nose at the wafting odour whenever he moved.

'Yes, you did sweat quite a bit, though I can't smell it, and I usually pick that up easily.' Hope sniffed the bedding, shaking her head. 'I can only just smell it. Your nose is definitely working overtime, but once you get up, I'll change the sheets again. Come on, swing your legs over the side, and stand up. Don't move too fast.'

With a bit of effort, Conrad swung his legs across and sat on the edge of the bed. He felt as weak as a kitten. If he took it slowly, he should be able to make it to the lounge room and sit on the sofa.

He rose slowly. Hope wriggled in under his arm to support him if he needed it. The first step was wobbly, and his head spun. Once the vertigo settled, he walked out of the room under his own steam. He reached the sofa and virtually fell onto it. Damn, he felt weak.

Hope appeared in front of him a few minutes later, with toast and some weak tea. She also had a couple of painkillers for him.

'Take the tablets after you've eaten. You have to take them with food.'

Conrad nodded and nibbled his toast. His mouth watered at the delicious smell, and he had to stop himself from eating too fast. He wanted to keep the food down. If it went in too fast, he guessed it would come out just as quickly.

Hope watched him as he ate, probably using her nursing experience to tell if he was going to throw up or not. After a few minutes, she seemed to be happy with what he was doing and returned to the kitchen to make her own breakfast.

Conrad was going well. The food he ate stayed down, and his head seemed to be less heavy. He absent-mindedly scratched his arm, pulling his fingers back fast when he scratched something raised. He crooked his arm toward him and glanced at the area. It was where he had injected himself. While it was red and raised, it didn't look too bad. It definitely wasn't inflamed. It was itchy, though. Just like a sting or bite would have been.

'Hope, do we have anything for mosquito bites?'

Hope appeared with a tube of ointment. Conrad squeezed a little out and massaged it into the itchy area.

'I must have been bitten at some time. Hey, maybe that's what is making me ill.'

Hope put her hand to his forehead. 'Hmm, you're still overly warm, but I'll think you'll live.' She looked at his arm, and the small red dot. 'I saw that yesterday before I went to work. It looks better now, but it could be what's making you ill. Well, if it is, the painkillers will fix it up.'

Conrad nodded his head to agree with her. He finished his toast and tea, took the tablets, and lay back on the couch.

A knock at the door roused him. He hadn't realised he'd fallen asleep.

Bill walked in, closely followed by his mother. 'Sorry Conrad, your mum insisted on coming over when she heard her little boy was sicky-poo. I tried to stall her, but you know what she's like when the mother hat goes on.'

Chloe sat next to Conrad and did the Mother Temperature Test. The lips to the forehead. A thing all mothers do.

'Mum, please. I'm not a little boy anymore. Hope is looking after me really well. I'm just a little under the weather, I'm not dying.' Conrad hated when his mother fussed over him.

He noticed Bill and Hope standing back with smirks on their faces. They were enjoying this. He loved his mother, but this was embarrassing.

'Mum … stop … please!'

Chloe sat back, a little dejected. 'I'm just trying to make sure that you are okay. When Bill told me you weren't well, I wanted to come over straight away but he wouldn't let me. You know how I am when you get sick.

With all the germs going around in the air, you never know.' She started to fuss again.

Conrad grabbed her hands gently and put them back in her lap.

'I'm okay, Mum. I've had something to eat and drink, and Hope has given me some tablets, which will help my headache. Okay?'

Chloe nodded and sat back.

Bill murmured something to Hope. She laughed.

'Okay Bill, what was that? What's so funny?' Whatever it was, it was about him.

'I just said to Hope it's probably "Man Flu". She agrees with me.' Bill laughed.

'Great. Now you want to get in on the act too, huh.' Conrad felt a little picked on, but even he saw the funny side of it.

'Seriously, are you feeling better? Your temperature seems to have gone down, which is good. I wouldn't be attempting the painting.'

'No, I don't think I'll get into that today, and maybe not tomorrow either. I have to get well enough to go back to work. I think I'll just take it a bit easy for a couple of days and see how things go. I keep falling asleep, so maybe my body is telling me what it needs.'

'Yes, that's exactly what he needs, more rest and fewer people. Let's leave him alone, shall we.' Hope ushered Bill and Chloe out the door.

Hope reappeared a couple of minutes later. 'Come on, you are going back to bed for a little while. Let those tablets take effect and do some good.'

Conrad smiled. 'Oh good, are we going to be playing Doctors and Nurses? Are you going to be a naughty nurse for me?' He was joking, of course, but felt he had to put up a good front. He felt weak, battered and bruised, and totally incapable of doing what he suggested.

'Naughty Nurses, hey. There's not much wrong with you if you are thinking that way already, is there? Do what the nice nurse tells you, and get into that bed, now … and you are not getting up again until you've had at least four hours of sleep.'

'Yes, Nurse Hope. Anything you want, Nurse Hope.'

He climbed into bed, feeling the cool covers slide over his fever-affected body. Blackness engulfed him as soon as he lay back.

****

The next couple of days were a blur for Conrad. He woke, showered, brushed his teeth, ate and went back to bed.

On his last day off, he woke with no headache, pains or any sign he'd been seriously ill.

He felt fit as a fiddle. He would tackle the painting that needed to be done and maybe even take Hope out for dinner. She deserved it after putting up with him for the last three days.

Conrad got himself out of bed. He dressed in his old comfortable jeans and an old t-shirt he could paint in.

Hope wasn't in bed. She must have risen earlier to get some things done before he rose and she had to take care of him.

Conrad walked into the lounge room and heard Hope softly sobbing. He walked up to her and held her. 'Sweetheart, what's wrong?'

'I was just thinking, that's all. What would have happened if you were really sick, what if you had died?'

He hugged her to him gently. 'Oh, my silly girl. I'm not going to leave you anytime soon. Look, I'm okay. I feel great.'

She lifted her head from where it lay against his chest. A wet mark on his t-shirt showed the evidence of her tears. 'I know you think I'm nuts for thinking such things, but I do.'

'There's no need to. Wipe your eyes. Everything is okay.'

He leant over to the coffee table, plucked a few tissues from the box lying on top and dabbed her eyes. He gave her the tissues so she could do it herself. 'I know how much you love me, and the last few days prove it even more.'

'I know I shouldn't get so upset, but I do. I suppose it's the hormones.'

'Yeah, that's it. Blame those pesky little hormones. Don't they always bob their horrible little heads up at times like this?' He was happy men didn't have the problems women had. He didn't think he'd be able to live with himself. The slightest sad moment and Hope would burst into tears.

Hope tilted her face to him and smiled. 'Thanks for understanding, Conrad. I know my crying must get on your nerves, but I can't help feeling the way I do.'

Conrad didn't need to answer. He pulled her a little tighter and let her sob. She would eventually stop by herself. She just needed to know he was there for her, like she had been there for him in the last few days.

When Hope's sobs faded, Conrad rose from the sofa and made them both a cup of tea. It was funny, but whenever any type of crisis happened, it was always the best type of drink to have. It was calming, and best of all, it worked on both of them.

He sat with Hope until she stopped crying. She wiped her eyes dry and drank her tea. Conrad watched her closely. It tore his heart out to see her sobbing, but maybe what he'd done would fix this problem. He fought with himself. Should he tell her or should he hold his news back? He didn't know if it would work, and more importantly, he didn't know how long it would take either. It wasn't worth getting her hopes up only to have them dashed the next month again. They'd had too many of those times, when each attempt failed. Three years of pain and hoping. No. He wouldn't tell her, not until he was sure what would happen.

It was up to him to get her up and moving. She liked helping him with things around the house, although he really preferred to do them by himself.

He stood up, walked over to the paint pots and brushes, and started getting things ready.

Hope wandered over to his side and put her arms around him. He bent his head and kissed her on the forehead.

'Come on. Let's get at least some of these walls painted. I'll get the paint, rollers and brushes ready; if you spread the paint cloths out, so we don't get paint on the carpet. Then you can help me cover the walls with this delightful colour,' he said, holding a can up of magnolia coloured paint. 'Later on, I'll take you out for dinner. I think you deserve it, after dealing with me for the last few days.'

Hope smiled back at him and grabbed the paint cloths.

CHAPTER SEVEN

Rufus wandered back to his cave. He looked forward to seeing his new little family, and thinking about the parting comments the Great Siam had made. One of his kittens as a present for his two-legs pet. Would that work? Could he use one of his own kittens as a way of finding out what was going on in the two-legs cave? Rufus knew he would have to put the idea to Princess, his beloved queen. She would be none too happy about it either. Of course, he would have to wait until the kitten was old enough, but that would give him time to see if the serum had worked on his two-legs.

His pet did give such nice rubs, especially in those hard to get to areas, Rufus thought to himself. If he did what the Great Siam suggested, he was sure the kitten would have a good life. Hmm, would he send a female kitten or a male kitten? Rufus supposed time would tell, and the right kitten would show itself.

He grinned a little at the thought. One of his kittens would be the first to travel back to the other world. He felt quite pleased and proud of himself. As he strolled around the last corner before reaching his cave, he had a jaunty step in his gait.

'I'm home, Princess, my queen.' Small mewls and squeaks caught his ears. Rufus followed the sounds and found his new family, with Princess fast asleep in the middle of them. Rufus approached cautiously, as Princess had been known to be cranky for a few days after giving birth. From what he could see, she'd birthed a good-size litter. He could see three males and at least two females. Princess's tail flicked as he drew closer.

'So you're finally home.' Yes, he'd been right. She was a little tetchy. He coughed lightly and backed off. 'Yes, Princess, my love, I'm back. I see you've had a beautiful litter of kittens. Can I come closer and have a good look at them?'

'Yes, I've had the little darlings. So, where have you been? Traipsing around the two-legs planet, bringing more spoilt, whining feline queens and their misbegotten offspring back here?'

Oh, Bast, she's in a real mood.

'Umm, no. I haven't brought any new additions to our colony back with me this time. I've just returned from giving the Great Siam my report. Did you have a hard time giving birth?'

'It was difficult this time, Rufus. Sorry, I know I shouldn't be cross with you. I knew you were the Siam's messenger when you asked me to be your mate. The birthing didn't go well. Come closer and see your new kittens.'

Rufus moved forward slowly and nuzzled the little bodies lying next to Princess. The males seemed to have the same colours and markings as him, and the females had the same, but necks and underbellies of white. 'Three males and two females that I can see,' he observed, 'is that the whole litter?'

'What! Five not enough for you? No, there's one more under my tail. She won't stay with the others, and even though her eyes aren't open yet, she keeps trying to get away. I've already had to pick her up and bring her back a few times. She made it halfway across the cave last time.'

Rufus gently picked up his mate's tail in his mouth, placing it above the kitten he found underneath. Like the other females, she had a white neck and underbelly. She was also twice as big as the other kittens. This little girl was going to grow into a very large feline.

'My, she's big, isn't she? But so pretty too.' He purred looking at her, a truly beautiful kitten.

'Yes, she is, and it's probably the reason there were two stillborns. Both were males.' Princess said sadly, 'I wish you could take her to the two-legs planet when she's weaned. She's going to be trouble if she stays here. Just look at the size of her.'

Rufus looked up sharply from the kitten. 'You'd want one of your kittens to go to the two-legs planet? Why?'

Princess mewled softly at Rufus. 'Look at her, Rufus. Even now she is trying to explore, and she can't see yet. Don't you think it would be the best thing for her? Maybe you could talk to the Great Siam about letting you take her when she is weaned?'

Rufus purred. 'You've just made a decision for me, Princess. The Great Siam has already suggested the same thing. Did he know about this kitten? Have you already made the same suggestion to him?'

Princess looked down at the litter sheepishly. 'I may have, or one of the other queens may have. This little female has been the talk of the caves lately. It may have reached the ears of the Great Siam somehow.'

Rufus leaned forward and licked her head. 'It's okay, Princess. I can take the little one with me when it is time. I'm sure my two-legs pet back on the planet will take good care of her. What have you named her?'

'Well, I don't know if you're going to like it or not, but I've named her … Wanderer, due to her escaping so frequently. What do you think of her name?'

Rufus chuckled to himself. 'I think Wanderer is a wonderful name. It describes her well. Well done, my queen. She and I are going to have to work hard together. I'm sorry to hear that you had two stillborns, but look at the wonderful kittens you have still.'

A satisfied purr rumbled through his queen's throat.

Rufus bent his head again to lovingly wash her neck. When he finished, he nuzzled the kittens again. He was so proud of Princess and the kittens she'd borne. He was sure there were no more beautiful kittens on Catatopia than the ones he was looking at now. He gazed at Princess, knowing he had the most understanding and beautiful mate any feline ever could. He snuggled down beside her and began to tell her of all what had been happening to him since he had last seen her.

CHAPTER EIGHT

Conrad woke early. He felt well rested and alert. Just as well; today he had to return to work, and glad that the headaches, and aches and pains of the last few days had vanished. He and Bill were rostered on the afternoon shift, starting at three o'clock in the afternoon.

Just enough time to get some shopping done, clean up and get his uniform ready. Bill and his mother had come over a few times in the preceding days, to check on him. They were totally amazed when they'd found him and Hope painting the rooms. He'd offered them some brushes so they could help, but they both declined and made their way back home. Conrad knew Bill had an aversion to any kind of work he didn't have to do.

He slid out of bed carefully so he wouldn't wake Hope. After doing the painting, she had enjoyed being taken out for dinner. Conrad had let her pick where she wanted to go. Hope decided on a little Chinese restaurant, not far down the block. They had enjoyed a nice, relaxed meal before returning home and settling down for the night.

Conrad lightly stroked her hair as he watched her sleep. He hoped the serum had worked its way through his blood, and changed something that would enable him to give her the child she desperately wanted.

He tiptoed out of the bedroom, slowly closing the door behind him.

Conrad showered and washed his hair. Somehow, being sick for a few days had increased his sense of smell. He could easily smell the perfume in the soap and shampoo he used. Even through the closed door of the bathroom, he could smell the paint they had put on the walls the previous day. He supposed as long as he didn't come across anything too rotten or powerful, an increased sense of smell wasn't a bad thing.

After getting the morning ablutions over and done with, he made himself breakfast and readied his uniform for the day. He was in the middle of ironing his shirt when Hope stumbled out of the bedroom. He placed the iron to the side and moved to the kitchen to make her a cup of tea.

'How do you feel this morning, love?' He handed her a mug of tea.

'Good.' She sat, stretching her arms out. 'I think I really needed that night out. I enjoyed dinner, and what made it better was I didn't have to cook or do any cleaning up.' She took the mug of tea from him and sipped carefully.

Conrad bent down and kissed her on the forehead. 'Nothing you didn't deserve, sweetheart, I'm glad you had a good time.' Her mood was better than it had been the day before.

'So, what's on for today?'

'Well, Bill and I have to be at work for a 3 pm start. We have a bit of shopping to do before that. Do you want to come, or would you like to stay home?'

'I'll come with you. There are few female things I have to pick up, which you don't like to do.'

That was true. Conrad was okay for most things to do with shopping, but when it came to shopping for female needs, he became totally confused. He preferred she do that for herself.

'Well, finish your tea then, and we'll be off as soon as I've finished ironing my uniform.'

Hope nodded, disappearing into the bedroom with her mug of tea in hand.

When she reappeared, they both headed out the front door.

****

Conrad pushed the cart in front of him as he and Hope wove their way around the shopping centre. He was about to walk forward after stopping to let some old ladies cross the aisle in front of him when he noticed Hope had stopped a couple of shops behind him. She was staring into the window of a pet shop at a kitten.

Conrad pulled up the cart beside her.

'Conrad,' she used her little girl voice on him, 'can we get a kitten?'

Conrad knew he was in trouble whenever she used that voice. She knew he was helpless to resist anything she asked for.

'Sweetie, yes, we can get a kitten one day, but not from a pet shop. You know these people keep the backyard breeders going. If we're going to get one, it'll be from a rescue shelter or from a properly registered breeder. I'll look around for one, okay.'

'Okay.'

Her dejected voice told him it was anything but okay.

'But …' she looked up at him with puppy dog eyes. 'I'd like a big fluffy one. The ones who have little tufts on their ears. I like the look of them. It'd be really nice to cuddle up with one like that.'

He laughed to himself. Maybe he could bring Fluffy home from the building. He had those tufts on his ears. 'I'll see what I can do, but you've heard the reports of breeder's cats going missing. It may take a little while to find one,' Conrad paused as he looked into her eyes, 'one we can afford.' Fluffy was looking better. He at least would be free, not the thousand dollars a breeder would charge him. Maybe he could have a look through the kittens at the nearby rescue centre as well. With luck, they may have one.

Hope's face beamed at him. 'Oh, you are the most wonderfulest man ever.'

'Yeah well, just you remember that next time I do something wrong.'

Conrad glanced at his watch. 'Heck, we have to move. I want to eat something before I go to work, and I have to be gone in an hour.'

The two of them left the shopping centre, loaded the car with everything they had bought and drove home.

CHAPTER NINE

Helga and Herbert had been busy the last three days. Only one day had elapsed after the injections of the infertility subjects and four of them were back complaining of headaches and aches and pains in their joints. Two of the subjects were sent home with placebo tablets and told to see their doctor. They had been in the control group, and the symptoms were psychosomatic. The other two, however, were running high fevers and vomiting.

Helga and Herbert placed them in the hospital area and treated them for the fevers by giving cooling baths and asprin.

After two days, the men started showing signs of recovery and were in better health on the third and fourth day.

Helga took their medical statistics on the last day, okaying them to be released home that day. She and Herbert had taken blood samples throughout their stay and had compared them to the initial blood samples they had given before they were injected with the serum.

The results were interesting. They could see on the second day the human cells had been attacked by cells from the serum. However, the cells hadn't been destroyed but had merged. This was what they had hoped would happen.

'Why was it only these two men who had the reaction?'

'Have a look at your medications sheet. These men are the ones who needed the sedative to calm them down. Obviously, it didn't calm their systems enough to prevent their human cells from recognising the introduced cells and attacking them.'

'It must be the increased heart rate which causes the reaction. We haven't had any word from the other subjects who were given the serum. I think it may be beneficial to phone the other subjects to check if they have had any reaction at all.'

Herbert nodded. 'That would be a good idea. After all, they are men, and you know how we men hate going to the doctor!'

Helga grinned at him. Yes, it was entirely logical. She'd make it sound just like a check-up call, so she wouldn't spook them into thinking something was wrong.

While Helga made the calls, Herbert completed the last call on his patients. 'Hello. As you know, you are over the worst stage. We've taken observations while you've been in here, and are sure there won't be any further problems. Now comes the slightly unpleasant bit, although it may not be.' Herbert grinned. 'I require a sample from both of you. This will be matched against the samples you gave when you first volunteered for this test.'

Herbert gave both men a plastic container, supplied them with some magazines, and pulled curtains around their beds.

'Call me when you are done.' he instructed and left the room.

Herbert met Helga later in the laboratory. He carried two sample jars.

'Have they gone home now?'

Herbert nodded. 'Each gave a sample. I don't think it was too strenuous on them.'

Helga shook her head. 'You men and your magazines, but you only get them for the articles. Sure.' She paused for a second. 'I've rung the other subjects, and none of them have had any problems. Some of them reported they have an increased sense of smell.'

'That's an interesting development; an unexpected side effect.'

They found the original samples given by the two men and prepared the slides with the ones recently received.

Helga used one microscope to see one of the samples, and Herbert used the other.

Both their heads rose simultaneously, with large grins on their faces.

'We've done it, we've done it. The sperm are moving and complete. Quick, let's get the electron microscope warmed up. We need a closer look.'

She and Herbert raced to the electron microscope and turned it on. The look of absolute joy showed on their faces. Could they really have fixed the problem of human infertility? All the years they and other scientists had been trying and experimenting, only to be let down, time after time, again and again. Could they really have accomplished it this time?

'Right, let's have a look at the cell structure.'

They prepared the slides needed to gain a closer look. Both of them held their breath as they focused the microscope. The view they had was the original sample on one side and the secondary sample on the other. The heads of the sperm in the secondary sample were fully developed, whereas they were stunted or misshapen in the first sample. Tails were visible in the secondary sample, where the tails in the original were short or missing altogether.

It was a total victory. The sperm had been rebuilt. One last test was required. Would the new sperm fertilise a human egg? They could only take fertilisation to the division of the egg for six stages. It wouldn't be allowed to go past that stage. There were strict rules and regulations about experimentation on human embryos.

Helga retrieved a human egg from the cryogenic chamber they were kept in. The solution in the dish would nurture the egg for the time it was needed. Herbert was the expert in this field, and Helga handed the dish to him. He prepared the sperm, and when everything was ready he piped the selected sperm into the egg. He withdrew the pipette, placed the lid on the dish and settled it under the microscope.

He and Helga sat back and waited. If anything happened, they would see it on the screen in front of them.

After a short time, the egg shivered. Helga and Herbert looked up expectedly. The egg shivered again and split into two. The egg had divided itself. The experiment had worked. They continued to watch. After what seemed to be a long time, the egg divided again.

Helga and Herbert were overjoyed. The serum had worked. A cure to the human infertility problem had been discovered. They looked at each other, held each other's hands and danced around the laboratory. They had done it, and it had all started with a comment made two months before.

****

Genetic modification wasn't anything new. The technique had been around for decades. Sugar cane, canola, beans. All had been genetically experimented with. Even livestock had not been exempt. What was required was the addition of another gene, or chromosome, to fix or improve the original gene.

Tests attempting to fix the problem of mankind's infertility had all failed because in a lot of the men the problem had been caused by a mutated common cold virus. The genetic imprint itself wasn't at fault, but the damage done by the virus was.

Another virus was needed to combat the mutated virus causing the problem in the first place. As hard as they searched, nothing could be found, until a chance comment by one of their assistants caused the head scientists to rethink the application.

The young woman had been playing with her cats. One of them liked its catnip toy and went into raptures whenever he played with it. Her other cat hated the toy; wouldn't go near it. She'd asked Helga if she knew the reason for one loving it and one hating it?

Unsure, Helga researched the data available, finding the assistant was right. Not all cats had a love of catnip. A gene within the cat's DNA was the reason. Helga too wondered if the mutation in man could be fixed with a genetic implant from another species.

She'd mentioned the thoughts she'd had to Herbert, and they began researching the genes of other species. Time after time they tried. Mice, rats, even pigs. Each time they failed, until they came to the feline species. There are many breeds of cat, but which had the different gene, and which breeds didn't?

Helga knew she'd seen a Maine Coon cat around the building, so she went looking for him. He was a magnificent specimen. Large, very furry, and extremely intelligent, as she found out. He seemed to know when she was coming for him and easily escaped.

Helga enlisted Herbert's help. After he'd received a good scratching and clawing trying to contain the animal, they had their test subject.

First, they tested him for like or dislike of catnip, finding he did seem to like it. They then drew his blood so they could screen his DNA against that of another feline, who didn't like the herb. The young assistant was given permission to bring her two cats into work, and blood was taken from them.

When the samples were compared to each other, it was found one of the woman's cats had a remarkably close tie to that of the Maine Coon. Both had identical markers in many areas. The other cat, the one who didn't like the catnip, was found to have fewer similarities.

During this process, the scientist were surprised to discover the Maine Coon's DNA showed up a variation of a gene which neither of the other cats had at all.

This variation was singled out and examined against the strand they possessed of the mutated virus that caused sterility in man. It was an exact opposite.

Theoretically, treating the mutant virus strain with the strand components from the Maine Coon's DNA should, by all rights, nullify the initial virus.

In order to get a decent amount of fresh DNA, they decided to take it from the sperm of the animal. The cat itself wasn't very cooperative with the harvesting method at all. Herbert gained another deeper set of scars for his trouble.

Shortly afterward, the cat escaped through a slow closing door. Herbert gave chase, but the cat had vanished in the maze of corridors.

Petrie dishes were prepared with both strands, placed into the incubator, and would be examined on a daily basis.

If this worked, it fixed the problem of the virus-borne sterility, and every male child would be given an inoculation. The mutated gene would be wiped from the surface of the Earth. They had done it with smallpox. There wasn't any reason they couldn't do it again.

After twenty-four hours had passed, the dishes were examined. In one of the dishes the strands had doubled in size. Under the microscope lens, Helga could see the cat strand had annihilated the virus strand.

It was a success. Just to be sure, they left the dishes in the incubator for forty-eight hours more. When they were examined, nothing had changed. The mutated virus was dead. The Maine Coon DNA strand appeared the same as before.

The time had come to make a serum that could be injected into human subjects and monitor what happened. Regardless of unknown risks, Helga and Herbert were sure they would be able to get volunteers for the test.

CHAPTER TEN

Conrad and Bill arrived on time, ten minutes before they were due to start their shift. They changed over with the daytime security crew and were updated on what had happened in the previous days.

'Hey Bill, look at this. Four men were admitted to the hospital wing. Two left later that day, but two were kept in for observation. Do you think they may have had the injection?'

Bill walked over and had a look at the report book. 'Go to the next day, see if there's an update.'

Conrad flipped the page.

'There,' Bill pointed to the entry, 'Two males still in hospital section.'

Conrad flipped the page again and again. 'Looks like they left yesterday afternoon.'

Conrad looked at Bill. 'I wonder if they had the same complications I experienced. The time scale is the same, sick on day one and two, then okay on day four.'

Bill shrugged his shoulders. 'I suppose I could have a quick look up in the labs, and ask Helga or Herbert if they are around. I'm due to go out on the first check in about thirty minutes.'

'I hope they haven't gone home yet.'

'No, neither of them leave until about six pm. Plus I can't see them logging out on the computer.' Bill scanned the computer terminal to be sure.

'Great, time for a mug of tea then.' Conrad walked over to the kitchenette.

'Hello, look who's turned up to see you.' Bill opened the door.

Fluffy walked in, tail in the air, jumped into Conrad's chair, and began washing.

'G'day Fluffy. Had a good long time off or did you spend time with the other guys on duty?' Conrad gave the cat a stiff rub behind the ears.

Fluffy started trilling. Conrad had never heard Fluffy meow like other cats. He had a quiet, gentle purr, relaxing to anyone who could hear it. Conrad noticed the purr was louder today. Maybe his hearing had increased as well. He'd noticed he hadn't turned the TV up lately.

'Is your purring louder today, Fluffy, or is my hearing a little better?'

Fluffy stopped his licking and sniffed Conrad. He sniffed Conrad's crotch, sat back and trilled loudly.

Conrad looked at him and knelt, so his face was in line with the cat's. 'What's up, Fluffy? Can you smell something? I haven't been doing anything bad. I've just been a little ill lately.' Fluffy headbutted him in the nose. Now Conrad was curious. Fluffy had never butted him before, but then, he'd never had his head this low.

Conrad ignored the feather-tickling sensation in his head and picked Fluffy up. He sat down, settled the cat on his lap and went to work, reading the printouts in front of him.

Fluffy appeared to have other ideas. He squirmed his way out of Conrad's arms, sitting on top of the papers, trilling the whole time.

Is he trying to talk to me? 'Fluffy, get off the paperwork.'

He tried to move him off, but the cat stood, moved forward on the desk, and glared at him, the trilling getting louder, if that were possible.

'Stop playing with the cat, Conrad. You've got work to do.' Bill's annoyed voice sounded from across the room where he was focused on a computer screen.

Conrad shook his head. 'I'm not playing with him. I'm trying to move him, but he just glares at me. Take a look. He's acting weird.'

He saw Bill glance across and sit back in his seat. 'He's never done anything like that before. It looks like he's trying to tell you something and as loud as his trilling is getting, I'd say he's yelling at you. I wonder what has him so upset.'

As if a window opened, words boomed through Conrad's head. 'I'm trying to talk to you, you stupid two-legs. Why can't you understand proper language?'

'Yeow.' Conrad's hands flew to his head, and he pushed himself away from the desk.

'What's wrong with you now?'

'The cat … Fluffy … I heard him speak in my head.' Conrad, seriously concerned, stared at the cat.

'Yeah, right. Sure. The cat just spoke to you.'

'No. He yelled at me. He called me a stupid two-legs.'

'You can't be serious. Cats can't speak. They're just stupid dumb animals.'

Fluffy's ears flattened against his head, the fur along his back raised, and his tail puffed, resembling a feather duster. Conrad watched as he stood up, stalked along the desk, leapt onto Bill's lap, and swiped him across the face, claws out.

Bill yelped, and half jumped, half fell from his seat. Fluffy landed on the floor with a soft thump, turned and began washing.

Bill pulled his hand from his face to find it smeared with blood.

'I don't think Fluffy likes being called a stupid dumb animal, Bill. I think he understands us.'

Fluffy jumped back up on the desk, walked back to his place in front of Conrad and sat, glaring at him.

'Hey, don't get mad at me, I didn't call you stupid. So, how does the mind speaking thing work? Can I speak to you the same way, or is a one-way thing?'

Fluffy gave a huff and stared at him. 'Pay attention, young two-legs. I and my kind are not stupid, or dumb. You two-legs are the stupid ones. You can't mind speak at all unless you have a little help. Luckily, I am here to teach you. Now, pay attention. I want you to mind speak your answers to me. If you can.'

Conrad concentrated. He often spoke with himself but had never tried to talk to another creature before. Could this be another effect of the serum?

He noticed Bill had sat back down in his chair and was dabbing at the scratches on his face.

'Why did you attack Bill like that? Why did you hurt him?'

Stronger, young two-legs. Talk stronger, I can barely hear you. You are whispering like a three-week old kitten.

Conrad tried shouting the words in his mind. This telepathy thing wasn't easy. He really had to concentrate on what he was doing.

'Ah. I did hear you that time. Maybe it will just take a little time, as it does with kittens. I hurt the older two-legs because he insulted me. You would have done the same. I have seen two-legs outside, fighting with each other because one insulted the other. I suppose he did not realise we can speak. Tell him I am sorry I hurt him.'

'Bill, he says he's sorry, but you insulted him when you called him dumb and stupid.'

The cat stepped onto the desk, walked over to Bill, and leapt into his lap. Bill pulled his head back, but Fluffy just sat there, purring softly. Bill hesitatingly stroked the cat's head. Placing his paws on Bill's shoulders and raising himself so his face was on an equal level with Bill's, he trilled again, then glanced at Conrad.

'Fluffy's saying he's sorry. He wants to clean the scratches for you.'

'What's he going to do, lick them clean?' Bill laughed nervously.

Fluffy trilled at him again.

'Don't tell me. He just said yes, that's what he's going to do.'

Conrad grinned. Bill needed no other answer. He picked the cat up, depositing him back on the desk. 'No offense, kitty cat, but I'll clean my own face. I don't need you to do it for me. I know where your tongue has been, and I don't want those germs on my face!'

Fluffy trilled, again looking to Conrad to translate. 'He said—suit yourself, but don't blame him if they get infected.'

'Hmm, I think I'll go to the hospital floor and find some disinfectant. That way they won't get infected. It's time for the first grounds patrol anyway.'

Bill picked up the keys and the radio and left the room.

'You can obviously understand me, so now let's work on you. You are trying too hard to talk. It is giving you a pain in your head, which is making it hard for me to understand you.'

The attempts at telepathy were giving Conrad a headache. 'Couldn't we just try this a little later, and work on it bit by bit?'

Fluffy cocked his head to the side. 'Okay, but we must keep working at it. I want to find out how, and why, I can finally talk to you. Also, before we go any further, my name is not Fluffy, it's Rufus!'

'Your name is Rufus … really! Cats have their own names—that's amazing. In that case, my name is Conrad. Of course, you already know the other man's name is Bill.'

Rufus trilled in response.

Conrad rose to grab some painkillers; his headache was quickly becoming a migraine. Rufus curled up in the corner of the desk, placed his tail across his nose, and went to sleep.

****

As Bill made his way around the building, checking doors and windows, he thought about Conrad's telepathic ability that had 'suddenly' arrived. If Fluffy hadn't brought it on, they would've never known.

As he reached the third level, he heard the sounds of a party. Opening the door, he was in time to see Helga and Herbert dance a jig around the room. Other workers milled about, celebrating. Entering the room, he crossed the floor toward the dancing pair.

'What's the party for? Has something been successful?'

Helga had grabbed him and jitterbugged her way across the room with him. He managed to extricate himself from her grasp and stood staring at the pair. Had they gone mad, or were they insanely happy about something?

'Yes, the infertility serum worked. Two men came in with fevers and stayed a few days. We ran their blood work and semen samples and compared them to the initial tests. The virus is gone. They are now fertile, and able to procreate.'

Bill watched and grinned as Helga did another dance around the room, this time by herself.

'Hey, that's great, but do you know if there are any side effects?'

Herbert walked Bill over to the electron microscope to show him the sample.

'All we can see is the virus that was here,' Herbert pointed to the previous samples, 'is not present in the sample taken a week later,' indicating the later samples. 'There does seem to be an increase in a couple of the senses. Sight and smell appear to be sharper than they were before, at least on the two men who presented.'

'But you have no idea what the children born will look like, or even if they will survive.'

'No, we don't,' answered Helga, as she rejoined them. 'All participants will be brought in each month for observation. When their partners become pregnant, they too will be observed.'

Bill glanced back at the microscope photos. He'd talk to Conrad before he mentioned anything to the two scientists, especially about the telepathy that seemed to have developed in his case.

'That's great. It'll be good to see people happy once more because they can have children. Congratulations to the pair of you.'

Bill shook their hands and left the room, leaving the two of them to continue their celebrations. He would clean his scratches later.

CHAPTER ELEVEN

Bill opened the door and walked into the security room.

'All okay up there, Bill? How's your face feel?'

'My face feels damn sore.'

He picked up his mug to make some tea. Conrad held his out to be refilled too.

'Did you happen to stick your head in the door to see what the scientists are up to?'

'Yes, I did, and I have good news. Let me fix the brews and I'll tell you all about it.' He grabbed the proffered mug, filled them both and returned to the desk.

Conrad waited as Bill sat down. 'Okay, what the news?'

'Well, the two men who came in did have the same symptoms as you. They also had a heightened sense of smell. But, the best news of all, both men regained their fertility. Herbert showed me the slides, and the immobile are now mobile.'

Bill had barely finished when Conrad let out a huge 'Whoop' and started dancing around the office.

'I'm going to be a daddy. I'm going to be a daddy.'
Conrad crossed the floor in two steps, hugged Bill and
planted a kiss on the top of his head. He picked up Rufus
and waltzed him across the room. Rufus wriggled and
struggled, Conrad placed him back on firm ground, and
sat down.

'Do they know anything else? Will the babies be
okay? You know, ten fingers, ten toes?'

Bill shook his head. 'I asked that as well. They have
no other information. It's going to be a wait-and-see
operation. Cross your fingers there aren't any surprises.'

'I'm going to start trying straight away. Hope's been
really down in the dumps lately because of the baby
thing. She's going to make a great mum.' Conrad smiled
at the thought.

'You do that. But have you thought what to tell her if
she does get pregnant?'

'When, not if. I'll tell her what happened, I injected
myself with the serum, and it worked. I'll tell her the
truth.'

'And when she hits the roof, starts accusing you of
being irresponsible, injecting yourself with something
unproven, possibly endangering yourself and her, what
are you going to say then?'

Conrad shrugged his shoulders. 'I suppose I'll have
to cross that bridge when I get to it. Hopefully, she's so
happy with being pregnant, she won't think of it.'

Bill nodded in agreement. 'I suppose it may happen,
but I still think, no, I know. She's going to say
something. So, how are things going with the telepathy
mind thing with Fluffy?'

'Um—turns out he doesn't like being called Fluffy.
His name is Rufus.'

Conrad noticed Rufus peering at Bill, the fur rising on the back of his neck. He was sure Bill didn't want another swat across the face.

'Rufus?' Bill shrugged his shoulders. 'Okay. One name is as good as another.'

The cat calmed, sat down, lifted a paw and groomed it.

'Well, we had a rest, and my headache went away. It's going to take practice, but we'll get better at it, won't we, Rufus?'

Rufus trilled his response and leapt onto Conrad's knees. Conrad began scratching the furry head and Rufus settled down in his lap, enjoying the attention. He purred softly, and Conrad smiled down at him.

'I'm glad the headache is gone, because in ten minutes it's your turn to go for a look around. Rufus will be staying here with me. You need your attention on what you are doing out there, not on language lessons with a cat!'

Rufus hissed.

'He needs to be able to do his job, Rufus.' Bill smacked his head with his palm. 'Geez, look at me, I'm having a conversation with a cat. How crazy is that?'

'Oh, I don't know, Bill. Plenty of people have conversations with their animals. The only difference is I know what he's saying.'

Rufus looked up and gave a louder purr.

'*Don't worry, my friend. I'll get there. It's so new. My brain isn't ready yet.*' He ruffled the furry head again. '*We'll try again soon, I promise.*' Glancing at his watch, he picked up the contented cat, rose, turned, and placed him back on the seat. 'Okay, I may as well head off on the round.' Conrad grabbed the radio and keys and reached for the door. 'You two play nice while I'm away. *Rufus, leave Bill alone and don't upset him.'*

Rufus gave a hiss.

Conrad concentrated. *'Please don't get Bill mad. I know you'd like to talk to him like this, but he can't hear you as I can. So please be nice to him. No more scratches.'*

Rufus gave a small mewl, jumped off the seat, and stuck his face in the food bowl. Conrad took this to mean yes and left the room.

He had a few things to think about as he walked around the building. What would Hope think about him taking the untried serum? Would she be upset, or would she just be happy to be pregnant? Would she want to abort the child if she found out? Would it be better if he didn't tell her until the child was born? What would he do if there was a problem? If there was a choice between Hope and the baby, who would he pick? Conrad knew the answer to that one, he would choose Hope. He couldn't live without her. Her smile, her laugh, her caresses. She would be the one he'd choose. To lose the child would be devastating, but not at the expense of his young wife. There would always be a next time.

He pulled himself out of the maudlin thoughts. Nothing would go wrong. He would have Hope and the baby. Conrad laughed to himself, picturing future life as a father, and Hope, a loving mother. A family would dry the monthly tears from her eyes. Conrad started whistling as he walked. Yes. Today was a good day.

The rounds took about an hour to complete. He didn't go to the floor the medical suite was on. Bill had visited the floor not long before so they wouldn't be counting on seeing him up there. Plus he didn't want to give himself away. As he arrived back at the security room, he saw Helga and Herbert exit the front door. They both had a spring in their step and smiles on their faces. Conrad waved to them as he entered the room. They waved back and continued on their way.

Conrad smiled. Rufus was asleep on the desk, and Bill played a game on the computer.

'Don't let the bosses catch you doing that, Bill. They wouldn't be impressed.'

'Nah, they've all gone home. I watched them leave. All okay out there?'

'Yeah. Nothing to report. Helga and Herbert have gone home too. They still look pretty chuffed with themselves.' He looked at his watch. 'Nearly time for us to leave as well.'

'Yep, you can go home and start making little ones. I can tell you're excited about this, you're like a cat on a hot tin roof. No offense intended, Rufus.'

Rufus opened one eye, gave Bill a disdainful look, and settled back down to sleep.

'Oh come on, Bill, you can't blame me. I thought I'd never be able to have kids, and the woman I love would never be a mother to her own children. This is going to be a whole new life for Hope and me. Of course I'm excited.'

'Conrad, don't get me wrong, I'm glad you have this chance, but it's not all beer and skittles. It's hard work bringing up children. You worry when they're sick, then you worry if they're going to be safe walking to school. When they get older, you're scared about that first time he or she brings home that "special" friend. That grey hair comes from somewhere, and it usually has to do with kids.'

Conrad laughed at Bill's concerns. 'Yes, but isn't it great I'll be able to have those thoughts and worries. I know it's not going to be easy. A week ago I never thought I'd be able to.'

Bill raised his hands in surrender. 'Okay, I give in. Just make sure they know their Uncle Bill is always there for them too.'

****

'Hope, I'm home and I'm famished. What's for dinner?' The air was thick with delicious aromas. Conrad's mouth began watering before he got to the kitchen. Hope stood at the bench, chopping vegetables and herbs.

'Air pie with no crust, just the way you like it.'

Conrad's smile turned to a frown.

Hope laughed. 'No, just joking. Rhubarb pie is in the oven, and rump steak, mushrooms, onions and potato on the cooktop. One of the ladies at work was just giving the rhubarb away, so I grabbed some to make a pie. We can have it with some ice-cream a little later on.'

'Oh, my darling. You know a way to a man's heart, straight through his stomach. Steak and mushrooms, yum!' Conrad grabbed Hope and spun her in a circle. 'Guess what you're getting tonight?'

Hope giggled and kissed him. 'I had hoped you would say something like that. I think we need some "together" time, so what do you say to an early night?'

'I'd say hello early night.' He reached for her, but she stopped him with an upraised palm.

'No you don't, mister, not unless you want burnt offerings for dinner. Besides, I'm afraid it'll just be cuddling tonight. I still have a few days before my time finishes.'

Conrad frowned, he'd forgotten about that.

'Now, go get changed. Dinner will be ready in ten minutes.'

When he returned, Hope had laid the meals on the table and was waiting for him.

Conrad ate while discussing his day, and asked Hope about hers.

'A woman came in today. She said the scientists at the university are experimenting with a fertility serum. Have you heard anything about it?'

Conrad wasn't sure how to answer. 'They're experimenting with all sorts of things there. Did the woman say anything else?' He stuffed a forkful of steak into his mouth so he wouldn't have to answer.

'She said her husband had been really sick for a few days and was admitted to the university's hospital. They took care of him, sending him home a few days later. She described his illness. It was strange because it sounded exactly like what happened to you.'

Conrad wasn't sure what to do. Should he tell Hope the truth or bend it a little? He decided to bend was best. 'Yeah, I saw the reports. The docs did have a couple of men in the medical section, but they were released in a healthy condition. It must be something going round.' An idea occurred, one that could explain the possibility. 'Hey, wouldn't it be something if I got my fertility back after being sick? You know, one cold takes it away, and years later, a fever brings it back.'

'That would be fantastic, though it's probably hoping for a miracle. We'll have to accept we will never be parents to our own children,' she paused for a second while looking at him, 'and that's-not-your-fault.' She jabbed at him with her fork.

'It doesn't stop us from trying, though, does it?' Conrad's eye twinkled, and he smiled.

Hope laughed. 'No, it doesn't mean we have to stop trying, practice makes perfect.' She grinned back at him.

'I'm looking forward to bedtime already. I suppose there's nothing on TV anyway. As I've been a bit under the weather, we'd better make it an early night.'

Hope giggled as he clasped her hand in his and led her to the bedroom.

CHAPTER TWELVE

Time passed swiftly for Conrad. Mind language training from Rufus, work, and blissful nights with Hope quickly filled the passing weeks. After four weeks, Rufus informed him his mind language skills were "*better*" and he should be able to hold a proper conversation with a member of the feline race. Conrad asked Rufus if he would like to visit his home, but Rufus declined, saying *"he had other jobs to do."*

Conrad wondered what 'other jobs' a cat could have, but didn't push the point.

One day while talking with Rufus, Conrad told him about Hope, *his queen*, as Rufus put it. The cat sat quietly, listening to Conrad, as he told him of the problems they had to overcome in regards to life, especially children.

'I don't know what my life would be like if I couldn't give my queen kittens. She is everything to me, but I'm sure she would choose another tom if I couldn't do what was expected. Is it not the same for two-legs?'

'No, it's not. I mean, I have heard of it, but I don't think Hope would leave me because I couldn't give her a baby. She knows it's not my fault. I'm glad to see you are calling us humans now, instead of two-legs.'

'Yes well, as I teach you proper language, I too learn your words. I think you speak well enough now to go on a little trip with me. Are you willing?'

'Sure, I'll go on a trip with you, but where?'

'I wish to take you to where my queen is. I want to show her to you.'

'How far away is it, somewhere in the building?'

'No, my home is not in the building. We can go when the circle on the wall tells you it is time for no more walking.'

Conrad thought about it. 'Oh. The circle on the wall is a "clock".'

'Clock'.

'And, yes you are right. It tells us the time to knock off for the day. If your home is not close, I will have to tell Hope I will be late.'

'A new word. This is good. We do not have "clocks" where I live. Yes, you should tell your queen you will be late.'

Conrad was intrigued as to where Rufus lived. He called Hope to let her know he would be a little late, saying he was taking a short trip to a friend's house. Well, it wasn't actually a lie. After all, Rufus was a friend.

Once Bill returned from the last patrol, they could both leave. Conrad started getting ready to leave for the day. A minute later, Bill walked in the door.

'Anything to report, Bill?'

'Nope. All quiet out there, but I have heard something from Helga and Herbert.'

Conrad stopped packing his bag. 'And …'

'One of the injected men has been back for a check-up, and he brought his wife. They did the usual test for pregnancy, and there are two happy people tonight. The wife is pregnant!'

Conrad smiled. 'Oh, that's great. So the serum worked for him. I wonder if it's going to work for Hope and me, lord knows we have been trying hard enough.'

'You never know.' Bill slapped on the shoulder. 'So, are we ready to go?'

'Yep, let's go. Rufus is taking me to meet his queen, but he says it won't take long. I've told Hope I'll be late.'

'How are you going to get home?'

Conrad hadn't thought of that. He and Bill always shared a car. He could catch a train, but they were few and far between. 'I'll take my chances on catching a train or a bus. I know they're unpredictable, but I've got hours until the so-called service stops for the night.'

'Okay, but if you get stuck, give me a call, okay. It's too far to walk, and it's dangerous out there at night.'

Conrad nodded. 'Will do, Bill. Come on, Rufus, let go meet your queen.'

Conrad opened the door and Bill, he and Rufus walked out.

****

Conrad waved goodbye to Bill in the car park, then turned to Rufus.

'Okay Rufus, show me where you live.'

'Mind speak only. You will have to place your hand on the door behind you.'

Conrad glanced behind him at the door. There was no place for a key and no handle either.

'Sorry Rufus, but I don't understand. How does it open? There is no handle or place for a key?'

'I said, place your hand on the door. There is no key and no handle as you understand them. The door is unlocked by your body.'

'My body?'

'Yes. The injection you took contained something not known to humans, and it is now in your blood. The lock inside the door will enable you to open it.'

Conrad placed his hand upon the door and heard a quiet 'click'. The door opened a small distance. He pushed it further open.

'Oh boy. It did open. Okay Rufus, after you.'

Rufus entered the darkened stairwell and waited as Conrad followed him and closed the door.

'Stand here a while. Let your eyes adjust to the darkness.'

Conrad was about to explain that humans couldn't see at all in pitch-blackness when he noticed he could see a little. The longer his eyes had to adjust, the better he could see.

'Heck, I can see in the dark. Rufus, is this another side effect like being able to talk to you?'

'Yes, Conrad-human, it is. The humans you call scientists captured me and took my essence from me. They mixed it with something else. Now you have it in your blood, you can do, see, hear and understand everything a feline can.'

'Normal humans can't open this door, can they? I know I have tried before to find some way to open it, but I couldn't see a way to do it.'

'No. To open the door, the correct blood must be

present. Follow me, and I will take you to the big box, which will take us to Catatopia.'

'What is Catatopia?'

'Are you going to question everything I say, human? Just come with me. I will present you to The Siam, then I will take you to meet Princess, my queen.'

Rufus led him down the stairs and toward a cabinet approximately two and a half metres tall and one and a half metres wide.

'Walk and stand inside, Conrad-human. You will see two glowing buttons on the wall. Press the higher one.'

Conrad did as instructed. Two glowing buttons sat at the height of his knee. He pressed the higher button. The next moment, his body experienced a heavy compression, much like he experienced diving, as if invisible walls were pressing against him. He found it hard to breathe, and his eyesight flickered. The feeling lasted only a few seconds, but it unnerved him.

'Conrad-human, welcome to Catatopia. You can step out now.'

CHAPTER THIRTEEN

Conrad stepped out into a room filled with neon lights, benches, tables and lino-covered floors. Seats sat pushed under the tables, and a refrigerator stood against the wall.

'So, this is Catatopia? Are you joking? Come on, Rufus, where are we really?'

'You are on Catatopia, my home planet.'

'Planet? This isn't Earth?'

'No, Conrad-human. We have left your planet, and travelled to mine.'

'But the lights, benches, even a fridge. This is all man-made?'

How was this possible? Man had gone to the moon and no further, as far as he knew. Walking around the room, human occupation was evident. A thick layer of dust covered everything, as he found when he placed his hands on one of the benches. Opening the fridge, he quickly closed it again. The sludge in the bottom smelt terrible.

'What the hell happened here?'

'The humans left a long time ago. I was only young when the last pair left.'

'So, what's it like outside this room? Will I be able to breathe the air?' Conrad was jittery. There was no reason not to believe Rufus, but he was having a hard time realising he was standing on another planet.

'Yes, you can breathe the air, but the colours of my world may seem a little different. The sky here is different to your planet's sky. Come, we must present ourselves to the Siam.' As they started walking, Rufus paused. 'Try not to get the Siam upset. He can get nasty.'

Conrad followed Rufus out of the room into a landscape looking very Earth-like, except for the colours of the sky, grass, and trees. Dust, hanging in the air, changed the colour of everything. Conrad had been caught in a red dust storm on Earth as a child, and that experience mirrored what he saw now. The red haze changed the colour of everything.

They walked along a street with houses on both sides. At every door sat cats, lots of them. Some sunned themselves; some with kittens, and others watched them walk past.

Turning a corner, they walked toward a large building. Letters attached to the brickwork over the doorway spelled a name. New Earth Council Chambers. Automatic glass doors stood locked open on either side. Entering the building, Rufus walked to a room guarded by an alley cat. Rufus placed his feet ahead of him and bowed his head.

'I wish an audience with The Siam.'

The red tabby disappeared into the room. Conrad heard yowling. He reappeared. 'You may enter. The Siam will see you.'

Rufus entered the room, but when Conrad followed, the guard cat sprang at him, hissing and spitting. 'You are not allowed, two-legs. No two-legs are allowed to see the Siam.'

Conrad saw Rufus turn around.

'Do what I did and he should let you through. He is young, yet he knows what you are. He has been told to keep the two-legs out.'

Conrad shrugged, knelt and stretching his hands out in front of him, bowed his head. 'I seek an audience with The Siam. I do not mean any harm.'

The guard cat sat and scratched himself. If it weren't so important, Conrad would have laughed, but confusion emanated from the cat. A few seconds passed before it looked at him and walked into the other room. This time the yowling continued. Conrad could also hear Rufus's voice in there. Then silence. The ginger cat walked back to his post. 'You may enter, two-legs. The Siam will see you.'

Conrad rose and walked into the room. A large Siamese cat sat on a pillow on a chair. He'd thought Rufus was a large cat, but this Siamese dwarfed him. Conrad looked at Rufus for guidance. Rufus was in the paws out, head bowed position, so Conrad followed suit. The Siamese stared at Conrad until he dropped his eyes.

'Rufus, my little soldier, has told me you can understand and speak. Is this true, two-legs?'

'Yes, I can speak and understand you, Great Siam. I thank you for allowing me to meet you.'

'Excellent. Rufus, you have trained your pet well. He is courteous.'

'Thank you, Great Siam. I am honoured.'

'Two-legs, what is your name?'

'My name is Conrad, although Rufus calls me Conrad-human.' Conrad hoped all this would be over soon; his knees were hurting.

'Very well, Conrad-human, you may stand if you are in pain.'

Damn, he had forgotten the cats were mind-readers.

Rufus hissed at him. 'Be quiet, we can hear you.'

Conrad was about to rise when he felt a paw on his head. He looked up in surprise.

The Siam stood in front, sniffing him and patting him on the head with his paw.

Conrad rocked back and sat on his heels.

The Siam walked over to Rufus. 'Rise, my little soldier. You have done well. It couldn't have been easy to teach a two-legs to speak properly.'

'Siam, he can talk because he has my essence. The others who have taken my essence will also be able to be taught.'

'That is no matter. No two-legs will ever live on Catatopia again. They cannot. Something in the air makes them very weak, and they cannot survive.'

'Great Siam, may I ask some questions?' Conrad interrupted, wanting to know more about how the cats had come to be here.

Rufus hissed at him.

'What have I done wrong?'

'You do not ask the Siam questions, Conrad-human. He has attendants who will answer those for you.'

'It is no matter, little soldier. I will answer the Conrad-human's questions. It is interesting talking to a two-legs. They speak in a funny way.'

The Siam sat down in front of Conrad. 'Ask what you will, and I will do my best to answer.'

Conrad thought hard. 'Great Siam, how did the ca—, I mean, the felines come to be here?'

The Siam sat looking at him. It was unnerving being stared at by a Siamese cat. It wasn't because they never seemed to blink, it was as if he was trying to read his mind.

'Yes, that is true Conrad-human. I am trying to read your mind. Do you not know anything about us? Your mind is not clear, and appears filled with many other thoughts.'

'I know nothing of this planet. All I know is humans must have been here before, as it's obvious from the buildings and felines here.'

'Yes. Two-legs, as we call them, were here a long time ago. They brought our forebears with them. Also other animals, horrible larger four-legs, who chased us; making our lives miserable.' Conrad could tell from the thoughts The Siam meant dogs.

'They built these caves we now live in. Very comfortable. We do not get wet or as cold as we would if we were outside.'

'Where do you get your food from? Do you catch it, or do you have felines here who prepare food for everyone?'

The Siam stood and walked toward him. 'Bow your head, Conrad-human.'

Conrad did as requested, then pulled his head back as razor sharp claws raked his face. 'What the hell was that for?' Conrad sat up, cradling the scratched area with his hand. Unintentionally, he had yelled out loud, and both Rufus and the Siam hissed at him.

'We only speak the proper language here, not incoherent two-legs language. Now, ask your question properly and be mindful. My claws are sharp. I can, and will, hurt you.'

Conrad stood. 'I came here as a favour to Rufus to meet you. If this is how you treat visitors, it's no wonder you are living here by yourself. This place stinks of crap, just like you!'

'Oh hell,' he heard Rufus think.

He turned and started walking out when Rufus raced in front of him, stood on his hind legs, placing his forepaws on Conrad's knee. 'Please don't go, Conrad-human. The Siam was not aware how different humans are. He has never seen one.' Conrad reached down, picked up Rufus and turned around. He stroked Rufus's soft coat to calm himself, as much as to calm Rufus. He could tell from the cat's panting he was scared. Would the Siam hurt him if he walked out? Conrad wondered.

'Yes, Conrad-human. The Siam would have me clawed badly, and it is highly doubtful I would be able to give my queen kittens anymore. She would leave me for another tom.' Rufus somehow managed to keep this speech from the Siam. 'Yes, I will teach you how to do this. Please come back, and continue talking to the Siam.'

Rufus was begging. Conrad couldn't refuse him. 'Okay, I will, but only so you won't be hurt, okay.'

Rufus answered with a quiet trill.

Conrad turned around, walked over to a chair and sat down. 'Okay, Rufus tells me you have never seen a human. I will let the insult go. How do you eat?'

The Siam jumped on the table next to him. Conrad pulled his face out of the way of those claws. 'There are boxes in the wall. We push buttons and food appears. This was set up by the two-legs before they left.'

Conrad was amazed. Humans had built this town, but receptacles that produced food from thin air were unheard of on Earth. If they could do it here, why couldn't they do it there? Hunger and famine would become a thing of the past. Everyone would be able to eat.

'Would you allow Rufus to show me one of these boxes?'

'Yes, I will allow him to show you the food boxes. Now I would ask you something.'

'Sure, what would you like to know?' Conrad was intrigued.

'You just picked up one of my best soldiers, and he did not struggle or howl. How did you do this?'

Conrad was a little confused. 'Do you mean how did I pick him up, or why didn't he howl?'

'Why didn't he howl?' The Siam growled deeply, sounding impatient.

'Rufus knows I am not going to hurt him. I have picked him up many times. I also pat him quite often.'

'What is this "pat" thing? Do it to me, but do not raise me.'

Conrad considered saying no, but after a look at Rufus, changed his mind. 'Okay, I'll pat you, but you should know; pats are usually reserved for reward.'

Conrad reached over carefully, stroking the Siamese from his ears to the base of his tail. The Siam purred loudly. Conrad could tell the purr was from delight, not fear.

'That feels good, Conrad-human. What else do you "reward" Rufus with?'

Conrad slowly moved his hand under the Siam's jaw and scratched his chin. 'Oh, this is wonderful, Conrad-human. Show me other "rewards".'

Conrad gently scratched him around the ears, making his way down under the feline's body. Suddenly, the purrs turned into a hiss. Conrad jerked his hand back, but not before the Siamese left a deep scratch on the back of his hand.

'Patting below is not a pleasant reward. You will not do that again. I do, however, like the ear and chin rubs.' The Siam sat up again and gave himself a quick wash. 'That is all for now. You can find your answers to any other questions from other felines. It is a kitten story, and everyone knows how we are here.'

Conrad understood they had been dismissed.

Together they bowed to the Siam and walked from the room.

****

'Well, that could have gone better. What a bad-tempered cat.' He examined his face with his fingers, the scratches stinging as he touched them. He could feel the dried blood where it had run down his face.

Rufus stopped walking and sat down against a wooden white picket fence. 'I did warn you. That is how the Siam is. He expects the best of his people, and he doesn't tolerate failure.'

'Are you scared of him, Rufus?'

Rufus fluffed himself and started licking his fur. He stopped and looked at Conrad. 'To be truthful, yes I am. He commands a great many people here, Conrad-human.

If I do something to displease him, he could hurt my precious Princess, any of my kittens, or me. I don't want that to happen.'

'Rufus, I understand, though I think you could easily take him. You know that, don't you?'

'Yes, I know that. If I did fight him and win, I would have to take on his job. I am happy doing what I am. I am happy travelling to your planet and finding new felines to bring here. I am happy to be with you and even Bill-human. I want at least one of my kittens to be able to experience that life as well.'

Conrad nodded. He understood too well. He wouldn't like to be stuck in just one place like the girls he had seen in offices, all crowded into little grey cubicles. That's why he liked his job. He could walk around, and within reason, go where he wanted to go. He had freedom. It was understandable. Rufus didn't want to lose his. 'Hang on. You said you brought back felines.'

'Yes, Conrad-human. Two helpers and I have brought back many new felines. Kittens and queens. We needed new blood in our lines. Is that a problem?'

Conrad shook his head. If he said anything back on Earth, they would never believe him. 'Yes Rufus, it has created a problem. People are missing their breeding cats. Many others are not able to get kittens for pets. The breeders have locked their remaining cats up even tighter than before.'

Rufus paused in thought. 'Should we replace them, or tell them they have to go back? They are so happy to be here. It will make them sad if they have to return.'

Conrad had an idea. 'Would felines born here be willing to replace those taken?'

'It would be an idea, but the Siam would have to be informed, and only he could say yes or no.'

Conrad pondered the idea. It was a possibility for a later time. He didn't want to confront the Siam again so soon.

'So, if it's a kitten story about how you arrived, you know the story and can tell me, can't you?'

'Yes, I can tell you. I needed permission. No human is supposed to know, but, as you are special, I can tell you. But I have a better idea. Let a kitten tell you the story.'

Conrad smiled. He'd like to be told the story by a kitten. 'So where is your house, sorry—cave?'

'Just around the corner …' Rufus stopped in his tracks.

'What's wrong?' Conrad looked ahead. A small kitten stumbled toward them. 'Oh, how cute. Gee, it's tiny.'

'Yes, she is tiny, and she is one of my kittens.' Rufus bounded up to the kitten, cuffing it and yowling loudly.

Conrad ran to catch up, rescuing the kitten by picking her up, away from Rufus's over-affectionate fatherly ministrations.

'Rufus, don't box her like that, she's only little.'

Rufus's reply was something he couldn't make out. He figured it was a form of cat swearing.

He hoisted the tiny furry bundle high to get a good look at her. She had a shocked look on her face. She started spitting and hissing, biting his fingers with her tiny teeth, which Conrad found rather sharp.

He placed her back on the ground, sticking his bitten finger in his mouth. 'Hey, I was trying to save you from your dad.' Conrad directed his thoughts at the kitten.

'I need no protection, you you, … Father, what is this furless thing?'

Rufus was mewling in a funny way. Conrad was concerned until he caught the thought … Rufus was laughing.

'He is a human, Wanderer. What you have heard of as a two-legs.' Rufus kept laughing.

'Hu … man?' Wanderer tried to grasp the unfamiliar word in her small mind.

'I'm sorry, Conrad-human, but it is so funny. Her mother did say she was like me.' Rufus tried to stifle his laugh. 'What are you doing so far from home, Wanderer? You are too young to be away from your mother.'

'I sneaked away, Father. I want to see what is out here, but they keep me guarded by Spook.'

As she explained, another cat raced around the corner, stopping suddenly and tripping over his paws when he saw Conrad.

'Wow, a two-legs.' The cat gazed in wonder. 'Wanderer, naughty kitten, come back here away from the two-legs before it gets you.'

'Oh, Spook. You spoil everything. My father is here. The two-legs is with him.'

Spook looked from Conrad to Rufus. 'Wow, I gotta tell Princess about this.' In the shake of a tail, Spook disappeared back around the corner.

Conrad watched him leave and turned to Rufus. It appeared he was just as confused.

'That was Spook, was it?' Rufus directed the thought at his daughter, but Conrad heard it as well.

'Yes, Father. He turned up one day and started playing with us, so our mothers let him stay. He can be such a pain.'

Conrad couldn't help but laugh. Wanderer spun around, startled by the unusual sound. 'She sounds like a human child. Just goes to show, there's not much difference in the young of different species.' All he heard from Rufus were more of the guarded grumbling thoughts.

Rufus picked his daughter up by the scruff of the neck and continued their journey.

'Let me carry her, Rufus, it'll be easier.' Rufus placed Wanderer on the ground. Conrad picked her up. He heard Rufus give her a command not to bite.

He cuddled the soft bundle to his chest and followed Rufus. Wanderer started licking him and cuddled into his warm chest. 'Hmm, I like this hu … man. You taste nice, not like us, but nice anyway.'

He began to lightly pat her. Even though she tensed at first, soon a contented rumbling purr emanated from her small chest. They rounded a corner and headed toward a house he would be happy to live in. 'Is this where you live, Rufus?'

'Yes. If you don't mind, I should let Princess and the other queens know you are coming in, although Spook has probably already told them. You'd better put Wanderer down. I'll take her in.'

Conrad didn't want to put the kitten down, but understood Rufus wanted to show Princess he hadn't hurt her. He placed her on the ground next to her father, and Rufus directed her inside with a light push of his paw.

Waiting outside until called in, Conrad glanced at the surrounding houses. Cats appeared on the paths, fearful and curious at why a two-legs was here. He read many thoughts directed at him.

After a bit of yowling from inside the house, Rufus appeared and invited him inside.

****

'Princess, this is Conrad-human, from the planet I have travelled to. Conrad-human, this is my queen, Princess.'

Princess sat up from where she had been laying and walked over to him. She sniffed his legs but jumped backward when he squatted. She hissed a little, but when Wanderer placed her front paws on his knee, she came forward, cautiously.

Conrad moved his hand over her head and patted lightly, then continued a stroke down her back. She held herself rigid, but relaxed within seconds. She purred in contentment as he continued to stroke her long coat.

Wanderer placed herself under his other hand. He tickled her under the chin.

'He-he-he. That tickles hu-man.' Conrad smiled as Wanderer trilled her happiness. He felt a movement on top his other hand, the one he was stroking Princess with, to find she was pushing down on his hand. 'Stoke me there too. I want to feel it as well.'

Conrad complied. He was enjoying himself, and so were they. Looking across to Rufus, he noticed the male cat becoming upset. He withdrew his hands from both Princess and Wanderer, hearing two disappointed mewls.

'You are here to meet Princess, my queen. Not to give pats to every feline here.' Rufus sounded cross, and maybe a little jealous as well.

'Okay, Rufus. Can you show me this food machine you use? I'm very interested in it.'

'Follow me.'

Conrad followed Rufus as he walked through the house. There had to be at least seven families of cats in here, all with kittens playing in each room. In their food room, interestingly enough, the kitchen, was a frazzled-looking Spook, teaching some kittens how to use the food machine. Conrad and Rufus stopped and watched.

'Okay Bibs, you press this button here with your paw.' The kitten Spook spoke to stood on his back legs and pushed as hard as he could with his little paw. The machine started whirring. A sealed silver foil bag dropped out of the lower chute. The kitten picked it up, carried it away to a corner, ripping it open with his tiny teeth. A meaty smell emanated from the package. The kitten quickly gulped down its contents.

Conrad clapped his hands. 'Well done, little Bibs.' He knelt next to the machine and ran his hands over it. 'That's a clever design. What happens with the bags once the contents have been eaten?'

'Watch what Bibs does next.'

The kitten, having finished his meal, picked up the ripped packet, carried it to a square-shaped receptacle set into the floor and dropped it in. Another whir and what sounded like a whoosh of fire. Conrad walked over to it and looked in. The packaging had disintegrated.

Conrad was amazed. This was high-level technology. Packaging and food created from what seemed thin air, and the rubbish able to be disposed of easily. While Conrad stood admiring the machines, he noticed something else he hadn't paid attention to. There was no smell of excrement in this house. It was incredibly clean in that regard.

Rufus seemed to have understood what his thoughts were projecting and helped him out with the answer. 'We have a small box for that too. Kittens are taught to use it when they first open their eyes.'

'This is amazing, Rufus. Man put all this in here, yet back home it isn't in use anywhere. I think I need to be told how all this came about.'

Rufus trilled. All the kittens came to him and sat down. Spook sat down beside the food machine and stretched out. Conrad crossed his legs and sat, joining the little group.

'Who would like to tell the two-legs the story of how we came to be here?'

No paws raised, and no kitten came forward until Wanderer walked in front of Conrad.

'I will tell you.'

'Please do, Wanderer, I'm very interested.'

Wanderer looked at her father. He nodded for her to start the tale.

CHAPTER FOURTEEN

'Many years ago, before the Siam was a kitten, this world was peopled by a two-legged furless creature. They came from a place far away through the metal box. They brought many things with them to build our caves, our food machines, and other things. Our ancestors came with them, as well as large smelly four-legs that chased and tried to bite us. They also brought flying things, which we are not allowed to eat.'

Conrad thought to himself. *Dogs and birds.*

'They worked hard with more machines for a long time, nearly one of our lifetimes, but then they became sick. The ones who were sick went back into the metal box. They did not return. However, the feline people thrived. Lots of kittens were born and with each litter, they became smarter. The two-legs trained them to do jobs, how to work machines with buttons and they learnt quickly.'

Conrad leaned forward, intensely interested.

'The bad mean four-legs got sick and died. The winged ones the two-legs set free. They still live outside. Soon, there were only two of the two-legs left, a male and a female. All the time the two-legs were here, they never had kitten two-legs. Finally, after making sure all food and other machines in the caves worked, the last two-legs left.'

Conrad sat back. 'Rufus, do you know which humans were the last to leave?'

'Yes, Conrad-human, I do. I was still a kitten at the time, and one of the last to be trained on the machines. They are the ones who caught me in your world. The ones who made the essence that is now in your body.'

Helga and Herbert, it had to be. 'Could they speak as we speak to each other?'

'No, they couldn't. I am sure we can only speak because you carry my essence within you.'

Conrad noticed Wanderer still sat in front of him. 'Thank you, Wanderer, you told the tale well. I understand more than I did before.' He reached down and picked her up, cuddling her into his chest and stroked her tiny body. She trilled with contentment.

'I did well?'

'You did.'

'Are you going to stay here with us? I like it when you touch me with your paw. I like it when you make me go up high.'

'No, I won't be staying. I have to go back to the other world. My queen is back there. I know she would like you very much.' Conrad glanced at Rufus.

'Do you think Princess would let Wanderer come back with us, or is she too young to leave?'

'We would have to ask her, although as Wanderer is already going outside the cave, maybe it would be okay.'

'NO! You can't take Wanderer. She is my special job, Princess said so.' Spook jumped in front of Rufus. 'You can't take her away. If she goes then, I have to as well.'

'Spook, you have all the other kittens. Who will train them if you leave?' Rufus tried to reason with the upset feline.

'There are others who can do that. Wanderer is special. I need her, please don't take her away.' Spook tried to crawl onto Conrad's lap to get closer to Wanderer.

Rufus looked at Conrad. 'What do you think, Conrad-human? Would your queen be upset if Spook came with us as well?'

Conrad knew there would be no problem. Hope would love to have them all, but it wasn't practical. A kitten and an older cat would be okay. Spook did seem to be attached to the kitten. 'As long as Princess says it's okay with her, then it'll be okay with me.'

Spook purred. 'Thank you, Conrad-human. I promise to continue to take care of her.'

Rufus stood up. 'I suppose we should go and ask Princess what she thinks.'

Conrad stood up as well. They walked back through the house to where Princess lay sleeping. Rufus nosed her awake.

'Stand back, she doesn't wake well.' Rufus stepped back a little, and Conrad followed suit.

Conrad watched as Princess woke. First one eye opened and then the other. 'What do you want?'

'Princess my queen, we need to ask you something. Please wake up.'

Princess rose, pulled herself into a sit, and gave her fur a few licks. 'Okay, what do you want to ask me?'

Conrad dropped to his knees. 'Princess, my queen would like a kitten. Rufus and I wondered if I could take Wanderer with me when I returned to my planet? Do you think she is old enough to go?'

Princess gazed at Conrad, and he dropped his eyes. 'She has been ready for a while. I can't keep her within the cave. Even Spook has a hard time keeping up with her. If you can tell me you will look after her, I will let her go with you.'

Conrad nodded back at her. 'Yes, my queen and I will look after her. Felines are very special to two-legs.'

A movement caught his eye. Wanderer walked between Rufus and himself. As he watched, she climbed onto his lap and settled down.

'You made yourself comfortable fast, didn't you?' Conrad clasped her in his hands, cuddling her to his chest.

A loud yowling came from behind them. 'You said I could go too. If you are taking Wanderer, you have to take me too.' Spook drew himself up on Conrad's knee as well.

Rufus looked at him. 'Behave yourself, Spook, and get off my two-legs.'

Spook looked down. 'Please Rufus, let me come with you. I can help look after Wanderer.' He looked imploringly at Conrad. The look broke Conrad's heart.

'Okay Spook, you can come too.'

Spook stood up on his lap, placed his front paws on his shoulders and head-bumped him. 'Thank you, Conrad-human, I promise to be the best feline I can.'

He leapt off Conrad's lap and sat next to Rufus, a big smile on his furry face.

Conrad stood up, still clutching Wanderer to his chest who had settled down to sleep. 'I suppose we should be off. We still have to get home somehow, once we return.'

Rufus walked up to Princess. 'I'll be back soon, my queen, it won't be long.' They bumped heads, and she washed his face a little with her tongue. Rufus returned the favour.

'Are we ready, or do you want to stay, Rufus?'

'No, I'm coming.' With one last lick, Rufus turned and walked to the door. They left, Rufus leading the way to the cabinet that would return them to Earth.

CHAPTER FIFTEEN

Okay, how do we get out of here without the guards catching us? Conrad held Wanderer close to his chest while he dug into his pocket for the mobile phone. They'd walked out of the transporter, into the inky blackness.

'*Rufus, Spook, stay close. Don't wander off.*'

Conrad turned the phone on and used the torch app to get some light. He only hoped the phone had enough of a charge left to get them out of the lower basement.

'*Rufus, am I able to open the door from this side?*'

'*Yes, you can. There is a small handle for you to pull on.*'

Conrad lit the way. His eyesight was keener, but none of them could see anything when there was no light at all. He hated the phone most days, but he was glad to have it now. With the two older cats following close behind, and Wanderer in his arms, he climbed the stairs. Rufus was right. A handle had been attached to the inside of the door. He grasped it gently, the door lock clicked, and Conrad pulled it open.

The car park lights were on, so Conrad switched off the torch application and replaced the phone in his pocket. Knowing where the cameras were placed gave him an advantage. Once outside, he again used his phone to call Bill. With three cats in tow, taking public transport was out of the question. The phone ring tone sounded twice before Bill answered.

'Hello, Bill speaking.'

'Hi, Bill. It's Conrad. I've got a favour to ask. Can you come and pick us up?'

'Sure Conrad. Hang on, who's us?'

'Umm, I've got three extra passengers of the feline variety.' Silence followed for a few seconds. *Surely Bill wouldn't let him down?*

'If one of them is Rufus, he'd better stay in the back seat. Your mother wasn't too happy with the scratches on my face last time. Who are the other two?'

'A kitten called Wanderer, and a protective fluffy black and white named Spook. Hope wanted a kitten, and Spook comes with the kitten. She'll go gooey over both of them.'

Wanderer looked up at him when he mentioned her name and purred. Spook stood on his back paws and reached up Conrad's leg, digging his claws into his pants.

'Spook, stop that. You'll ruin my uniform, and your claws are digging into my leg.'

'Sorry, Conrad human. Your furless covering is so thin.'

Bill had been speaking, but Conrad hadn't heard a word. He'd have to become adept at talking with his mind and with his mouth at the same time. 'Sorry, what was that Bill? I just had to stop one of them using me as a pincushion.' He glared at Spook, who dropped his head to gaze intently at the concrete path.

'I said I'll be there soon. I'll meet you around the corner, near the plantings. Make sure your friends make use of it. I don't want any 'accidents' while they're in the car.'

'Good idea. See you soon.' The phone bleeped as Bill hung up, and power in the phone ran out. Conrad led his little group to the place where Bill would be picking them up.

'This place smells wrong. It doesn't smell like home.'

Conrad stroked Wanderer's silky fur. 'Don't worry little one, you'll get used to it. When the day comes again, you'll see there's quite a bit of difference. There's nothing to be afraid of. Not while your dad, Spook and I am here with you.'

He stopped at the raised garden beds. The two adults jumped on top of the concrete walls and sniffed their way into the beds. Conrad carefully placed Wanderer down, watching as she scampered to be with her father and Spook. *'How do I say this? Rufus, Spook, Wanderer. Bill is coming to pick us up in the car. You need to relieve yourselves in the garden bed.'*

The three cats all turned to him. He swore they had questioning looks on their furry faces. *'You know, do your business?'* Conrad thought of a cat toileting, first digging a hole, positioning itself, then covering up the leavings.

'Conrad-human, you didn't need to do that.' Rufus turned his back. *'We aren't savages. We do know how to take care of that part of our business.'* He walked further into the bed, behind a small bush, and Conrad heard the scraping of soil.

'Isn't there a hole in the ground to use, like we have back in our cave?' Wanderer's thoughts only faintly discernible as if she was embarrassed by the mental picture she'd received from Conrad.

'See Rufus, I wasn't wrong. Sorry, Wanderer and

Spook, there isn't a hole in the ground. You have to do it the way Rufus is. Dig a small hole in the dirt, do your business, then cover the mess over again.'

Spook led Wanderer into the planted area.

Conrad heard him quietly instructing her on what to do. There would be a few differences for the two new arrivals to learn. Another would be food. Conrad didn't have a food machine like they had on Catatopia. He'd have to do some shopping on the way home. They only needed enough for the meal tonight, he could get extra tomorrow.

Rufus walked back and sat beside Conrad on the wall.

'Sorry Conrad-human, I forgot they wouldn't know what to do. You did well in your instruction. We might also have another problem. Spook and Wanderer have never seen what you call "a car". The machine may frighten them.'

Conrad understood Rufus's apology. He doubted the cat had ever needed to apologise before. Whenever he talked with Rufus, he'd always felt like the 'undercat'. *'Have you ever been in a car, Rufus?*

A brown and black striped face looked up at him and hissed. Conrad leaned back. *'Gee, okay. No need to swear.'*

The other two rejoined them, sitting next to Rufus. Spook pulled Wanderer to him with a paw and began washing her face and neck. Rufus followed suit and groomed.

Conrad laughed to himself. He wondered what the people walking past would think of him two large cats and a kitten sitting on a planter. It was a pity his phone had run out of power. The three of them together would have made a cute picture. There was always time for that later.

'*Spook, Wanderer. Rufus has reminded me you don't know what a car is.*' Conrad flashed them a mental picture of his car. '*It has a loud noise that may scare you when you are inside. I don't want you to be scared. Nothing can hurt you.*'

At that moment, Bill pulled into the curb and beeped the horn. Spook immediately sprang in front of Wanderer, arching his back and spitting ferociously.

Wanderer sprang to the only place she felt safe. Straight onto Conrad's shirt and dug her claws in.

Conrad yelled in pain but instinctively cradled the kitten. '*Hush hush, it's okay.*' '*Wanderer, please take your claws out of my skin. You're dicing me to pieces.*'

'*It's a monster, Conrad-hu-man. It wants to eat us.*' She hid her head in Conrad's hand. Her little body trembled, and she cried in fright. Conrad tried to soothe her, but the kitten curled tighter into his chest, becoming a small furry ball.

'Bill, turn the engine off. The car's scaring the bejeebers out of the cats.'

The driver side door opened, and Bill poked his head out. 'What? I can't hear you over the engine noise.'

Conrad grimaced in pain as Wanderer stuck her tiny needle-like claws into his hand and chest once more. 'Turn the flamin' engine off. The little one's terrified, and the other one is ready to throw himself under the tyres to protect her.'

Bill must have heard the urgency in his voice, because he reached in and turned the motor off, before walking over—slowly.

Conrad noticed Spook kept his eyes on Bill, not letting his fur rest. *'Spook, Bill is a friend. He's not going to hurt us. He's stopped the engine. It's dead now. It can't hurt you or Wanderer. Calm down ... please.'*

As Bill came closer, Conrad could hear him talking in low, soothing voice. 'It's okay kitty, I'm not going to hurt any of you. Don't be scared.' He approached Spook, and reaching his hand out, lightly brushed the side of the cat's face. A low rumble sounded from Spook's chest. Bill withdrew his hand. 'I suppose you'll have to get to know me before we can be friends.' He nodded at Rufus. 'I see the car's engine didn't bother you, hey.' He stretched his hand toward Rufus and scratched the cat under the chin. Rufus purred in satisfaction.

'Thanks for coming, Bill. I wasn't sure what else to do.'

'No problem, but where have you been? Hope's been over, worried sick. She said you gave her a call, saying you were going to a friend's place. I know you meant Rufus, but Christ man, how far did you go?'

Conrad chuckled. 'Bill, you wouldn't believe me if I told you.'

Bill crossed his arms on his chest. 'My eyes have been opened a lot lately.' He pointed to Rufus. 'To start with, a talking cat. So come on, where have you been?'

Conrad shrugged his shoulders. Well, why not. 'Okay, I've been visiting Princess, on the planet Catatopia. I've stroked and been slashed by the claws of the leader, the Great Siam,' he raised the hand with the scratches across the back, 'and I've seen technology, created by humans that you wouldn't believe. Food from thin air, a rubbish incineration unit, not to mention what the toilet does.'

Conrad began to enjoy himself. He could tell Bill fought with believing what he'd been told. Bill stood in front of him, his lower jaw dropping further and further down. 'You went to another planet?'

Conrad nodded.

'Really?'

Conrad tried hard not to laugh at the incredulous look on Bill's face.

'How?'

'We used the transporter in the third basement of our building.'

Bill looked at him intensely. 'There is a transporter that takes you from this building, the one we work in, to another planet?'

'Yep.'

Bill nodded, turned around slowly, walked a few paces, and turned back to face Conrad. 'Yep, you're right. I don't believe you.'

'So can we still get a ride home?'

Bill stood grumbling to himself. 'Yeah, I'll still give you a ride home. So it's Rufus and the other furry one here? Hang on, you said three.'

'The other furry one's name is Spook, and this little one here,' he uncurled his hand from against his chest, cradling the kitten, 'is Wanderer.' Conrad had never seen such a change come over a man. Bill took one look at the kitten, and all tension and anger left his body.

'Oh Conrad, she's beautiful.' He reached forward, but a rumble to his side stopped him in mid-reach.

'Spook, stop that. He's not going to hurt her.'

'Why does he keep doing that?' Bill dropped a glance toward Spook.

'He believes it's his job to protect her, and he is extremely protective. Here, you can hold her.'

Conrad carefully handed Wanderer over into Bill's hands. He watched as Bill stroked her with a single finger. Wanderer lapped every caress up, her purrs becoming louder and louder. 'Oh, she's wonderful. Are you going to give her to Hope?'

Conrad nodded. 'That's the idea. I'm sure Hope won't mind taking on Spook as well. With both of us still working during the day, Spook can look after Wanderer, and neither of them will get lonely.'

'What about Rufus here? Is he going to stay with you as well?' Bill pointed to the cat, still sitting in the same position. He hadn't moved.

Conrad shook his head. 'No, he'll meet Hope, stay with us tonight, and come back to work with us tomorrow. I've been told he's got a job to do, and he can't do it while he's with us.'

'Okay. We'd better set off.' He gently handed Wanderer back after rubbing her against his face. 'You'd better hold onto this one so she doesn't get too scared. Do you want to sit in the front or the back? The bigger ones will have to stay in the back of the car. I can't have them walking around and getting under the pedals.'

'I'll stay in the back with them. I'm sure Rufus will be quiet, but Spook and Wanderer have never seen a car, until now.'

'Right, I'll go and open the doors. You have a talk to them and ask them to behave themselves.' He left smiling after giving Wanderer a parting stroke under her chin.

Conrad nodded. *'You hear that? We're going to get*

into the car now. You need to lie down and not walk around. Otherwise someone could get hurt.'

'We understand, don't we, Spook?'

'Yes, I understand. We have to get inside the monster and not walk around. Conrad- human, are you going to be holding onto Wanderer?'

'Yes, Spook. You don't need to worry about Wanderer. She'll be safe with me. The drive won't take very long.' Conrad looked up from talking to the cats. Bill waited by the car, the back door open, ready for them to get in.

Rufus led the way, confidently strolling across the footpath, and leapt onto the back seat. Spook followed, but baulked at jumping onto the seat. Conrad picked him up and placed him next to Rufus, before sitting down and putting on his seatbelt.

Bill closed the door, walked around the car, got into the driver's seat and started the engine.

Conrad waited for the wailing to start from all the cats, but all kept quiet. He placed his free hand on Spook. The cat trembled with fear but didn't make a sound. 'It's okay, Spook, this won't take long. You're doing great.'

'Thank you, Conrad-human. I'm trying hard not to be scared.'

'Bill, we need to stop at a shop so I can get some food for the cats. Is the one around the corner from us still open?'

'Yep, it's still open. Five minutes and we should be there. I'll nip in and get supplies. You need to stay here with them. Anything else you'll need?'

Conrad thought for a second. 'Yes, I'll need some kitty litter too.' He leaned to the side so he could get his wallet. Opening it up, he pulled out a few notes. He could see the neon signs of the shop up ahead, and Bill pulled into a parking spot out the front. Conrad handed him the notes, and within minutes Bill returned with a full shopping bag.

He handed Conrad his change. 'I got a couple of toys for the little one, from her Uncle Bill.' Fishing in the bag, he brought out a dangly toy.

Conrad laughed inside. Wanderer had stolen Bill's heart. The man was in love with the ball of fluff. Bill restarted the car. A few minutes later, the car pulled into Conrad's driveway.

'Thanks for this, Bill. I really appreciate your help.'

'No problem, Conrad. I'm sticking around to see Hope's face. She's going to love the little one.' Bill stroked Wanderer's head again with his finger. 'Maybe your mum and I can babysit one day.'

'I'm sure we can arrange that, Bill. Let's get them all into the house.' 'Rufus, Spook. We're at my cave. Time to leave the car and meet my queen.'

He waited until both cats had jumped from the car and stood beside him, then walked up to the front door, opened it with his key, and walked in.

****

'Hope, I'm home.'

Conrad waited. He heard pots and pans clanging in the kitchen. 'Uh-oh, I don't think she's in a good mood.'

'I think you're right there, boy. Maybe I'll make myself scarce.' Bill stepped back and was about to leave when Conrad pulled him back.

'No, you don't. You said you wanted to see her face.' Plus Conrad knew she wouldn't get mad at him while Bill was standing beside him. *Yep, I'm a coward.*

Hope barrelled out of the kitchen toward him. The cats hid behind his legs. Even they were aware of her mood.

'What time do you call this? I had a special dinner ready and everyt—'

Conrad could tell she'd seen Wanderer. Her whole demeanour changed.

'Oh my Lord, you got me a kitten, and a fluffy one like I said I wanted.' She bent down, putting her face close to Wanderer's face. 'It's so cute. Please, can I hold it?' Hope held her hands out for Conrad to place the kitten into them.

He wasn't about to disappoint her. As he handed Wanderer over, Spook and Rufus appeared from behind him. 'Her name is Wanderer, and she's a very special kitten.'

Hope's eyes rested solely on the kitten in her hands. She hadn't noticed the other two standing behind him. 'And this is Rufus and Spook.'

Hope looked down. 'Another two, and they're both gorgeous. Are all three for me?'

Conrad chuckled. 'Spook comes with Wanderer. Rufus is her father and will be returning with Bill and me when we return to work.' Conrad caught himself before telling Hope Rufus had wanted to meet her.

Bill, standing beside him, grinned like a Cheshire Cat. As Hope knelt to pat the two adult cats, Bill leaned toward Conrad. 'Wouldn't have missed that for anything in the world. Damn, is she happy or what? Wanted one, got three.'

Conrad laughed. 'Well, now you've seen it, you can go home, can't you.' Bill looked at him with a small scowl on his face.

'Spoilsport. I'm waiting for when she wants to sit down and cuddle all three at the same time. Rufus ain't going to like that.'

Conrad directed his thoughts toward Rufus. *'Rufus, if my queen wants to pick you up, you're not going to scratch her, are you?'*

'You have no worries, Conrad-human. Your queen is safe as long as she keeps giving the chin rubs, oh, that is sooo nice ...' Rupert broke off all thoughts as Hope massaged the fur behind his ears.

'Conrad-hu-man, Wanderer's thoughts broke into his mind, *your queen smells nice, like my mother. When is she going to have her kittens?'*

'Kittens?' Conrad spoke out loud with shock. He glanced down at Hope, who was looking back at him. Bill looked askance at him.

'What about kittens? Are there more coming? I think the ones we have now will do. We can't hog them all to ourselves.'

Conrad ignored Bill's glance. 'Hope darling, why don't we sit on the sofa? That way you can put Wanderer down, and give the others some attention as well.'

'What a wonderful idea. I can have a blanket of fur.' Hope turned and walked toward the couch. Rufus and Spook followed willingly. Bill started to follow, when Conrad restrained him lightly, with his hand on Bill's arm.

'What's up? And what why did you blurt out ... kittens?

Conrad shook his head, still not believing what Wanderer had told him. 'Wanderer just told me, Hope has kittens.'

Bill shrugged his shoulders. 'Yeah, she does. You just gave them to her.'

Conrad shook his head. 'No, I mean Wanderer says Hope is carrying kittens. She's pregnant.'

CHAPTER SIXTEEN

'Pregnant? You sure? With kittens?'

'Of course it won't be kittens. Wanderer doesn't know any different. She thinks Hope smells like her mother. Pregnant females must give off a scent, and Hope seems to be doing the same.'

'Excuse me. Are you two going to stay out there, or are you going to come in here with us?' Hope's voice carried from inside the lounge room.

'We'll be there soon sweetheart, just talking work stuff to Bill.'

'So, this is fantastic Conrad. Congratulations.' Bill punched Conrad on the arm. 'Even though the shot made you sick as a dog, it's worked.'

Conrad felt the smile spread across his face. 'Yeah, it's great. But we can't let Hope know how we know. We'll have to keep mum until she tells us herself.'

'Hmm sure. Still, though, good on ya. 'Bill punched him again. 'Can I at least tell your mother?'

'No, you can't tell her. You know how women are about things like this. Sorry Bill, Mum will have to find out the news the normal way.'

Bill pouted. 'Damn. I would have got brownie points if I told her beforehand.'

Conrad smiled and patted him on the shoulder. 'Don't worry. You got brownie points with me. Now, before Hope yells at us again, we'd better go play with the cats.'

Conrad sent Bill in ahead of him, as he watched Hope enjoying herself underneath, as she'd said, a cat fur blanket. Wander stood on her back legs, nibbling Hope's ear. Spook was being stroked with one hand, while Rufus lay prostrate, upside down across her lap, having his belly tickled. Their contented purring could be heard from where he stood in the doorway. Conrad laughed inwardly at the picture, as he too, walked into the room to join them.

'Having fun there, honey?' He glanced toward the kitchen. He hoped he hadn't ruined her special dinner by arriving late. 'Something smells nice. What have you been cooking?'

Hope glanced at him, but didn't stop giving her attention to the animals on and surrounding her. 'I made your favourite, but I don't know if it's still okay. It may be a little overdone.'

He walked over to her, leaned forward and kissed her forehead. He couldn't get any closer without kissing fur, as Wanderer had climbed onto her shoulder and snuggled in. 'Doesn't matter. I'll eat roast beef anyway it comes, especially if you've made your special gravy as well.'

Hope nodded. 'I did. I thought I'd make a special dinner, as I have some news to tell you.'

Conrad sat next to her on a small part of the sofa the cats hadn't taken over. 'Great. What kind of news?' He'd play along, letting her have the satisfaction of telling him. 'Did you get a promotion? I know you've been after one for a while.'

Hope shook her head as a smile crossed her face. 'Uh-uh. Nope, though that would have been great too.' She turned slightly and grasped his hands in hers. 'I got really sick today. Everything was okay then I started feeling queasy, and I had to run to the bathroom.'

Conrad's face dropped. 'That's terrible. You haven't caught anything have you? Did you see one of the doctors to get checked out?' His good mood left him. Damn, he didn't want her to get sick. What could be so good about that?

She laughed a light laugh, like little shards of glass tinkling against each other. 'Yes, I had a doctor check me out. That's when I found out.'

Confusion swam through Conrad's mind. 'Found out what?'

'We're pregnant, silly. I'm going to have a baby.'

Conrad's smile spread so far across his face he was sure his head would tip backward and fall off. Bill rose from his seat, crossed the small space between his seat and Hope's and kissed her lovingly on the cheek, cat fur and all.

'Congratulations, Hope, I'm so happy for you both. Conrad, your mother is going to love this. I'll go over and tell her now.' As Bill walked by, he tapped him on the shoulder. Conrad looked up. 'If you think you're going to get dinner, you'll have to dish it up yourself.

Once your mother gets here, it's going to be a long night.'

****

He watched as Bill walked out the front door laughing. He knew what would happen. Bill would tell his mother, she would come running over, and he would have to listen to renditions of what happened when he was born.

'*What is that nice scent Con-rad-hu-man?*' Spook's nose quivered as he sniffed the wonderful smells coming from the kitchen.

'*That's human food, Spook. It's called roast beef. Would you like to try some?*'

'*I would like some too please, Conrad-hu-man.*' Wanderer raised her head and looked in his direction.

'Hope, what do you say I dish up and give the cats a few meat scraps to taste?'

Hope rose from the couch. 'We can do that, can't we little one?' Hope rubbed the fur underneath Wanderer's chin as the kitten stuck her neck out further, enjoying the rub.

Conrad reached over to take Wanderer from his wife's hands. 'Maybe you can do it, but the kitten may be a little young to help dish up. I would really prefer not to have cat fur in everything I eat, but I realise it'll be a struggle with two long-haired cats in the house.'

Hope begrudgingly handed the kitten over and walked into the kitchen just as Conrad's mother came through the front door.

'Bill's just told me. I'm going to be a grandmother. Oh darling,' she grasped his face in her hands and kissed him, 'You've made me so happy. I'd given up hope. I thought it would never be.'

She released him and raced into the kitchen, giving Hope the same treatment. 'You must be so happy, Hope. Finally. I know how badly you've wanted a child. You will be such a great mother.'

'Mum,' Conrad called out, 'Hope's setting up dinner, do you want some while you're here?'

His mother fluffed her hands in the air. 'No. No. I've already had something to eat. You two go ahead. I'll sit at the table with a cup of tea. There are so many things I want to talk to you about, Hope.'

'Mum, maybe that can wait for a bit. Come here and I'll show you the other new additions to our little family.' As Chloe exited the kitchen, he saw Hope's eyes roll upward. He gave a slight shrug of his shoulders. What could he do? His mother was here, and she wouldn't be leaving until she'd said her piece. He heard Hope put the kettle on as his mother walked toward him.

He held out Wanderer for his mother to hold.

'Oh, how darling are you!' Chloe cooed at the furry ball in her hand and tickled a finger under Wanderer's chin.

'Wanderer, this is my mother. Please don't bite her.' Conrad had heard Wanderer's thoughts about this strange human, and her little mouth started to open.

'Oh look, another one ... another two! Conrad, are you starting a cattery? Three cats?'

Conrad chuckled to himself. 'No Mum. The big tabby is Rufus, and he will be joining Bill and myself back at work. The black and white one's name is Spook, and he is like the kitten's nursemaid. We had to take them both. They couldn't be parted.' Conrad winced as

Spook spiked his claws into his flesh at being called a 'nursemaid'.

'Spook, please. There's no other way to say it.'

The claws retracted, and a pair of amber eyes stared up at him. *'I am her protector, not a nursemaid, Conrad-human.'*

Hope entered the room, a plate of food in each hand, walked to the small dining table and placed the plates on it. 'Conrad, put the cat down, grab your mum's cup of tea, then come and sit at the table.'

Conrad did as instructed, placing Spook on the couch with Rufus, and took Wanderer from his mother, placing her with the two older cats. *'Please stay on the seat. I'll bring you some of the meat to try soon.'*

'We understand, Conrad-human. We will settle here until you are ready, and your mother has left.' Spook leaned over Wanderer, started washing her, and Rufus curled himself into a ball and napped.

CHAPTER SEVENTEEN

Three months on

Hope sat outside the waiting room thrumming her feet on the floor. Conrad sat next to her, nervous tremors coursing through his muscles.

'What if they find something wrong? What will we do?'

Conrad reached across and held her hand. 'Nothing will be wrong, and if anything does come up, we'll deal with it. You're nervous, but you have a right to be. You're carrying a special bundle in there.' Conrad stroked the small bump. 'Believe me, I'm as nervous as you are.' He gave her a lopsided grin. He knew she was anxious about the pregnancy, but his nervousness came from another reason. He still hadn't told her the truth on how he'd become fertile again. Bill kept him updated with news he'd heard on the third floor.

A couple of the subjects returned after a few months, bringing their wives with them. Tests had confirmed an abnormality with the developing foetuses. Bill thought it had been the same men who had been in an earlier time with the fever, the same type Conrad had experienced.

Conrad hoped they wouldn't be given the same result.

'Hello, Hope and Conrad, would you like to come in?'

With all his inward thinking, Conrad hadn't noticed the doctor standing beside them.

Conrad swallowed the lump in his throat. He was about to find out if the chance he'd taken was a good one or a bad one. He grasped Hope's hand as they entered the doctor's office.

The gynaecologist's room seemed comfortable enough. The usual posters adorned the sterile walls. Curtains and an examination bed completed the look. Conrad's quick glance around the room wasn't missed by the doctor.

'Conrad, are you anxious?'

Conrad cleared his throat, though he still sounded a little hoarse. 'Just a bit, doc. It's the first time I've been in a room like this, and it's a little daunting.'

The doctor chuckled. 'I suppose it would be, for a man. Just as well you aren't the one having the baby.'

The doctor turned his gaze to Hope. 'Now Hope, how far along do you think you are?'

Hope looked at Conrad. He shrugged his shoulders. She shook her head and looked back at the doctor. 'I think I'm around the four-month mark, though it could be a little under that.'

'Okay,' the doctor made a notation on the paperwork in front of him. 'Have you had morning sickness?'

Hope laughed. It was a joke now, but it hadn't been a couple of months back. Hope had been extremely ill. Not go to the hospital ill, but still sick enough for Conrad to be worried.

'I did have extreme morning sickness, but it disappeared a few weeks ago.'

The doctor hmmmed, and made another notation. 'I suppose being a nurse you'd have known what to do to limit the symptoms.'

'Yes, I knew what to do, but because we've had trouble falling pregnant, I didn't want to jeopardise my chance of carrying to full-term.'

'Wise decision, Hope. Dependence on drugs at such an early time in the pregnancy can have serious consequences, but I'm sure you know that.'

'I do.'

'Very well, hop up on the examination bench. I'll have a feel of your belly, and we can have a look with the ultrasound.'

Hope rose, and Conrad attempted to, but she gently pushed him back into the seat. 'I'll call you when we are doing the ultrasound. You don't want to be there for the other part of it.'

Conrad realised what Hope was telling him. She didn't want him there while the doctor 'examined' her. Truthfully, he was glad she'd made the call because he didn't want to be there while some other man, it didn't matter the other man was a doctor, put his hands on his wife. 'Okay, I'll stay here. You yell when you want me to come in.'

'Good. Thanks for understanding.' She bent over, kissed him, crossed the floor to the examination table, and pulled the curtain closed.

Conrad tried to become interested in the posters and artwork on the arctic white wall, but couldn't help listening in to what was going on behind the curtain. He could have 'tuned' out his hearing, but he didn't. He wanted to know what the doctor was saying.

'You can come in now, we're about to do the ultrasound.'

Following the doctor's beckoning, he strode over to the examination table and sat in the chair indicated. To his side stood a stainless steel table with a monitor. His nervousness and excitement grew. He was about to see a child he and the love of his life had created.

He watched as the doctor smeared a colourless goop on Hope's tiny bump, and placed the sensor on the lubricated flesh.

Changing his view to the side, he watched as the computerised view inside Hope began to form.

'We should be able to see something soon, it's just a matter of finding where baby is hiding. At four months, he or she won't be very big.'

The picture began changing, and slowly, a small face revealed itself. 'Well, hello there little one. Let's see if we can get a better reading.'

The doctor slid the sensor around to the side of Hope's tummy, giving a slightly wider view than had shown before. Straight away, a little body came into view. A tiny, slightly triangular face showed on the monitor. The eyes were shut but looked slightly slanted.

The doctor hmmed again and moved the sensor further to the side. Another face showed, this one rounder than the first, but with the same slightly slanted eyes.

'You have twins.'

Twins! Two lovable bundles. They had not one, but two babies. Conrad was overjoyed and clasped Hope's hand tighter.

'Doctor, is that normal? The eyes being like that, I mean?' asked Hope.

'I wouldn't worry, Hope. It could be the babies are laying in such a way the features are distorted to the sensor. I want to find a leg or arm to measure so we can determine correctly how far along you are.'

The sensor slid a little further over Hope's belly, and again the image changed. Little arms and legs filled the screen, and as Conrad watched, something else came into view from one of the babies. Something thin and longer than a leg.

The doctor saw it too, and Conrad heard a sharp intake of breath.

'Doc?'

'Later, Conrad. I'll take the measurements needed, and then you and I will have a little talk.'

'Is there anything wrong? Are my babies okay?'

The doctor smiled at her. 'Nothing to worry yourself about, Hope. There are a lot of things that show up in early pregnancy that don't mean anything. It could have been the umbilical cord has become trapped between the baby's legs. At such an early stage, I think we can assume it will move as the baby turns around.'

Conrad caught the hesitation in the doctor's voice. This was something that didn't happen often, but neither of them wanted Hope to worry.

When the examination was over, the doctor handed Hope a disposable cloth. 'Here, you'll be able to clean it up better than I could. After that, get dressed, take a seat and I'll take a blood sample. Conrad and I will leave you in peace. We'll just step outside for a minute.'

Conrad rose and following the doctor stepped out of the room. As soon as the door closed, the doctor rounded on Conrad. 'Why didn't Hope tell me you were part of the University's Fertility Program?'

Conrad dropped his gaze to the floor, ashamed.

'She doesn't know, does she!' The doctor pushed Conrad in the chest with his finger. 'Did you think you wouldn't need to tell her?'

Conrad sat down heavily in the seat behind him. 'You're right, she doesn't know. I haven't had the right time to tell her.'

The doctor sat down beside him. 'You've had four months.'

'How could you tell? Are the babies going to be deformed?' Conrad didn't know what he was going to do. He truly hadn't thought about anything like this when he injected himself. 'Was it the faces and the eyes?'

The doctor glared at him. 'Yes, that and when one of them waved its tail around.'

Conrad gulped. 'A tail?'

The doctor nodded. 'Yes, a tail. Not an umbilical cord at all.' He stood, and paced away a few steps before coming back. 'I'm going to take the blood sample and send it to the scientists in charge of the trials. They are also going to have to see Hope.'

Conrad's heart skipped a few beats. Even the scientists didn't know he'd taken the serum. He reached up to the doctor and touched his sleeve. 'They don't know either.'

'What? How can they not know?' The doctor sat in the seat beside him, a look of incredulity on his face.

Conrad took a deep breath and quickly told him what had happened. Hope would be wondering why they were taking so long.

The doctor listened, shaking his head at the story. 'Am I to tell her what has happened, or will you do it?'

'I'll do it. She needs to know. I only hope she understands why I did what I did.'

A second later, Hope opened the door. 'Are you two coming back in anytime soon?

'Coming now, Hope.' The doctor answered. 'Conrad and I just had to have a little talk.'

A confused look crossed Hope's face.

'Later, lovely lady.' Conrad tried to assure Hope all was okay.

'Something is wrong with the babies, isn't it?'

'No love, nothing is wrong. We just have to see another doctor. One of the ones at the university.'

'Because you work there?'

'Yes, something like that.' Conrad kissed her forehead and followed her back into the room, sitting in the same chairs they had before.

'Just the one more procedure to take care of, Hope. I heard Conrad telling you about seeing the university doctors.' He cinched the elastic strip around her upper arm, lightly slapped an area to bring up the blood vessel, took the sample, and placed a piece of gauze over the top. 'I'll send the results of this sample, and everything else I've done today, to them.'

'Am I or the babies sick?'

'No Hope, there is nothing wrong with you or the babies. Be happy you are finally pregnant and about to become a mother.' He looked at Conrad. 'I'm sure your husband is going to be a big help to you throughout the pregnancy.'

Hope stood, as did Conrad. The doctor shook their hands. 'The university doctors will take terrific care of you, Hope.' He walked to the door and opened it for them. 'I'll email them the results I have at the moment, and the blood sample will be sent to them via a medical courier. I'll give them a call and tell them to expect you.'

Hope walked out into the hallway. As Conrad followed her, the doctor grasped his arm. 'Time to 'fess up, Conrad. While I understand why you took the serum, I hope your wife and the scientists at the university have the same understanding. I suggest you tell Hope what you did before you get to there.'

Conrad hung his head. Yes, he'd been a coward not telling Hope what he'd done. He prayed she'd understand. He hoped the scientists would understand. This could cost him his job, his marriage, his life.

CHAPTER EIGHTEEN

'What did you and the doctor talk about, Conrad?' Hope buckled herself into the car seat.

Conrad shrugged his shoulders. 'He wasn't happy with something I'd done, and also something I hadn't done.'

'What hadn't you done?'

Conrad didn't know how to answer. So often he'd run this conversation through his head, and every time the result had been the same. Hope, devastated and crying her eyes out, asking him how he could have even thought of doing such a thing. Hadn't he thought about the consequences? Hadn't he thought about her?

'Can we get a couple of drinks first and maybe some chips, and go feed the seagulls?'

Hope gave him that glare only women could achieve. 'Conrad Richard Adamson. What have you done?'

He glanced quickly at her. Yes, she still had that look. 'I promise I'll tell you. We need to get out of traffic first. I'll grab a couple of drinks and some chips, and we'll sit down at the lake.' He snuck another peek at her.

She'd crossed her arms and was staring out of the window. Yep, he was dead meat on a stick.

Stopping at the closest shop, he parked the car, got out and walked into the food shop. He'd decided to buy Hope a huge block of chocolate. He knew it was her favourite, and he'd used the chocolate ploy before when he'd been in the doghouse. Opening the car door, he slid in behind the wheel and handed the chocolate to her.

'Got you a pressie.'

Hope looked at the proffered chocolate, then looked at him. 'It won't be that easy this time, Conrad.'

He squelched an inward shiver. Damn, he hadn't seen her this angry in a long time. Starting the car, he drove to their favourite spot by the lake.

'I'll grab the blanket from the back of the car, and we'll sit at "our" place.'

'No, we'll sit right here, and you will tell me why the doctor, who has seen us through everything, all of a sudden decides he can't help any longer, and I need to be seen by a couple of scientists.'

Conrad wrung his hands in his lap. There was no way she was going to move from the car until he'd said something. 'Hope, I want you to know what I did, I did for you. You wanted a baby so bad, and I couldn't afford the IVF or any of the other procedures, not on the money I make.'

Silence.

'Hope, please say something.' Fear began its slow crawl up Conrad's spine.

'I will say something when you tell me what you did.'

There was nothing else to do. He had to tell her the complete truth. 'The scientists made a breakthrough in their fertility trials. Bill and I were working, and he told me what he'd heard. I ran up the stairs to get put on the trial list, but there wasn't anyone in the room, they'd all gone home.'

'What did you do?' Hope whispered, sitting forward, leaning toward him. Her face had lost colour.

'I searched the fridges, found the serum … and injected myself.' In a way, he was glad he'd finally let out what he'd held secret for so long. Conrad let the tears fall down his cheeks as he lowered his head. He reached out for Hope's hand and held it gently in his. He looked up and saw tears cascading down her cheeks as well. 'Hope, all I could think of was that I could give you a baby one day, something of you and me.'

'Oh, you silly, silly man.' Hope sniffed back a few tears. 'Was that why you were so sick? You could have died. Didn't you think of that?' She grasped his hand in hers.

Conrad shook his head. 'I didn't think of anything but being able to give you a baby. You always cried so much because you could never fall pregnant. It ripped me apart inside. I was scared of losing you to someone who could give you a child.'

'Oh, my stupid, loving, man. Don't you know there could never be anyone for me but you?' She leaned over the centre console and hugged him hard. Tears of sadness became tears of joy.

'I'm so happy you aren't mad at me, Hope. I know what I did was insane, but for you, I'd do it again in a heartbeat.'

'Why didn't you tell me earlier?'

Conrad gave her a sheepish look. 'I was scared to.'

Hope placed her hands on her hips and cocked her heads sideways. 'Am I really that terrifying?'

'Umm, yeah.' Conrad winced, as Hope punched him playfully on the arm.

'Come on, let's go have that picnic.'

****

The seagulls had enjoyed their cold chips. Hope was back in a good mood and kept patting and rubbing her tummy. Conrad noticed her grimacing ever so often. 'Hope, are you okay? You keep squinting your eyes.'

'I don't know what it is. Maybe the stress of having that disagreement or something, but I have a terrible headache.'

'Sweetheart, it's been a tough day for you. If you have a look in the glove box, there are some aspirin in there. Take a couple, or if you can wait, we can ask at the university for some. We don't have far to go, just a few minutes.' Conrad hoped it was a headache and not something else.

Hope shook her head. 'No, until I see the university scientists, I don't want to take anything. I made it through the morning sickness without needing drugs. A little headache isn't going to make me start.'

'Okay, it's not far now. You can see the research department from here.' Conrad may have been putting a happy tune to his speech, but inside his gut was squirming. Hope had forgiven him and understood his actions. Would Herbert and Helga be as understanding? He'd find out soon.

Conrad directed the car into a parking spot reserved for the security section. He hoped it wasn't the last time he'd be parking there. 'Well, here we go.'

Hope clasped Conrad's hand. 'My god love, you're shaking. What's wrong?'

'Herbert and Helga don't know I took the serum. I refilled the vial with distilled water.'

Hope took a deep breath. 'They're about to find out, aren't they.'

'I only hope I'm not sacked. I can't afford to lose this job.'

Hope turned him to face her. 'Conrad, if I can understand why, then I'm sure these very smart people can understand too.'

The way Hope spoke made him feel proud of her. She was a mother lion facing down a predator. She would protect her man, and he was that man. He could do no less. Together they would show a combined front, able to weather anything, as long as they were together. Yes, he was proud of her.

****

'Are you sure you took the serum?' Herbert sat across the table from Conrad and Hope. 'We've received the phone call and all the results the doctor found, but we can't understand how you could possibly be one of the trial subjects.'

Conrad took a deep breath and felt the quick hand squeeze from Hope. 'The night before the trials, I took a vial from the fridge, injected myself, then filled the same vial with water and put it back.'

Herbert looked at Helga and shrugged. 'I don't know how this is possible?'

'Can you remember which fridge it was?'

'Sure, I remember. It was the fifth fridge in the row. The serum was on the third shelf.'

Helga nodded to herself. 'That's the one that tipped over shortly before the trials took place. The vial that broke must have been the one you refilled.'

Herbert nodded slowly. 'That scenario is entirely possible.'

'So,' Conrad swallowed the lump of nervousness which had lodged in his throat, 'will you admit my wife, Hope, and I, into your trials?'

'We will have a look at Hope and inform you of our decision.' Changing her direction of speech to Hope, Helga continued speaking. 'You have already been through one examination today, are you sure you want to have another?'

Hope stood and pushed her chair back from the table. 'Yes, I'll do another. I just want to know what's going on.'

'I can understand that, Hope. Come with me, and I'll collect your particulars.'

Conrad rose to follow, but Herbert intervened. 'No, you stay here. We must first have a talk.'

Okay, this was the talk he'd been dreading. He was going to be fired.

'Did you get sick after injecting yourself?' Herbert began asking questions.

'Ummm, yes, I was very sick for about four days.'

'I see.' Herbert made notes on a sheet of paper. 'Have you experienced anything unusual since then? Bad headaches, or something similar?'

Conrad caught himself before he answered. He'd have to keep back the telepathy. He didn't know why, but he sensed it needed to be kept between him and Rufus.

'I've had some awful headaches, but my eyesight and hearing have improved remarkably.'

'Yes, yes,' muttered Herbert. 'Can you hear the conversation between Helga and your wife?' Herbert pointed the pen in the direction of the examination cubicle Hope had walked into.

Conrad concentrated. 'Yes, I can hear Helga speaking.'

'Good, what is she saying?'

'Hope, do you understand what has happened, how you became pregnant?'

'Helga,' Herbert yelled at the top of his voice. 'What did you just ask your patient?'

Conrad clapped his hands over his ears. Such a loud sound in close proximity hurt like hell.

Helga's reply came back, just as loud. 'I asked whether she understood how she'd become pregnant.'

'Thank you.' Herbert raised his voice again, then looked back at Conrad. 'Okay, so your hearing has picked up. Now for your second test. A mouse has died somewhere in this room. Find it.'

Conrad had forgotten the increase in his sense of smell. Now that Herbert had mentioned it, Conrad recognised the smell of decaying mouse. Standing, he sniffed his way around the large room, stopping ever so often to zero in on the smell. He finally traced the increasing scent to a corner of the room. Moving a small cupboard, he found the decaying rodent caught in a trap. He bent over and picked it up, then replaced the small cupboard back into place.

'Very good. I heard the snap of the trap yesterday, but couldn't remember where I'd put it.'

Conrad cleared his throat. Herbert looked up at him. 'Are you going to have me fired?'

Herbert made a steeple with his fingers. 'Give me one good reason why I shouldn't? You took something you had no right to. You could have caused serious injury, even death to yourself or your wife. You are an extremely irresponsible young man.'

'Yes, I did all those things, and yes, I am irresponsible. I need this job to support my wife and new babies. I need to keep paying for my house, and if you allow me to keep working here, you can observe me at any time.'

Herbert sat nodding to himself. 'Yes, yes. I can understand this, and I agree, you will be useful being here most of the time.' He mused a few seconds longer. 'Okay, I will not report you. Count yourself lucky.'

'Herbert, you need to see this.' Helga parted the curtain and called out. Her voice indicated urgency.

Conrad and Herbert looked at each other and hurried over. Helga had repeated the ultrasound. The image on the screen needed no added description. The face of a kitten, with tiny folded ears at the top of its head, filled the screen.

'It's happened again. Just like the other two. Definite feline features.'

'How about the other one? Does it have the same features?'

Helga moved the sensor. A rounder visage appeared, more human looking than the other child, but the human ears showed a definite point and the eyes did appear ovoid.

'So one has strong feline features, the other not so much.' Herbert paused. 'What about the rest of the body? Are you able to pick it up?'

Again, the sensor moved, this time to the other side of the small bump in Hope's abdomen.

Conrad moved to Hope's side and clasped her hand. Wanderer hadn't been entirely wrong when she'd said on that first night that Hope was pregnant with kittens.

Helga searched, sliding the sensor back and forth. Finally, after a few minutes, little human feet appeared. 'They are very active at the moment. I need them to quieten down so I can do measurements.'

Conrad concentrated hard. He wasn't sure if it would work, but he'd try. *Little ones, you need to be still, not move.* As he'd done with Wanderer, teaching her the human language, he sent a mental picture to his babies, picturing them laying still.

'Excellent. They must have heard you, Helga. We should try that with the other patients.' Herbert slapped her on the back lightly.

Conrad watched the screen as his children did as requested. Tiny legs and feet stilled. His children were telepathic.

Measurements were taken and noted. Hope's grasp strengthened as all of them watched another appendage come into view.

'Wow, he's a big boy, isn't he?' Conrad remarked.

Herbert shook his head. 'That's not what you think it is. With what Helga and I have seen before with the other patients, we believe it is a tail.'

'A tail? My baby has a tail?' Hope's grip on Conrad's hands became crushing.

Helga removed the ultrasound sensor. 'Hope, do not stress yourself, it isn't good for the babies.'

'How can you expect me not to be stressed! At least one of my children looks like a cat. With a tail, and both have pointy ears.' Hope's voice became louder and shriller. 'You say this is happening to someone else as well. Why? Why is this happening to me?' She sat up and rounded onto Conrad. 'Did you know this would happen? Did you?'

Conrad stepped back. 'No, this is the first I have known about this. I didn't know this would happen.'

Hope burst into tears. 'I've wanted a baby for so long, and now I'm having twins, and I find out they're kittens?'

Conrad held her tight to him while she sobbed against his chest. He kissed the top of her head gently. 'Sweetheart, does it really matter?' What a stupid thing to say, of course, it damn well matters. It matters to her that her babies aren't entirely human. 'After all, you love cats, don't you? You love Rufus, Wanderer, and Spook. You've said so many times they are like your children.'

Hope pulled her head away from his chest. Had he been able to talk her around, even if it was just a little? Could she look at this as being something good? 'Yes, I love Wanderer and Spook, and sometimes they are just like human children, getting into trouble.'

'When you have contained yourselves, please get dressed and meet us back in the other room,' Herbert barked.

Hope gave a smirk. 'He doesn't have a very good bedside manner, does he?'

Conrad smiled, at least she wasn't crying anymore. He could understand how much of a shock it had been. 'Maybe he's not good around emotional women.'

Hope punched him on the arm. 'Yes, seems to be a man thing, doesn't it.' She slid off the examination table after Conrad found a paper towel she could wipe the ultrasound gel off her abdomen. 'You go outside, I'll just be a minute.'

Conrad held her at arm's length and looked into her eyes. 'Are you sure, I can stay here if you want me to?'

Hope waved her hand in the air. 'No, it's okay. I'll just get myself together. I'll only be a couple of minutes.'

'Okay, if you insist, but I'll be only a metre away, just on the other side of the curtain.'

Hope pushed him out. 'Yes, I'm sure.'

Conrad closed the curtain behind him.

****

Hope leaned back, bared her midriff again, and stroked her bulge. Did it really matter what the children looked like? As long as they were healthy, nothing else really mattered. She was pregnant, and she was having twins. Even if there had been a problem, she would have still wanted the baby. The little lives inside her were a mixture of her and Conrad, and somewhere along the line, a cat.

'My little ones, I don't care what you look like, even if you have fur, pointy ears, and a tail. You are mine. I'm your mother, and will always love you. You are two precious little souls, and I will always protect you.'

Hope straightened herself out, wiped the drying tears from her cheeks, opened the curtain and strode out into Conrad's arms.

****

He smiled down at her. 'I heard what you said to the babies, and I agree totally. It doesn't matter to me at all. I'm their daddy, and I'll protect you and them.'

She smiled up at him. 'Let's see what they can tell us.'

Together they walked into the other office and sat down.

Herbert cleared his throat. 'Ahem. What we have been able to ascertain is that when Conrad injected himself, he had a high-stress level, and had been exerting himself.'

Conrad nodded. 'Yes, that's right. I had run up the stairs and was sweating heavily.'

'It appears that under stress, there is a side effect. The other two patients were also highly anxious when given the serum, and they too experienced the fever.' He looked toward Conrad. 'When we became aware of the effect, we called in all the trials who had been given the actual serum and tested their spouses. All were pregnant. All foetuses appeared normal. The limbs are slightly longer, but apart from that one difference, all were okay—except for the two who had the fever.'

Conrad now understood why Herbert had asked him the questions at the start. The other two men also had the increased senses. He wondered if they also had the telepathy. 'So the wives of those two men also have pregnancies with feline features?'

'Yes, the other two pregnancies are the same as yours.' Helga paused, looking at Hope, a pained expression crossing her face. 'We will give you a choice, as we gave the other two women. If you do not wish to keep the children or continue with the pregnancy, we will allow a termination.'

Hope sprang from her chair, knocking it backward. She wrapped her arms around her stomach. 'You are not touching my babies. I don't care if they have fur or tails. They can be pink and purple as far as I'm concerned. They are my babies and no one will take them away from me.'

Helga stood up. 'Hope, please don't judge us. We don't want to take your babies, and I'm so glad to hear you want to keep them. Please sit down again, it was only an offer.'

Conrad held his hand out to Hope and coaxed her back into the chair. He kept holding her hand as Helga and Herbert continued.

'When we constructed the serum, we used parts of the feline DNA. A gene within the DNA had a cancelling factor on the virus, which had caused the infertility problem. As no other animal is affected by the flu mutation causing the infertility, we had no choice but to test it on humans first.'

'That's when I took the serum. The night before you were to have the trials.'

'Yes. We didn't realise what had happened as there was an accident in the lab the next morning. Only one vial had been broken. That vial must have been the one you used.'

'So, because you used a gene from the feline DNA, all the children will be cat-like?' Conrad could tell Hope was trying to understand what had happened. As a nurse, she knew more about the human body than he did. He decided to sit back and let her ask the questions. He already knew where the feline DNA had come from. He'd let Hope know later.

'Not as far as we can tell. Like I said before, the other pregnancies are progressing well. Ultrasounds taken show no "changes" in the foetuses, apart from slightly longer limbs.'

'With everything that has happened, am I to understand that all medical situations are to be handled here?'

'Yes. When the children are due to be born, a qualified obstetrician will be brought in. I believe you already know him. He's the doctor you saw today.'

'Fine.' Hope was happy to know someone qualified would be around, and she wouldn't be subjecting her children to academic scientists. 'How long is gestation? Are you assuming the normal nine months?'

Herbert and Helga shrugged at the same time. 'Truthfully, we have no idea. We suspect the gestational time would be a normal one, but as your and the two other pregnancies are slightly different, we suspect the gestational time may also be different. We will give you a phone number to call when labour begins, but in the meantime, we wish to see you every two weeks until the seventh month, and then every week after that until delivery.'

Helga rose and left the table. Herbert took Conrad and Hope's details to enter into the trial database. When Helga returned, she brought with her information sheets and dietary requirements.

'We prefer the test subjects to eat a specific diet, and refrain from any type of drug taking, even aspirin. If you feel unwell, please call us and return here to be treated.'

As they all rose, Herbert stopped them before they took a single step from the table. 'I hope you understand the need for secrecy. Until the babies are born, we have no idea what they will look and behave like. With so many infertile people in the world, there would be a rush on the treatment. Before we can give it out, we need to be sure of the end result.'

Conrad wasn't sure he liked the term 'end result' when he knew they were talking about his children, but he did understand the need for secrecy. He glanced at Hope and read the understanding in her eyes. 'Yes, we understand. No one will hear anything from us.'

'Excellent. We hope to see you soon.'

Conrad placed his arm around Hope and guided her from the room, through the building and out into the car park. As they walked toward their car, Hope started laughing.

'What's so funny?' Conrad asked.

Hope pointed to the car. 'Someone is waiting for us.'

Conrad looked up at the car. Sure enough, sitting on the roof was Rufus.

'Why are you here? This is not the time for you to take your exercise.'

Conrad still hadn't been able to convey the concept of work to Rufus. *'We needed to see the scientists. Hope's babies are different'.* Conrad sent an image of a cat/human hybrid to Rufus telepathically.

Rufus hissed. *'What is that? It is not a cat and not a huuuman.'*

Conrad caught the feeling of disgust Rufus communicated back. He was shocked. *'Why do you think that is bad? These are going to be my children, my kittens.'*

'Is this happening because my seed was used?'

'Yes, the gene they used from your seed is strong and has affected the way the babies will be.'

Rufus hissed again. *'The Great Siam must hear about this. He will not be pleased.'*

'Rufus doesn't seem to be happy at all. I wonder what is wrong with him?' Hope stretched out to pat him, but Rufus backed away and hissed at her.

'Rufus, behave yourself. How would you like it if I was rude to your queen, like you are being now? Remember, Hope now carries your genes too.'

Rufus shook himself, gave a growl, but walked forward toward Hope. He allowed himself to be stroked for a minute or two, then leapt from the car to the ground. He rubbed himself against Hope's legs, and walked off.

'Your queen seems to have accepted my apologies. I will leave to report to the Great Siam.'

Conrad watched as Rufus stalked off, tail high in the air.

'He didn't seem too happy, and why on earth did he hiss at me?'

Conrad opened the door and stood to the side. 'He probably smelt Herbert and Helga on you. Where do you think they got the cat gene from?'

Hope half sat on the car seat, her mouth agape. 'Oh. He wouldn't be happy then. Poor Rufus.'

As Conrad climbed into his own seat, Hope turned to him. 'So if the feline gene came from Rufus, I wonder if the children will have his colouring or ours?'

It was Conrad's turn to have his mouth agape. That was another thing he hadn't thought of. 'I suppose in five months or so, we'll find out.'

CHAPTER NINETEEN

Rufus grumbled to himself all the way back to Catatopia. His pure blood being mixed with the two-legs, it was unthinkable. He was happy for Conrad-human to finally father kittens, but he didn't expect his essence would be tainted by the two-legs blood. The Great Siam would not be happy at all, but what could they do?

Another problem he faced was the inability to bring any more pure bloods back. The distance they had to cover had on the two-legs planet had become too great, and he'd already lost queens and a kitten to the roaring metal monsters the two-legs called "cars". He needed the humans' help, but after the recent revelation, he wasn't sure the Great Siam would allow such a partnership.

With so many thoughts in his mind, he nearly walked past the Great Siam's cave. Rufus pulled up as one of the guards called out to him.

'Hey, you with your head in the clouds. The Great Siam wants to see you.'

Rufus focused on the job at hand, steeled himself and strode confidently into the building. Before he entered the door, he stretched his paws out before him and touched his head to his legs.

'Great Siam, it is your soldier, Rufus. I request an audience with Your High Furriness.' Rufus knew the term was pompous from a discussion he and Conrad-human had, but the Great Siam liked it, so everyone had to bow before him.

'Come, my little soldier. You are late in giving me news of the two-legs planet.'

The Great Siam scanned the empty space behind Rufus. 'I cannot see any new queens or kittens, has something happened?'

Rufus readied himself for the anger outburst he foresaw coming his way. 'I'm sorry, Great Siam, I haven't been able to bring any more back to add to our blood lines. The distances are further than is safe, no more counted in only a paws time, but in two or three light times. The metal machines that roar on the hard black ground take the lives of those who wish to join us here. I'm sorry, Great Siam, but I can do no more without help from our two-legs friends.' Rufus bowed his head to his paws again, waiting for the raking of claws from the Siam.

'Rufus, my little soldier, you have done well. Our caves are becoming crowded. I have been thinking of sending some of our youngsters to the two-legs world. Would you think this possible?'

Rufus sat up, stunned at the words he heard. 'I'm sure something can be worked out. You do not mean for our youngsters to be left to fend for themselves, do you, Great Siam?'

'No. They must be housed as you have been and your daughter is. I believe for this we will need the assistance of your two-legs.'

'I will ask him, Great Siam.'

The Siamese leapt from his seat, landing in front of Rufus. He pushed his face against Rufus's and snarled. 'You will not ask him, you will tell him. It is an order, and he will not disobey.'

Rufus nearly laughed. The Great Siam was getting a little too big for his dainty paws if he thought he could order the two-legs around. 'Of course, Great Siam, I will inform him of your wishes.'

'Hmmm, so you shall. Is there any other news you bring for me?'

Rufus hung his head. 'You remember the trial I had when the two-legs attacked me and took my seed?'

'Yes, I remember. You fought them bravely, but they succeeded.'

Rufus wasn't sure how to say what had happened. 'My two-legs obtained some of the mixture they made with my seed and injected it into himself. His queen is now pregnant with kittens.'

The Siam cocked his head to the side. 'I do not see the problem.'

'Two-legs don't have kittens like our kittens, they have two-legs kittens.'

'Yes, this I understand. What are you holding back, Rufus?'

Rufus sighed deeply. 'The two-legs queen is pregnant with a two-legs kitten cross. My blood line now runs in the bodies of the two-legs kittens. Not only one, but many of them.'

The Great Siam laughed out loud. 'Ha-ha-ha-ha. Oh, my little soldier, you need not be worried. You will not be punished, it was not of your doing. If anything, maybe your blood in the bodies of the two-legs kittens will make them proper people, who will be smart and be able to at least speak properly.'

The Siam didn't care. Rufus shook his head, stunned at what he was hearing. He'd never understand what ran through his leader's head.

'You are not appalled by what has happened?'

'Not at all, I think it is a great moment. It is something we can make use of later, when the huuuman kittens are older.' He took a few steps back toward his seat, then turned to face Rufus again. 'You are dismissed. See your queen. When you are next in the two-legs world, tell your human what he must do.'

Rufus knelt with his paws forward and head on his legs. 'I will, Great Siam.' Standing, he walked backward until he had left the room. Walking around the corner of the building, he sat and smoothed down his ruffled fur. One day the Siam would go too far, and Rufus would make his stand. Once he thought he was presentable, he trotted off to see Princess. He missed her more every time he left. Maybe it was time for someone else to take over, so he could stay home with his queen.

****

'Are you sure Hope is okay with all this? Bill asked as they turned the corner into the underground car park.

'Yep. They gave her the option of terminating, and she nearly ripped their heads off.'

'And when you got home?' Bill drove down the ramp and parked in the area kept free for Security personnel.

'Got home, all was okay. She picked up Wanderer and told her everything that had happened.'

'Did Wanderer understand?'

'She did after I told her in what the cats class as "proper language".'

Bill released his seat belt, Conrad did the same, and both stepped out of the car. 'So Wanderer doesn't understand our language yet?' Bill spoke across the roof of the car.

'No, neither does Rufus. As far as they are concerned, we just make wailing noises.'

Bill laughed. 'That's funny, because that's what we think they do.'

Conrad laughed with him.

As they were about to enter the lift reserved for them, Rufus stepped from the shadows. *'Conrad-human, we need to talk.'*

'I'll be up soon Bill, Rufus wants to talk.'

'Okay, but don't be long. We left a little late today.' He glanced at his watch. 'You've got a quick five minutes.'

Conrad waved his acceptance. Bill entered the lift and the doors closed.

'What's up, Rufus? I wasn't sure you were going to talk to me again, after the last time I saw you.'

'You are my human, and I will always talk to you. I didn't like what the other two-legs have done to your queen, but I am told by Princess it doesn't matter what the kittens are like, your queen will love them all the

same.'

Conrad had to smile. Hope had said virtually word for word the same thing to him. Maybe the females of all races and species felt the same. *'I don't think that's the only thing on your mind. I sense you are uneasy about something.'*

'You are right. I can no longer find suitable queens and kittens to take to Catatopia. All the purebreds are too far away. I need your help. Also, the Great Siam wants our kittens to come to your world, but they must be placed with people who will care for them.'

Conrad looked at his watch. The five minutes had flown by. 'Rufus, I'll think about it and attempt to come up with a workable plan. Right now, I need to start my exercise. Bill is waiting for me.'

'I understand. Let me know when we can talk again.' Rufus turned and walked toward the door to the basement. He stopped before opening the door. 'Please make it soon.'

'I'll do my best.' Conrad watched as Rufus rubbed against the door; it opened, and he walked through, the door closing silently after him.

'How on earth am I going to get new blood lines for them, and distribute kittens into good homes?' Conrad shook his head in frustration.

A short elevator ride to the upper security room later, Conrad opened the door and looked around. Bill was the only occupant. 'The other two take off already?'

'Uh-huh. Tonight is drinks down at the pub on the corner. They wanted to get an early start.'

'So, anything to report?' Conrad placed a seat in front of the lift override buttons and grabbed his mug to make his first cuppa for the shift.

'Nothing much, just the usual comings and goings, but there is a message for you to call in at the research department at your earliest convenience.'

'That's Helga and Herbert's department, isn't it?' Conrad wondered what they wanted him for.

'Yep, that's the one. I would suggest you grab the keys and head on up. See what they want and then continue with the round.'

Conrad grabbed the keys and radio and headed out the door. Usually, he would take the elevator, but today he elected to walk the stairs. At least he could check the doors on the way up.

Arriving at the third floor, he walked down the carpeted corridor to the entrance door of the research lab. Herbert was waiting for him.

'Come inside please, Conrad.'

Conrad walked through, and Herbert closed the door behind him. 'Why am I here? What do you need me for?'

'You will see in a moment. Don't worry, it won't hurt.' Herbert directed him toward a small sterile room. 'Just through the door please, and take a seat. Helga will be with you soon.'

Conrad sat down and fiddled with the keys until Helga entered the room. She pulled out a chair and sat down. Through the open door, Conrad noticed Herbert urging all the other workers out the door. His enhanced hearing caught the sound of the research door being locked. Herbert entered the room, and he too chose a chair and sat down. 'Okay, now you have me worried. What's going on?'

Herbert looked at Helga and nodded his head.

'We want to know how you were able to open the door and operate the wormhole to New Earth.'

****

'New Earth. Sorry, I don't know what you mean.' If they'd had him hooked up to a polygraph at the moment, they'd be hearing buzzers going off right now. Conrad's heart thundered in his chest.

'Please, Conrad, don't lie. We built the cabinets and trained the cats how to work the machinery. We were the last to leave. Tell us how you are aware of it.'

'Why do you think I'd know anything?'

Herbert sighed, turned his tablet around so Conrad could see the video playing. The footage showed he and Rufus entering the cabinet, a bright flash and they'd disappeared.

'The evidence speaks for itself. We have known the cat has been going back and forth, and we've also seen all the other felines he has transported to New Earth. What surprised us was when you used the portal.'

Conrad hung his head. His secret was blown. 'How long have you known?'

'Not long. We only managed to get into the room the day you and your wife arrived here.'

Conrad looked up. 'How? There's no lock, and only those with the gene can operate the door.'

Helga smiled. 'I happened to follow you to your car. I saw the interaction between you and the cat. When the cat went through the door, I managed to slip something against the door jamb, stopping it from closing. You may not have noticed, but there is a movement-activated camera on the inside wall above the door.'

Conrad swore to himself. 'Yes, I've been to New Earth and met the cats. I hope you're not thinking of going back. I understand from what the cats told me you can't anyway. Something in the air makes you sick.'

Herbert leaned forward. 'The cats have told you? You can talk to them?'

If there had been a handy wall nearby, Conrad would have knocked his head into it. He hadn't wanted them to know about the telepathy. Begrudgingly, he replied. 'Yes, I can talk to them. They also talk to me.'

'Amazing.' Helga and Herbert muttered excitedly. 'When did this occur?'

He'd have to let everything out. If he kept quiet, they'd just keep asking. 'It happened after I got sick from the injection. I could see better, especially at night. My hearing and taste improved as well. The cat you see with me in the footage is Rufus. He taught me to speak. I had what I thought was a migraine, then I heard him yelling at me.' Conrad laughed. 'Did you know they think we are stupid and slow because we can't speak the "proper language"?' Conrad paused. 'Rufus hates you two with a vengeance because of what you did to him. I can't say I blame him either.'

Herbert shrugged. 'That doesn't worry me one bit. I now realise he was the "stray" we caught and used.' He sat back in his seat musing, before moving forward again. 'You have been to New Earth. How is it fairing?'

'The town is doing quite well. The grounds are a little unkempt, and garden beds have taken over and self-seeded, but there is no bad smell about. The incinerators work well.' Conrad remembered the food dispenser. He leaned forward in his seat. 'I was especially taken with

154

the food dispenser. If you can do that, why have you not implemented it here? There are so many hungry people who could use something like that.'

'Believe us, we would love to, but the molecules in the air on New Earth provide the food source. We tried a machine here and tested what came out. Apart from being inedible, the ingredients proved to be toxic. The war polluted everything. The ground, water, and air. The air on New Earth is pure, not contaminated by anything man has done.'

'But man has been on the planet. You have houses there. The building materials must have come from somewhere?'

'All materials needed for the expedition were transferred from this world. Nothing was manufactured there. As we were all scientists, we wanted to study the planet as it was. Unfortunately, as we found out, humans and canines are unable to occupy New Earth for long.'

Helga interrupted. 'We would like to take a sample of your blood and compare it to our blood to see if you have a gene we don't. If we find you have a special gene, it would mean another world we could inhabit. We could send people from overcrowded countries to a new life. Borders could be opened up, people could begin—'

Conrad stood up, his seat skittering across the small room before hitting the wall. 'No. Definitely not! The Great Siam tells me that no two-legs will ever set foot on Catatopia, and I think he's right.' Conrad leaned on the table. 'If man ever got onto that world, gene or no gene, they would rip it apart. What would happen the life forms there now? What would happen to the cats? They'd all be killed, a sacrifice to man's eternal greed to own more land, have more money.'

He began pacing the room. 'No, you can't take my blood for that. You are scientists, as you said, you didn't want the new world polluted like Earth, so everything came from here.' Conrad threw up his arms. 'So why start now? New Earth, as you call it, must remain a secret.'

Helga and Herbert looked at each other. 'Yes, you're right. Humans would take advantage. We hadn't thought that far ahead.'

Conrad strode toward the doorway. 'I'm willing to help in your research; after all, you are the people who made it possible for me to be a father. But,' Conrad took a few steps toward the table, 'I'm not willing to put New Earth at risk.' Conrad glared at each of them, turned his back and strode angrily out the door. He unlocked the main door to the department and leaned against the frame. Please let them come to their senses and not try to pull anything like that again. Calming himself down, he took a deep breath and began the well-trodden path of his circular route around the university's many buildings.

****

Conrad sat on the couch at home, reading his paper. Spook had snuggled against his leg and was fast asleep.

Hope leaned on the kitchen counter. 'Honey, what do you think about us setting up a rescue home for cats? We could take in those on the street if they were tame enough, or those whose owners became sick.'

'Wanderer, have you been giving Hope ideas?'

Wanderer curled herself around the coffee table, her tail lazily caressing the pine siding. *'I may have suggested something like that, but I'm sure she doesn't understand me. She can't talk.'*

'She may not be able to talk to you, but I think she can hear you.' 'What gave you that idea love?'

'Oh, it just popped into my head yesterday. I was brushing Wanderer, and I thought how nice it would be to have a few more around.' Hope stirred a pot on the stove, and leaned back on the bench. 'Then I thought about getting a bigger place, you know, with a bit more land, and being able to take care of those cats less fortunate. People could contact us if they needed to rehome a cat. Of course, we wouldn't let them go somewhere bad. Potential owners would have to prove they were good people.'

Conrad nearly choked when she said 'more land'. 'Don't you like it here anymore? Has something happened at work?'

Hope shook her head. 'No, nothing really, I just feel unsettled. I love being a nurse, but lately it just doesn't seem enough.'

Conrad laughed. 'My mother said you may feel this way. She called it "nesting".'

Hope frowned and straightened up, placing her hands on her hips. 'No, I know what nesting is, and this isn't it. I think I want a change in scenery and it would be good for Spook and Wanderer to have some land to run on.' She walked around the bench and scooped Wanderer into her arms. 'Every time they go out, I get scared they may get hit by some car. Or get kidnapped. Or something terrible will happen to them.' Lifting Wanderer higher, Hope rubbed her face in the kitten's fur. Wanderer purred heavily.

Conrad shrugged his shoulders. 'I suppose it wouldn't hurt to look, but what about our jobs?'

Hope flipped her hand. 'Oh, we wouldn't have to go too far away.' She grabbed a pamphlet from the bench. 'These houses have a few acres, and if we sold this place, we could own it straight away.'

Conrad took the pamphlet from his wife and looked at the picture. It looked lovely, green grass and trees. The address wasn't too far away either. He could still commute to work. He flipped the page over. A ramshackle house stood in an unkempt garden. He glanced back up at Hope. 'You want to sell what we have here, the house we have recently finished renovating, and buy this?'

Hope nodded excitedly. 'I'm sure it's not as bad as it looks. Maybe we can go there for a look on the weekend. You're not working this weekend, are you?'

Conrad knew when he'd been bested. If he didn't agree, she would keep on asking. 'Okay,' he sighed heavily, 'we'll take a look at the weekend.'

Hope jumped happily on the spot. 'Great, Mum and Bill are coming too.'

'What? You already asked them?'

Hope nodded. 'Yep, a couple of days ago. Well, I asked your mum, and she said yes, Bill probably doesn't know. He'll come anyway. He always does what she asks him to do.'

That was true, Conrad thought. What had started out as friendship had become something a little more serious. Conrad knew how much Bill cared about his mother. The older man hid it well, but Conrad had seen the looks pass between them. He was happy both of them had found happiness in each other.

If they did get a new place, it might also open up a way for him to help Rufus in getting the Catatopian kittens into good homes. Who knew, they might even get a few pure bloods in who may like to live on another world?

****

'Could this track be any rougher?' Conrad eased his car over the larger bumps, trying to not damage the underneath of the vehicle on the rutted mud standing in rills.

'It is the country, Conrad. Not everywhere can be flat with sealed roads.'

Conrad grimaced as a loud knock resounded from underneath the car. 'If this track takes off my exhaust, I'm going to yell.' He looked in the rear-vision mirror to see Bill soundlessly swearing in his car.

'When we buy the place, you can flatten the track. According to the brochure,' she waved it under his nose, 'This place also has a machinery shed with a tractor.'

A tractor, how lovely. I wonder what condition that's in? 'Don't set your heart on getting this, Hope, we're only here to take a look. Nothing is set down yet. If the picture is anything to go by, the place will need a lot of fixing up.'

'I know, I know. But look how green everything is! It's beautiful. Wanderer and Spook would love it out here, and I could grow a proper garden, with vegetables and fruit trees.'

'Not until you got a toxicity report done on the soil, but you are right, it does look nice out here.' Conrad wondered why this place was so green and lush, whereas in town the grass had only started to grow again.

'We can make that one of the points when we buy it.'

Conrad did a double take. "When we buy it", not "if we buy it". He sighed again. He would have to be strict. The place was cheap, true, but if a lot of work had to be done and the place wasn't liveable, they'd have to keep the other house while they did repairs. That meant a mortgage, and he didn't want to have to do that again.

'Apparently there's another "shack" on the land. Maybe Bill and your mum could live there?'

Conrad groaned.

'Oh look, there it is, I can see it.' Hope bounced excitedly in her seat, pointing out the window.

Conrad swore under his breath. The place was a mess. Iron was missing from the roof, and he could see a couple of verandah posts leaning away from the house. 'Hope, I don't know if it's safe for anyone to go in. The place looks like a strong wind would knock it down.' He hadn't thought it possible, but the house looked worse than it did in the brochure. Conrad stopped the car a good distance from the house. Rubbish and loose building material lay scattered around, and he didn't want to chance getting more than one flat tyre out here.

Hope had the door open and the seat belt released in record time. She jumped out of the car and ran close to the house. Conrad swore as his seat belt stuck. He wrestled with it and finally heard the click. He leapt from the car.

'Hope, don't go any closer. It's dangerous.' Conrad rushed to her side. His mother and Bill arrived seconds later.

'What a flamin' mess,' Bill scrubbed his chin with his hand, and gave Conrad the "are you joking" look.

Conrad only had one answer. 'Yeah.'

Conrad's mother walked up beside Hope and placed an arm around her shoulders. She winked at Hope, who winked back. 'Oh, I don't know. A few nails here and there, a lick of paint and the place will look okay.' Both women giggled.

Conrad looked at Bill. 'Is there something we are missing here?'

Bill shrugged his shoulders. 'Don't know. It's your mum and your wife. Anything is possible.'

Conrad walked up to the two women. 'Okay, 'fess up. You two are like two giggling schoolgirls in the playground. What's up?'

Hope turned to Conrad's mum. 'Should we tell him?'

Mum crossed her arms and looked askew at Conrad. 'I don't know, you think he deserves it?'

Conrad grew impatient with the two of them. 'Look, I'm not in the mood for playing games. One of you tell me what's going on, or I'm going home by myself.'

'Hmm, he's got his grumpy pants on. We'd better tell him.'

Mum nodded. She stepped forward, placing an arm around her son's shoulders. 'Conrad, this is the shack. The real house is up there.' She walked him further up the hill, and turned him to the side. 'There's also no we're buying it, or no we aren't, because you already own it.'

Conrad's eyes grew wide. A huge brick house stood in front of him. Colourful, landscaped gardens surrounded it, and he could see rows of fruit trees around the back. He was confused. 'How can I already own this? It must cost a million dollars.'

A sob escaped from his mother, and he watched a tear run down her cheek. 'This was your father's house before we married. We lived here for a little while, but when he was killed, I couldn't live here anymore. I always expected to see him come up the track. You were so young, and kept asking when daddy would be home. That's when we moved into the city, where we are now. I've had it rented ever since.'

Conrad was stuck for words. He kept looking at his mum, then back at the house.

Bill clapped him on the back. 'Come on, let's go check it out. Not much point standing there gaping like a fish.'

Conrad could only nod as his mother and his wife grasped him by a hand each and dragged him up the hill.

'Your father wanted to leave you something, in case he never came back. He gave this to you in his will. I've been waiting for the right time to hand it over. At first, I thought I'd give it over when you and Hope were married, but you'd already bought the house in town across the road from us. You were so proud of getting it, so I changed my mind. Now you're about to become a father, so I think it's the appropriate time.' She spun around once they reached the stone verandah. 'I want my grandchildren to grow up in the beautiful countryside, running in and out of the trees, just like you did.' The tears fell like rain now, and Conrad gathered his mother in his arms.

'Dad will always be here, Mum. He's been a big part of your life, and a part of mine. He'll never be forgotten while we're around.'

Bill walked over. 'Chloe, I know I'm not a shade on Richard, but he was my best mate, and I told him I would care for you and Conrad for the rest of my life if needed. Conrad has his life with Hope now, and is about to have kidlets of his own.' Bill knelt on one knee in front of the woman he'd loved for years. 'Chloe Adamson, will you marry me?' Bill fumbled in his jacket pocket and pulled out a small box opening it to show her what lay inside. A ring, with a petite stone, sat on white velvet.

Chloe nodded, unable to answer, tears now falling for a different reason, as Bill placed the ring on her finger. She hugged him, and for the first time in public, Bill was able to kiss the woman he loved.

Conrad clapped him on the back. 'Bill, I've always wondered why you never did this sooner.'

Bill shrugged. 'Like your mum giving you the house, I could never find the proper time.'

Conrad laughed. 'Well, I wish you all the happiness in the world. You've always been a father to me.'

Bill looked at him. 'Yeah, not that you listened.'

Chloe shook her head. 'What are we waiting for? Don't you want to have a look inside?' She dangled the house keys in front of him.

Conrad stepped forward, opened the door, swept Hope off her feet, and carried her over the threshold of her new home.

****

Ideas began forming in Conrad's mind. They needed a way for Rufus to be able to bring the kittens to Earth safely. He couldn't keep using the university's portal. They'd already been seen. It wouldn't take long for someone else to see him using a door that magically opened. Catatopia needed to be kept a secret.

There was plenty of space to build a small brick shed on the new acreage. They only needed the portal to be able to connect to Catatopia. Conrad wondered if the scientists could help. After all, they'd built the one in the university's basement. In the meantime, he and Bill had begun tearing down the old shack. The building had become too rundown to save, but the council gave permission to build another house in the same position. This one would be for Bill and Chloe. They wanted to be close when the children arrived. Permission had also been given to construct suitable accommodation for rescue animals.

'I'm going to be glad to see the last of this come down. It's an eyesore and also damn dangerous.'

Bill stopped hammering off a board and looked at what already lay on the ground. 'Your dad would be sad seeing this demolished. It's a pity we couldn't save it.'

'Why?' asked Conrad, pulling off another board and throwing it onto the rapidly filling trailer.

Bill stepped off to the side and sat down on an old stump, bouncing a board in his hand. 'Your dad built this shack with his own two hands. He lived in it while the main house was built.' Bill became thoughtful and grew quiet. 'Conrad, do you remember your father? I know you were only a couple of years old when he left. Do you have any memories of him?'

Conrad shook his head. 'No, I don't remember him at all. I only know who he was from Mum's photos. She says we used to live here, but I don't remember this place at all. The only father I remember is you.'

Bill looked up. 'Really?'

Conrad smiled at the man who had been there for him for as long as he could remember. 'Yeah really. So now you've had your reminiscing, get up and help me tear this place down.'

'Gee, sentimental, aren't you.'

'Bill, I don't remember him. I know you and Mum do, but when my kids are born, it's you they'll be calling Grandpa.'

Bill chuckled and smiled. 'Grandpa huh.' He shook his head. 'I never thought I'd ever be called that.'

'Hope and I will make this place our own. I don't think the kids are going to have an easy time of it. You know what people are like with others who look "different". They're going to need a place where they can leave the world behind and be safe.'

'You think it's going to be that bad?'

Conrad nodded with a sad face. 'I do, Bill. Our children and the others in the trial group aren't going to have an easy start.'

'Don't be pessimistic like that. The human race may still surprise us and accept them, even though they're different.

'I hope you're right, Bill. That would make things so much easier.' Conrad bent and began pulling up the last of the old, grey, cracked floorboards. Two more trailer loads and the old shack would be gone forever.

****

'I'll take the first run, Bill. You sit back and put your feet up, old man.' Conrad felt sorry for him. Bill was great at odd jobs but hadn't done any real hands-on work in a long time. Pulling down the shack on the weekend had left him realising the muscles in his body hadn't been worked hard for a long time. He groaned making the smallest movement. Conrad had to drive to work because Bill swore he ached too much to press the accelerator.

'Thank you, you're all heart. Before you go, can you make me a coffee please?' Bill held his mug out in front of him. 'I think the walk to the kettle may kill me.'

Conrad did as asked, sitting the steaming mug in front of him. 'Don't exert yourself, Bill, and remember, it's hot.' Before he was out the door, he heard Bill swear loudly. Conrad wondered if the coffee was only on the desk, or if he'd spilt it on himself.

Taking the elevator and checking the doors on each floor, Conrad made his way to the research department on the third floor. He had checked earlier to make sure Helga and Herbert hadn't left yet. Opening the main door, he walked in, whistling as he walked the floor.

'Who's that?' a voice called from around the corner.

'It's Conrad, Helga. I need to ask you and Herbert a question.' Conrad walked in the direction the voice had come from.

Helga walked out of the clean room, removing her gloves and gown as she approached Conrad. 'What can I do for you?'

'The portal cabinet. Does it have to be in the basement or can it be anywhere?'

'That's an interesting question. Why do you ask?' Helga opened the bin and threw the rolled up items in, then closed the lid.

'Just wanted to know, that's all.'

'It's a delicate piece of machinery, Conrad. I'm not sure it can be moved.'

They weren't going to answer his question. 'So when you made it, you constructed it in the basement, did you?'

Helga stood in front of him and folded her arms. 'No, it was transported as a unit, then wired in when it was put in place. Again I ask, why do you want to know?'

'Because,' Conrad adopted the same stance, 'I want one of my own.'

Helga shook her head. 'No. Impossible. The blueprints were lost a long time ago. Another one can't be built.'

'I'm not asking for another to be built, I'm asking for the one in the basement to be moved to a place only I know about. What happened to the portals you used to transfer all the bricks, cement, and machinery to New Earth?'

'They were scrapped once they had served their purpose.' Helga turned on her heel and walked away.

'What is with the raised voices?' Herbert asked coming through the door. 'I could hear you as soon as I stepped out of the lift.'

Helga ignored his comment, so he turned to Conrad. 'Have you upset her?'

'Sorry, I think I have. Herbert, I need a portal cabinet that isn't monitored, so the cats and I can come and go as we need to. Helga says all the earlier cabinets used to transfer goods to New Earth were destroyed. Were they?'

'Ahh, I see now. Helga wanted the one in the basement destroyed. She said as no one could go back there, the portal was of no use. I disagreed, so she allowed the machinery to stay.'

'Why didn't you want the box destroyed?'

'I liked the cats, and I suppose, as a scientist, I was curious about what would happen in the coming years.'

'But I thought you couldn't go back anymore.'

'I can't, and neither can Helga. If we took one more trip, we would arrive dead on the other side. But someone else could go in our place and bring back the information we need.' Herbert walked around Conrad, looking him up and down. 'How many times have you been to New Earth?'

Conrad shrugged. He hadn't kept count. 'I don't know, a few times I suppose.'

'And you haven't felt sick or had extreme rashes break out over your body?'

Conrad recoiled. 'Damn no. I did feel a little queasy the first time Rufus took me through, but after that, everything has been alright.'

'It must have something to do with the gene we used, although we didn't become affected until we'd been there for a little while.' Herbert leaned back against the wall, his finger thoughtfully tapping his bottom lip. 'Conrad, you want the portal, we need a sample of your blood. Would you consider a one for one deal?'

Conrad became defensive. 'What would you do with my blood sample?'

'As I said before, all I want to do is to test your blood against ours. That's all.'

'And you wouldn't serumise it to allow others to go to New Earth?'

'No. I wouldn't do that, but I may need you to take some observations for me when you are there and bring me back the results.'

'I won't hurt any of the cats there. I won't take samples of blood or anything like that.'

Herbert shook his head. 'No, I wouldn't ask you to do that. No, just air, soil, foliage, that type of thing. We may find something natural over there able to cure the common cold, maybe even cancer? If you are willing to do that for us, I will let you take the portal cabinet. I will even come with you to install it wherever you want.'

'So it doesn't matter where the cabinet is for it to work?'

'No, as long as it stays within a hundred kilometres radius of the university, the portal will work.'

Their new home was definitely within the zone. With Herbert happy to wire it in, Conrad only had to find a place to put it, and he knew the perfect place.

'I will take your observations, Herbert.' Conrad extended his hand to shake on the deal.

Helga would be happy the portal was gone, and Herbert would be able to get a ready supply of any materials he may need from New Earth, and he would have the cabinet.

'When do you want to do this?' Herbert asked.

'About a month and a half. I still need to build the room the cabinet will go into. I'll need some idea of the electric connections for the room.'

Herbert waved Conrad to follow him and handed over a sheaf of rolled-up papers. 'This is the only copy of the wiring needed. Keep it safe.'

Conrad slapped the roll against his hand. 'I will, Herbert, I promise.' Papers in hand, Conrad strode out of the room, locking the door behind him as he left.

****

Conrad laid out the plans on the table. Hope, Chloe, and Bill surrounded the table as Conrad walked them through the Cat Rescue Centre, pointing to all the areas.

Hope placed her finger on the plan. 'What's this room? It doesn't have a name on it.'

Conrad looked over. 'That just another storeroom.'

'But we have the larger one over here.' Hope indicated the large seven-by-five metre room. 'What do we need a second smaller one for?'

Chloe jumped in with an answer, which Conrad silently thanked her for. 'Honey, you'll find out, you can never have too many storerooms.'

After lots of ahhing, and 'where is this going', everyone seemed to be happy with the plans. Conrad dusted his hands against each other. 'So, are we right to go?' he glanced at his watch. 'The builders will be here in about half an hour.'

'I can't imagine what this is going to look like when it's built.' Hope cooed.

'I can't imagine how much it's going to cost to feed them all. What is the maximum number you can have here at one time, Conrad?' Bill grumbled.

'We can have twenty cats, regardless of age. Wanderer and Spook aren't included in that number. Luckily, the government has given us a grant to set this up and to feed and vaccinate them all.'

'How about desexing?' Chloe asked.

'Helga and Herbert at the university have come up with a chemical prill that's injected under the skin, just as a microchip is. The prill renders the animal infertile. They tested it on a few alley cats, and it worked well.

Surgery is no longer needed, and it's not expensive either. Good for everyone.'

Bill looked down the hill and glanced at his watch. 'I don't know about half an hour, but the workmen are here.'

Conrad turned around and watched the procession of vehicles climb the slight hill. 'Gee, I hope it doesn't rain. Otherwise that track may get a lot deeper. I'll have to think of something to stop that happening.'

Bill sauntered down the hill and called back. 'I'll get them to leave all their cars at the bottom. They can walk up.'

Thank you, Bill. Conrad thought. His mind whizzed at a hundred miles an hour. So much had to be done in a short amount of time. He looked around him. The site had been pegged out, he and his mum had done that together. The concrete blocks and mortar sat to the side under a tarpaulin. A huge backhoe worked its way up the hill. Soon there wouldn't be grass; there would be a housing area any cat would love to live in. The smaller kittens had a communal area in which to play together, and the larger cats had rooms. Windows would look out onto the green grass and landscaped flowerbeds.

Trying to keep the layout similar to the houses on Catatopia wasn't easy. How do you make a normal house not look like a house? The toileting was another problem. Wanderer and Spook found it disgusting they had to dig holes or use the kitty litter. Eventually, they got used to it. He'd have the same problem with the cats coming from Catatopia. He'd have to totally retrain them, as houses here didn't have the incineration systems. They would be an excellent addition to all homes, especially as the mess had to be cleaned away by the humans. Maybe

Herbert would allow him to get them mass-produced if he went halves in the profits.

Conrad could see owners snapping them up fast, especially if they could be easily installed.

Time for thinking had passed. The backhoe sat revving its engine, ready to go. His mum helped him move the table out of the way, and they both watched on as the bucket descended and took a huge bite out of the ground.

'After this, I promise we'll build your house, Mum.' Conrad leaned to the side and pecked his mother on the cheek. 'Thanks for letting us get this done first.'

'Darling, living with you and Hope makes me happy. I don't think we're too cramped, do you?'

Conrad shook his head. 'No, not at all. I don't know what Dad thought when he built this, but there's plenty of room.' When his mum didn't answer, he looked at her.

Tears streamed down her face. She wiped them away with the back of her hand.

'Mum, what's wrong? Why the tears? I thought you were okay with being in the house again?'

Chloe sniffed back the tears and smiled. 'Yes, I'm okay with living here. It was the question you asked, about why the house was so big?' She sighed and wiped her eyes with both hands. 'Don't worry about me; I'm getting sentimental in my old age.' She sighed deeply. 'The house is so big because your father wanted lots of children. You don't know this, but I had trouble falling pregnant. When you finally came along after a couple of years, we were overjoyed. Then the war happened, and your father had to leave.'

'And that was the last time you saw him. Then I got a cold, and you found out I may be infertile when I grew up.' Conrad had to swallow back a sob. 'You wanted more than one child, and then you found out you may not have grandchildren either.'

Chloe could only nod. Conrad hugged her tight, and she cried into his shoulder.

Hope saw what happened and overheard a little of what had been said. She wrapped her arms around both of them. 'Don't be sad, Mum. You have me, Conrad and Bill, and now you know you will have grandchildren.'

Chloe laughed. 'I know, I'm such a sook. I don't know what's going on with me.'

'I think everything has just become a little much. It's all happening at once.' Conrad assured her. 'Let's go inside the house, and leave the builders to do their job.'

CHAPTER TWENTY

The Cat Rescue Centre was operational, the 'special' cupboard had been installed in the small storage room, and it had been tested. Before the portal had been disconnected, Rufus had entered and transported. The cabinet had been disconnected and moved to its new home.

Conrad had never seen Helga so happy. She actually danced with joy when he and Herbert manhandled the cabinet up the stairs, through the door and onto the back of a small rigid hire truck.

Once installed, an apple made its way to Catatopia and came back in one piece. A tree branch was the next item to be sent. When the branch returned, there was a little consternation, as the foliage was a reddish brown. Conrad realised it was a branch from the tree outside the building in Catatopia. Seconds later, Rufus appeared.

'Conrad-human, it is good to see you once again.' Rufus looked around and spied Herbert standing not far away. He hissed and arched his back, spitting his disgust

at seeing the man. 'What is this? Why is that human here with you?'

'Calm down, Rufus. Herbert needed to connect the machinery. He's not here to hurt you or anyone else.'

'Boy,' Herbert backed away, 'he really doesn't like me, does he! If you don't mind, I'll go wait outside.'

'Thanks. Bill will run you back to the university.' Conrad turned his attention back to Rufus, who was still visibly and audibly upset. *'Rufus, calm yourself. He'll be gone in a minute.'*

Rufus didn't relax until the hateful human was out of his sight. *'He will return to hurt the kittens.'*

'No, he won't. He's been blindfolded on the trip here, and the trip back. He doesn't know where this place is.'

Rufus looked up, sat on his haunches and began washing. Conrad could feel the cat's rage waning. He waited until Rufus regained his composure. That would only be when he'd finished washing.

'You took a chance coming through yourself, Rufus. You could have been killed or—how do I say this—not put back together the right way.'

'There was no danger. The green ball and the branch were unharmed. I was the next step, as you will be when you accompany me back.' Rufus began exploring the rescue centre. *'This is where the kittens will learn to live on this planet?'*

Conrad followed him around. *'The kittens will be housed together. They will be given the vaccinations needed to be able to live on this planet and not get sick. They will be taught by Spook and Wanderer how to act around humans, how to eat and use the litter box.'*

'Conrad-human, the kittens will not need to be taught how "to use the litter box". That comes naturally.

However, I understand what you mean. There are no food dispensers here, so they will have to trust their new servants know what to feed them. What is this "vaccination" thing?'

Conrad sent a mind picture to Rufus, and he howled with anger.

'Why do you need to plunge that into them? It will kill them. I cannot believe you would subject kittens to that torture.' Rufus ran back to the cabinet, but Conrad knelt and grabbed him. Rufus yowled and scratched.

'If I didn't have to, I wouldn't, believe me, Rufus. Please. The shots are needed because without them, the kittens could get sick and die. Your world is clean and pure, free from the diseases of this planet. I'm sure on your travels you have seen sick cats. Do you want your kittens to catch those illnesses?'

Rufus stopped fighting Conrad and sat down. *'I have seen cats very sick. I would not want my kittens to be like that. If it is needed, even though I think it is barbaric, I will allow it. I understand you mean only good.'* Rufus noticed the full-length window and walked toward it, bumping his head on the glass. *'Why is this air hard? It will not let me pass outside?'*

Conrad laughed. *'That's called a window. It lets us see the outside world, but keeps us dry and warm on wet and cold days. I will show you how to get out, in case you come back one day, and I am not here.'* He stood, letting Rufus follow him out of the enclosure. *'I've installed a door here for you. Spook and Wanderer also know where it is. You put your paw on this light,'* Conrad placed his finger on the photoelectric cell, *'and a small door will open, big enough for you and kittens, but not large enough for a human to get through. Like the door at the university, this will only open for those able to live on your planet.'*

Conrad had taken apart the basement door to find the apparatus responsible for opening. Once found, the basement became a room with a normal lockable door, and Conrad had a cat door, which would only open for certain cats.

He stood and walked out the human-sized door to the side of the cat door. Once outside, he waited for Rufus. *'Okay Rufus, give it a go. Place your paw on the light.'*

A second later, Rufus walked out of the enclosure. Spook and Wanderer met him on the outside.

'Surprise!!'

'Father, you're here. I have so much to show and tell you.'

'I am pleased to see you as well, daughter. I hope you haven't been causing Spook too many problems.'

'No Father. I haven't done anything badly wrong.' Wanderer gazed at the ground and washed her paws.

'Wanderer, what have you done?'

Spook came to her defence. *'She's only a kitten, Rufus, and she's been exploring as all young ones do. She occasionally gets herself into a little bit of trouble, but it's not usually bad.'*

'Spook, I understand you want to protect her, but she needs to know right from wrong. Wanderer, please tell me.'

'Umm, I couldn't find the new place for the litter tray and had to use a tree in the house, and then another time, Hope-queen went out, and I ate what was on the bench, and I wasn't supposed to. Hope-queen wasn't happy with me.' Wanderer continued to hang her head in shame.

Conrad heard the interchange. *'Rufus, don't worry*

about it. Wanderer has been a great little kitten, and Hope loves her dearly. Spook has been doing a great job.'

'I'm glad to hear it.' He walked the few steps to Wanderer and licked her head. *'Come, daughter, show me around. This place is much preferable to the old cave we used before, Conrad-human.'*

'I agree, Rufus, it's much better, and the kittens will love it too. We may even be able to "find" some purebreds for you to take home. That may take some time.' Conrad walked off toward the house as Wanderer scampered in front of him. He watched as Wanderer showed her father the cat door, and how to get into the house. Watching her with him made him long for children of his own. Hope was only six months pregnant, so she had at least three months to go before that would happen. He wondered what they'd be like.

****

Two days after Rufus arrived, he and Conrad made the first trip back to Catatopia. Conrad hadn't been back for a while and was interested to see if anything had changed. Surely the planet had periods of hot and cold. Rufus wasn't able to answer about the seasons, as the only change that happened was his coat grew thicker. Conrad assumed the temperatures had dropped to start the coat change.

Sure enough, when they stepped out of the portal on Catatopia, Conrad checked fingers, toes and other regions before taking another step; he could hear a howling storm outside. A quick glance through the dirty windows told him neither he nor Rufus would be taking a step outside until the maelstrom had calmed. 'Does this happen often, Rufus?'

'Occasionally, though as long as I have been alive, we've only had a couple of bad storms.'

Conrad wondered about the damage to houses. Surely the cats were unable to fix any damage caused? They weren't equipped to deal with such things.

'No, we move to another cave. There are many here, though with the new arrivals and the kittens already born, the caves have more families in them than before. That's one of the reasons for sending our young to your planet.'

'Do you mind if I take a look at some of the "caves" that can't be used because of damage?'

'Why?' Rufus gave his coat a couple of licks and looked back at Conrad.

'I may be able to fix the damage, giving you more caves to use.'

Rufus shook, his thick shaggy coat moving in waves around his body. 'If you wish, it does not worry us.'

The storm appeared to be easing, but the wind still blew hard. Conrad opened the door, only to have the doorknob nearly ripped from his hands. 'Damn, that wind is strong.'

'Yes. The winds can be very strong. The caves keep out most of the noise, but when it is a big storm, it is loud, as it is now.

Conrad again looked out of the window. Tree branches flew past, and he could hear the tiles rattling on the roof. 'I wouldn't be surprised if this wasn't close to a cyclone. I suppose we will be here for a while.'

'Yes. We will not be moving soon.' Rufus walked over to a corner of the room and curled into a ball.

'You're going to sleep?'

Rufus raised his head, annoyance showing on his face. 'Yes, I am going to sleep. There is nothing else to do until the wind has gone. Now, leave me in peace.' His head lowered and his eyes closed. One paw covered his eyes to keep the light out.

Conrad looked around. Folders and paperwork lay everywhere, on the floor, on top of cupboards and, as Conrad found out, in the drawers. He picked up a file, looked at his watch and started reading. They had all day to get the kittens back home. His watch showed 9 am. They had plenty of time.

Quiet filled the room. Conrad opened his eyes. Damn, he must have fallen asleep. He looked at the file his head had been laying on. No wonder, the reading material wasn't exactly action packed. He glanced at his watch: 3 pm. Damn, how had he managed to sleep so long? He looked over to the corner where he'd seen Rufus last. The cat was nowhere to be seen. Conrad jumped up and dashed for the exit.

Wrenching open the door, Conrad ran outside. The road was a mess. The storm had been a big one and had caused damage. Conrad made his way into town, to the house he knew Rufus and Princess lived. The further into town he walked, the worse the damage. Some houses had lost roofs, and a tree had fallen on one.

Conrad entered the houses where the most damage had occurred, searching for any inhabitants who may have been injured. In the house with the tree through the roof, he didn't find anyone. He searched all the rooms. Everyone appeared to have escaped. He made his way to the next damaged house. He could hear cries of pain.

Conrad entered the house and could hear Rufus giving orders. He turned to his left and entered what would have been the lounge. Rufus and a few other cats were trying to lift and push a large bough off a queen trapped underneath. 'Rufus, stand to the side, and I'll lift it off.'

'Thank Bast you are here. There are many injured and trapped. This is the worst storm we have ever seen. This is a time when we do need a two-legs.'

Conrad bent over, placed his arms around the bough and heaved upward. A hole gaped in the ceiling, and Conrad could see the sky above that. 'Can you drag out your friend?'

'She is clear, you can let the tree down.'

Conrad lowered his burden slowly. It rolled to the side and lay still. He'd have to remove it later. There was no way the other cats would have been able to lift it, or even move it. 'Rufus, we are going to have to go through the town, checking all the houses. We won't be able to take any kittens back today.'

'I agree, Conrad. We must help the others first.'

Conrad noticed Rufus had left 'human' off his name. He wondered if it was accidental, or if he'd finally gained the feline's respect. They hurried to the next house to help anyone who needed the extra strength only a two-legs could muster.

Working their way along and across the streets, Conrad lifted doors, more large branches, and fallen ceilings off luckless cats and kittens. A few had injuries that he could attend to, but a couple, including a kitten who'd been cut by broken glass, needed urgent medical attention. Conrad knew he wasn't able to give them what they needed. They had to go back through the portal.

Rufus explained what was to happen. The kitten's mother didn't want her baby to be taken to the two-legs planet, but Rufus explained what would happen if she didn't go back. The two adult cats were scared but wanted the pain to end. Both had broken limbs.

Conrad fixed up a box to carry the injured back through the portal. 'Rufus, how did Princess fair? Is she okay?' He'd sent him off to check after they'd checked most of the houses. Neither of them could hear any other cries of distress.

'She is well, Conrad. When the storm came, she moved all others in the cave, to the Great Siam's Cave.' Rufus smiled. 'The Great Siam wasn't happy with all being there, but even he wasn't brave enough to go up against my queen.'

Conrad laughed. Rufus sounded proud. 'I think I can understand why, Rufus. I don't think I would be brave enough to go against your Princess. She is a formidable mate.'

'Conrad, the caves are badly damaged. Many families will be unable to live as they had before.' Rufus was understandably worried.

'Don't fret, we will find a way to fix them. I will contact the two-legs who were here before. They may be able to tell me where the materials are to fix the caves.' Conrad didn't think they would have used all the materials when they made the town, and not kept some in readiness for repairs. Surely Helga or Herbert would know. For now, he needed to get the two adults and kitten back to Earth to be tended to.

'Rufus, if you want to stay here with your family, I understand, but I have to get these three back home.'

'Thanks for what you have done. You are a hero now, and we all owe you our thanks for helping us when we needed it. We now know not all two-legs are bad. I will stay here with Princess for a time. Please come back. We need the caves made liveable again.'

Conrad hoisted the box with the cats inside. 'I'll be back when I have news. Take care while I'm gone.' Conrad turned and walked out the door, down the street, entered the portal and pressed the light.

****

Reappearing in the new location, Conrad opened the door and rang the closest vet from the rescue centre. He told the vet on call what the problems were and said he'd wait. Setting up a few recovery boxes, Conrad placed all three felines in the same small room. *'You are about to meet a two-legs who cares for all animals. You must trust him. He cannot speak, but I will let you know what he says. Please do not be scared. He will not intentionally harm you.'*

One of the injured adults, a Burmese if Conrad knew his breeds, answered for the three of them. *'You have done much for us, and we thank you. If the two-legs can help stop the pain and mend our broken bones, we will all be eternally grateful. We have only heard bad things about your kind. You are not like that, and we trust you.*

Conrad felt humbled by their appreciation. They weren't the dumb animals some people thought they were. They were people in fur coats trying to live their lives, just as humans were. Conrad looked at his watch. Was it too late to ring Helga or Herbert?

The door opened behind him and Conrad spun around. Hope stood in the door, her eyes on the three wounded cats. 'When did these arrive? I didn't hear anyone come up the drive.'

'No, I had to go get them. Someone found them in a box on the side of the road.' Conrad hated lying to his wife, but she didn't know about his trips to Catatopia. Hell, she didn't know about Catatopia at all. 'There's two adults and a kitten. All have broken bones. I've phoned the vet, and he's on the way.'

Hope walked over quickly and examined the occupants of the box. 'Hmm, yes, I can see this one has a fractured foreleg.' She spoke softly to the cat as she carefully felt the broken limb. 'Shhh, brave one. I won't hurt you. I only want to help.'

'This is your queen?' asked the cat.

'Yes, why do you ask?'

'She carries kittens, but they are not as normal two-legs. They seem people, but also two-legs.'

'You are correct. They are two-legs, but also people. I sense your confusion, why they are like that is hard to explain.

'They are special?'

'They are. They are my kittens, and all kittens are special.'

The cat purred. *'You are right, hero. All kittens are special.'*

Hope must have thought the cat was purring because of what she did. 'Oh look, she's purring. I hope it means she's settling and isn't purring because she's scared.'

'No, I don't think she's scared. Can you have a look at the other two? The kitten has a large gash as well as something wrong with his leg, and the other one's back leg looks bent the wrong way.'

Conrad watched as Hope leapt into nurse mode. Her patient may be an animal, but from what Conrad observed, the species didn't matter. Her patient was injured, and she knew of only one way to care for her patients. With love and care.

Conrad heard the slam of a car door and saw the vet walk up the path to the building. Leaving Hope to do what she was doing, he walked to the door, gave the vet the same explanation he'd given Hope, and led him into the first-aid room.

****

Conrad stood at the top of the main street, tool belt around his hips filled with nails, screws and an assortment of another objects, a chainsaw at his feet, and viewed the damage. What had he volunteered for? The job would take weeks. He sighed. Standing around wouldn't get anything fixed, better to roll up his sleeves and get started.

He walked to the first house and pushed open the door. It opened and promptly sagged, one corner hitting the floor. He examined the hinges to find the screws had slipped out. A few dobs of glue and longer new screws would fix that.

Cats sat around him watching. 'Don't you all have something else to do?'

'No,' came the answer in a dozen voices.

Being watched by one person, usually Hope, when doing repairs was irritating, but being watched by twelve pairs of eyes became nerve-wracking. Conrad could hear some talking. 'If you want to help, you can pick up the smaller sized debris laying around and take it to the block at the top of the road.'

'How?' came the chorus again.

'You have your mouths to carry with, don't you?'

They conferred amongst themselves. Conrad mused. When people—humans—talked, the sound resembled a gaggle of geese, loud and grating on the senses. When the cats conferred, it sounded like a strong wind blowing through the tree tops. Audible, but pleasant on the ears.

'We can carry some things, others may hurt us.'

'I agree, do not carry anything that will cut your mouths like glass.' Conrad picked up a large piece of broken window. 'This can hurt tender mouths. Only take sticks and twigs. I will take away anything too large for you.'

Again they conferred, finally moving off from the huddle, each picking up something in their mouths, and began the walk to the area at the top of the street. Conrad watched as other cats joined the procession. As word spread, more joined the line, and Conrad watched the pile at the top of the road grow larger. He noticed larger rubbish being deposited on the pile, and watched astonished as eight male cats carried a large bough from inside one of the dwellings. Four carried with their mouths, the other four supported the branch across their necks. With the cats occupied, and doing a great job, he was able to complete small repairs quickly.

Herbert had given him directions to where the building supplies were kept at the far end of the town. Areas like broken windows needed to be boarded up so the weather wouldn't impact the inside of the houses. Conrad had to find something to board them up with. After he'd run out of broken ceiling boards to patch up some of the frames, he walked to the 'warehouse', as he called it. Herbert had assured him the building would be unlocked. Conrad was happy to find the doorknob turned easily, and the door opened.

He walked through the reception area and into the cavernous room next door, stopped and gasped. The building contained every bit of hardware and building material he would need. He couldn't have walked into a hardware shop back on Earth and had the amount he had to pick from here. Lumber, plaster panels, fixings, everything he would need. Even spare doors and windows leaned against a wall. Beside two huge metal roller doors sat a golf cart-sized vehicle and a trailer. His joy was complete. Conrad had been wondering how he would move the larger, heavier items.

He walked over to the cart. Sure enough, it was plugged into the solar batteries. He turned the key in the lock, and it hummed into life. Transport problem fixed, Conrad began loading supplies into the trailer.

CHAPTER TWENTY-ONE

Hope opened the door to the rescue centre. Her charges were healing nicely. Conrad had left the house a few hours beforehand. She wasn't sure where he went, but she trusted he wasn't doing anything wrong. He always returned in the afternoon, or at night, worn out. She'd asked him where he went, but the answer was always the same, he was helping friends with repairs.

She wished he'd stay home occasionally. The headaches were growing, and she wondered at how active the babies had become. They never seemed to settle down. With two inside it must be getting squishy. Hope stroked her expanding midriff, and the headache lessened. Sitting down at a table, she prepared breakfast for ten hungry cats and kittens. Word had spread about the rescue centre, and they'd had a few new faces join them. Hope loved and cuddled every one of them, sure she could never let them go, but realising she'd have to. All here would go to new homes, living better lives than they had before.

Hope placed the last plate of food in front of a small kitten when pain ripped across her middle. She cried out in surprise, dropped to her knees, and scared a few of her charges. She attempted to stand, the pain retreated to her back, and she crawled to a seat where she could sit down, perspiration beading her forehead. Were these contractions? They couldn't be; she was only six months gone. She still had another couple of months at least. The pain waned and disappeared. Hope took a deep breath and stood. She took one step, hesitated, then another. When no further pain gripped her, she carried on with her duties. She'd known about the pre-labour pains called Braxton Hicks women often experienced. Hopefully, that was what assailed her. Fifteen minutes later, another pain gripped her. She'd been ready for this one and leaned against the wall, supporting herself and breathed throughout the contraction. She knew this wasn't any Braxton Hicks. This was the real deal. When the pain dissipated, she made her way back to the house carefully.

She needed Conrad, and he'd gone god knew where. Sitting on the couch next to the phone, she began dialling his mobile phone but only received the 'Please leave a message'.

She screamed down the phone, 'Wherever you are, get back here. I'm in labour.' Hanging up, she tried dialling Chloe and Bill. The phone rang out. Hope cried in frustration. They must be out in the garden.

Wanderer and Spook jumped onto the couch beside her. Wanderer meowed, as did Spook. She wished she could understand what they said. Her headache had become worse, and she closed her eyes to block the light. Maybe that would stop her head hurting so much.

Laying her head on the armrest, blackness engulfed her.

****

Wanderer patted Hope on the face with her paw.
'She's not waking up, Spook, and the kittens inside her are calling. What can we do, she doesn't know how to talk?'

'We'll have to get the big two-legs who is in the cave down the hill. You stay with Hope-queen, I'll run down and speak to the two-legs.'

'Please Spook, make it fast. I'm worried.' Wanderer kept patting her beloved servant on the face.

Spook ran outside and pushed his furry legs as fast as they could go, down the hill. He could see the female two-legs Conrad had called Mum, leaning over digging in the ground. He ran up to her, placing his paws on her leg.

'Come, the queen needs you. Hope needs you.'

Chloe ruffled his head. 'Hello, Spook. Come down to play have you? You're talkative today.'

Spook shrugged her off and ran a short way back to the house, then returned to her and kept speaking. Growing frustrated with not being able to be understood, he grabbed her hand and tried to back up.

She stood, and Spook saw the worried look on her face. 'Bill, I think something is wrong. Spook is acting funny. He just grabbed my hand. I'm sure he was trying to guide me to the house.'

Spook saw Bill come running. The big two-legs bent down to look Spook in the face. Spook placed his paw on the two-legs wrist. *'Please, try hard to hear me. Hope needs help!'*

'Spook, is something wrong with Hope?'

Spook couldn't understand what the two-legs was saying, but the noise sounded like a question. He repeated the action of trying to drag the man up the hill by his hand.

'Chloe, can you get the car ready, and drive it to the top of the hill. Spook isn't playing. Something's wrong.'

Spook took off up the hill with Bill not far behind him. Spook thought he'd never run so fast before. He hoped Wanderer had managed to wake Hope. Dashing inside the house, Spook jumped onto the couch, landing heavily beside Wanderer.

The kitten cried in fear. *'I can't wake her Spook, and the kitten's cries are getting fainter.'*

'I've brought the two-legs Bill with me. He'll help her.'

Bill puffed in through the door. He shooed both Wanderer and Spook from the couch, shook the unconscious woman and slapped her face gently. Hope wasn't responding. Bill bent his knees, slid his arms under her legs and back and heaved Hope's body upward.

'Damn girl, you weigh a bit. I hope my back doesn't give out.' As he turned around, he saw Chloe park the car in front of the door, run around and open the back door for him to slide Hope in.

The cats danced on their paws, anxious with what was happening. Bill closed the rear car door and bent down to the cats. 'I'm not sure if you understand me, but you need to find Conrad. Understand me, find Conrad.'

Spook and Wanderer couldn't understand everything the two-legs Bill was saying, but there was one word he used that they did understand. Conrad.

'We must find Conrad. We have to go through the portal. He is in Catatopia.' Both cats raced to the centre, touched the diode, let themselves into the portal and disappeared.

****

Only seconds had passed before they were standing in their world. 'Where can he be, Spook? There are so many caves, how will we find him?'

'We ask the others to help. Someone will find him.'

The two raced off; Wanderer still only a kitten, her small legs struggled to keep up with Spook's ground-swallowing gait. She panted to a halt, her little chest sucking in as much air as she could. Spook noticed she wasn't behind him and backtracked, finding her gasping in the centre of the road.

'Come on, Wanderer. I can't do this without you.'

Wanderer shook her head. 'You go on. I need to catch my breath. If you take the side my house is on, I will take the other side.'

Spook danced, unsure of what to do. His job was to protect Wanderer, but he was torn between that and finding Conrad. 'Wanderer, help me, I don't know what to do.'

Wanderer stepped up to her companion. 'Spook, I'm not the helpless little kitten anymore. Finding Conrad is more important. Go, run fast and find him.'

Spook didn't need another push. 'Run as soon as you can, Wanderer, our pet needs us.' He sprinted off and slid around the corner, calling out at the top of his voice for all cats to take notice.

Wanderer drew in a deep breath and began to run again. She crossed the road and began passing the message that they needed to find Conrad, and it was urgent.

****

Conrad was about to hammer the last nail into a window frame about halfway up the street. He'd accomplished so much in the last few days.

A searing pain stabbed his leg, and he nearly brought the hammer down onto what or whoever had attacked him.

A nondescript tabby kitten hung off his leg. 'Hero, you are needed by the one called Spook. He is running through the caves trying to find you.'

'Spook is trying to find me?' Conrad picked the kitten off his pants leg and placed him on the floor. 'Thank you, little one. Rest here until you get your breath back.' The kitten's tiny chest heaved with exertion. Conrad ran out through the open door and into the street. Cats milled everywhere, all calling for their hero, saying he was needed. A familiar black and white blur careered up the centre of the street. Spook.

The cat leapt, hitting him in the centre of his chest. Conrad was knocked back, but held onto the furry bundle now firmly attached to his shirt.

'Conrad, your queen needs you. She isn't talking, and the big two-legs you call Bill has taken her in the metal monster. The kittens inside her are growing weak. We came to find you. You must go now.' Having delivered his message, Spook pushed himself off Conrad's chest.

'Something is wrong with Hope?' Fear grasped Conrad's heart and twisted it in evil claws. He sprinted down the street, every cat making way for him as he ran. He saw Wanderer as he sprinted past, but couldn't stop. She and Spook would have to return by themselves.

Conrad hit the portal building at a flat-out run. His chest hurt from the exertion, but he ignored the pain as he wrenched the glass door open. Entering the cabinet, he hit the return button and was gone.

A second later he appeared in the rescue centre room. His mobile phone began beeping as he stepped out of the box. Messages flashed across the screen at him. One from Hope, about ten from Bill and his mum. He selected Bill's number and listened to the message.

Swearing to himself, he ran for his car, dialling Bill's phone number as he ran. Bill answered. He didn't wait for Conrad to speak, instead bellowing down the phone, 'Get your arse to the university. Hope's gone into labour, and she's close to birthing your children.' Conrad heard Hope screaming in the background.

The phone went dead as Conrad reefed his car door open. He dropped the phone onto the seat, buckled himself in as he reversed the car out of the garage, narrowly missing the garden bed and some extremely large rocks. The car sped down the track to the road. Conrad was lucky no other vehicle was in the vicinity as he flew out of the drive onto the bitumen. He prayed hard there would be no police on the way to the university because he was about to break every road law ever made.

CHAPTER TWENTY-TWO

Conrad hoped Bill had informed security he was coming in. The roller door was up, and Conrad raced down the entry to the car park, threw his car around the corner and into a car spot. He remembered to lock it before he made a beeline for the elevator. It sat at the carpark level waiting for him. He ran into it and pressed the button for the ground floor. He'd have to catch another lift to the third floor. The doors closed slowly. Conrad, being impatient, kept hitting the button.

Finally, the elevator moved, but nothing moved fast enough for him. As the doors opened, he was out and running to the next set of elevators. One sat on the ground floor. He entered, bouncing off the back wall. The button for the third floor pressed, he waited, virtually running on the spot until they opened again. At least now he was on the right floor. His blood froze as he heard her scream, and a premonition of dread coursed through his veins.

The door to the research room had been held open by a chair placed against it. Walking fast, Conrad entered, heading straight for the back room where he could hear

195

voices. Bill stood in the door and turned when Conrad called him.

'Thank God you're finally here. She's been asking for you for the last four hours.' He tossed Conrad a gown and mask. 'You need to put this on, the scientists insisted on it.' He placed his hand on Conrad's arm as he made a move to go into the room. 'She's had a hard time of it, son. Don't be upset, she's okay, just very tired. I'm sure she'll be okay as soon as she sets eyes on you.'

'Thanks, Bill. Thanks for taking care of her.' *Thanks for doing what I should have.*

Conrad approached the bed. Hope saw him, and a tired smile crossed her face. Bill hadn't exaggerated. Hope looked like she'd been dragged backward by a truck over rutted roads. 'Honey, I'm sorry I wasn't around. I'm back now. Are you okay, are the babies okay?' Conrad caught himself before he said kittens. He really had to spend more time with humans.

A nurse in the room answered him. 'Your wife is okay, tired, but okay. The babies, however, aren't doing so well. They appear to be tiring, and as they are premature, the doctor would like to perform a caesarean. Your wife says she doesn't want to be operated on.'

Conrad could hear mewling. The babies, it could only be them. There was a difference with hearing something with your ears to hearing something with your mind. He caught flashes of the feeling of being squashed. They were scared. Conrad searched gently, touching them with his mind. He showed them a dark tunnel, then them coming into the light. He tried to place peaceful thoughts in their minds. The children calmed, and the fear dimmed.

'Conrad, I know I can give birth normally. I don't want to be cut open.' Hope was scared, and that was being communicated to the babies.

'Hush, love,' Conrad stroked her brow. 'No one is going to do anything you don't want them to. I'm sure things will be okay now. You need to stay calm. I know it's not easy, but when you are upset, it upsets the babies and tires them out.'

Hope listened to him. The pained lines on her brow eased.

'That's right, breathe deeply. Get all the air you can to those two little bundles you have inside you.'

Conrad could see the monitors. Hope closed her eyes. The sensors changed for the better. The babies calmed. The doctor walked in. 'Just need to check how far she's dilated.'

Conrad kept his gaze on Hope's face. She winced once, grasping his hand tightly as the doctor examined her. 'Everything's okay, love. Just relax.'

The doctor sat back on his stool. 'I don't know what you've done or said, but it worked. Everything is moving along well.' He glanced at the monitors. 'The babies have calmed too, and one of them is ready to be born. The head is engaged and coming down.'

Hope's face screwed up, and Conrad could see her whole body tense. The children's mewls increased. 'Breathe, love, breathe. It won't be long now.'

'I need to push, I can feel something coming out.'

The doctor moved up to the table and placed her in the birthing position. 'Yes, you're right, I can see the sack coming out now.'

Conrad still held Hope's hand but looked between her legs. 'Hope, I can see a head.'

'Hold it right there, Hope, I need to turn the baby to allow the shoulders out. Just pant if you feel the need to push.'

Hope panted, and Conrad found himself doing the same.

'Okay, with the next contraction, I want you to push.'

Hope looked at Conrad. 'We're about to have babies.' A smile lit her tired face, and tears of happiness ran down her cheeks.

Conrad squeezed her hand. 'Yes, and you're going to be a great mum.'

Hope squeezed his hand back, but the pressure didn't let up. Her contractions had started again. 'Push, love, push.'

Conrad peered at his new baby being born in front of him. Shoulders emerged, then with a rush, the rest of the body followed. The membranous sack hadn't broken, so the doctor tore it off, gasped, and nearly fell off his stool.

Conrad's child lay on the bed, wet and mewling. Slick brown, black and white fur covered the body, two small ears lay flat on the top of its head, and a tail disappeared between its legs. Conrad blinked once. 'Hope, we have a baby boy.'

Helga hustled forward, wrapping the baby in a blanket. Conrad could hear him mewling.

'Helga, let me hold him please.'

'We need to do the tests first.'

Herbert laid a hand on her arm. 'Let the father hold him first. The tests can wait a couple of minutes.'

Helga handed the small bundle to Conrad. A small feline but also human face looked up at him, and his heart broke into small pieces. With dark-brown almond-shaped eyes, Conrad could already see the connections being made in the child's mind.

'Hello, my son. I am your father, and this,' Conrad raised the boy's head so Hope could see him, 'is your mother.'

'He's beautiful.' Love beamed from Hope's face. 'And he's ours.'

Conrad held the baby closer to Hope, and she kissed him, running her finger across the top of his head.

Helga stepped forward. 'Can I take him now?'

Conrad nodded and handed him over. Immediately, the child began mewling. Conrad sensed the fear at being removed from his parents. Conrad sent a calming thought to the boy, who quietened.

Hope gasped in pain, and all eyes were back on her.

'Here comes number two.' The doctor glanced up at Hope. 'This is going to happen the same way, hopefully, head first and shoulders to follow.'

Hope nodded, her forehead creased with exertion and pain.

The child's head appeared rounder-faced, with more of a human appearance than the firstborn.

'Okay, pant.' instructed the doctor.

Conrad could see him moving the child.

'Hope, on the next contraction, push!'

Hope gripped Conrad's hand and pushed hard; the force showed in her face, turning it red. A baby girl wooshed out, the bag breaking as she was born.

'A little girl, Hope. We've got one of each.'

'I want to see her,' whispered Hope.

As before, Helga bundled the baby in a blanket, and handed her to Conrad. Her face was decidedly more human than feline, and her skin marked with a light red tabby marbled pattern. However she wasn't furred. Her ears bore tiny tips at the top of human ears, and her eyes were an electric blue. Conrad held her so her mother could see her.

'So sweet, and such lovely eyes.' Hope moved the little girl closer and kissed her. Conrad sensed the bond straight way between mother and daughter. Hope would be fiercely protective of both children, but the bond was stronger with her daughter. Helga approached after a few minutes to collect the baby girl. Again, a mewl sounded as they parted, and Conrad felt the loss.

Hopes eyes grew heavy. The doctor checked her over. 'All bar the placenta coming out, your wife is doing well. I've given her a shot to dislodge it, but she'll be asleep before it discharges.'

Hope murmured something, but neither of the men understood. Conrad leaned in toward her, trying to catch what she was saying.

'Very tired, so very tired. Can't hold my eyes open.'

Conrad looked at the doctor in alarm. 'Could something be wrong, doc?'

The doctor shook his head. 'No, Nothing unusual at all. Birth takes a lot out of a woman. Don't worry, Hope's okay. The best thing to do would be to let her sleep. Helga will clean her up, and she'll be placed into another room where she and the babies can be monitored.'

In another room, a phone rang. Conrad noticed Herbert leave. He hadn't noticed how many people were in the room when Hope had given birth. Oh hell, Bill and his mum had been in the room too. He doubted Hope would have told them the children may 'look' different because he certainly hadn't.

Helga walked past, and Conrad grabbed her sleeve. 'Do you know where Bill and my mother are?'

Helga nodded, smiled and pointed to the room where she had earlier taken the babies. 'Don't worry. Your mother was a bit concerned when she saw the little boy, but I explained everything to her.' Helga tapped his hand in a caring way. 'She's fine, and adores her new grandchildren.'

Conrad glanced at Hope, who appeared to be fast asleep. He brushed her hair away from her eyes, and she smiled. She had the face of an angel when she slept. A face that showed the innocence of her soul. She'd be a great mother to the children. Would he be a great dad?

Leaving Hope's side, he stepped softly into the room where the babies were. Doting grandparents had already bagged their first cuddles. Conrad leant against the doorframe, watching and listening to them talk for a few minutes. If he'd had any worries, they disappeared in the first minute. The look on his mother's face was pure love, and he'd never seen Bill's face so unlined and alive.

What he found amazing was that the babies were just as entranced with those who held them. Unable to speak as yet, they marvelled at the faces above them, a sense of security emanating from them. Chloe leaned her face forward and rubbed it in the little boy's fur. Delight shone from the child, and he mewled with happiness.

Conrad stepped forward, and his mother looked around. 'You're not upset with me, Mum, are you? I didn't know what to tell you, or even how to tell you.' Conrad pulled a seat forward and sat in between his mother and Bill, and marvelled at the two little beings in their arms.

'I was a little concerned when I first saw them, but now I understand what happened.' She gazed down at the precious bundle. 'Regardless of what you look like, we will always love you.' She stroked the baby's slightly furred nose, before giving her attention to Conrad. 'You know, all babies should be born with fur, they are so lovely to cuddle.

'Even if they don't have fur, they are lovely to cuddle,' added Bill. 'Look at her blue eyes. They are like her mother's eyes, only more intense.'

Conrad looked over. He hadn't noticed that, but Bill was right. His little girl's eyes were like Hope's, just more of an electric blue. He looked over to the little boy's face. His eyes were of the darkest brown, just like his dad's eyes. The brown of his fur was a cross between Rufus's colour, but also his own hair colour. The children were definitely a meld of their parents and the one who had made them possible.

'I only hope Uncle Rufus likes you too.'

Herbert burst into the room. 'I'm sorry to break this up, but the babies, even though a good size, need to go into the incubator. We have to make room. Another of the trial subjects has gone into labour, and they are on their way in.'

'Is the father another of the ones who had the fever?' Conrad asked.

Herbert stopped to think. 'Actually, I think he is.' He stepped out of the room and returned holding a chart. 'Yes. Yes, he is. Also one of his babies also showed a tail on the ultrasound.' Herbert tapped his top lip with his finger. 'I think I'll show this to Helga. This could be interesting.' Herbert started to walk away again, then stopped and retraced his steps.

'I'm sorry, I became sidetracked. You'll have to leave. You can come back tomorrow, but you need to leave now.'

Helga bustled in. 'Herbert, put down that chart and make sure the birthing room is ready for our next mother.' She turned to Conrad, Chloe, and Bill. 'I know cuddling the children is lovely, but they do need their sleep, and it looks like it's going to be a busy night. I don't wish to be rude, but can I have the babies back and ask you all to leave?'

Conrad stood, took his son from a caring grandmother and handed the child to Helga, who transferred him to the incubator. Walking to the next prenatal chamber, she opened it up and waited as Conrad gathered his baby girl from Bill before handing her over.

'Thank you. You are welcome back tomorrow. Please ring before you come in.' Helga stepped to the side and ushered them out with a wave of her hand. As they left the rooms, Conrad heard her mutter, 'I hope they don't all go into labour at the same time.' The door closed behind them.

The three of them made their way back to the cars. Conrad waved them off before driving off himself.

As he left the ramp and drove onto the road, he remembered that he and Hope hadn't discussed names. After all, they thought they still had three more months. Conrad's mind began ticking over as to what names he would like the babies to have.

****

'Hi, love.' Conrad entered the room and presented her with flowers and balloons, one saying Girl, the other saying Boy.

Hope took the flowers in her hands, pressed her nose into the bouquet and inhaled. She sighed, a happy smile on her face as she gazed at Conrad. 'I missed you.'

'I missed you too, love. I had to feed the inmates at the centre; they wanted to know where you were.'

Hope laughed, and Conrad's heart filled. He loved her laughter; it filled his soul with happiness. 'I'm sure they were happy just to be fed.'

Hope wasn't to know, but the cats in the centre had asked where and how she was. They knew she had been in labour, and asked about the kittens. Conrad had assured them she was okay, as were the babies.

'Have you seen the babies today?' Conrad wasn't sure what had been happening, whether the mothers were allowed to suckle the children as normal or if they were bottle fed?

'Yes, the babies are out of the incubators. Helga and Herbert seem to think the short pregnancy is because they are part feline, part human. They've been checked over, and both are what Helga and Herbert call "fully formed".'

'What an interesting term. As long as it means they're okay.'

Hope smiled and laughed lightly. 'They're more than okay. Your son has a huge appetite, just like you, and our daughter is a fussy little eater,' she paused in thought. 'A bit like me, I suppose.' She reached out and grasped his hand in hers. 'It's amazing feeding them. Our son feeds like a kitten, kneading my chest with his hands and our daughter lies there and suckles. Both feed well.'

Conrad had been worried about the children, but his mood picked up on hearing the good news. He half sat on the side of the bed. 'We can't keep calling the babies "son" and "daughter". We have to give them names.'

'I agree, Helga asked me this morning if we'd decided on any names. She looked shocked when I said we hadn't talked about it.'

'I know, Mum asked me the same thing this morning. She had a few suggestions, but I don't know if you'd like them.'

'What were they?' Hope pushed herself further up the bed and leaned back against the pillows.

Conrad wriggled into position, sitting cross-legged on the bed facing her. 'Well, for boy's names she suggested Richard, after my dad, Casey, Kitchener, she reckons we can call him Kit for short, and Dexter.' He could tell Hope didn't like the name 'Kitchener,' as her face has screwed up. He hadn't either.

'I don't like Kit. I mean, would we call the little girl Katherine, then shorten it to Kat, so we have two kids called "Kit and Kat"?'

Conrad snorted. 'I didn't think of that.' Okay, maybe she meant that one as a joke. 'So, we're down to Richard or Dexter.

Hope mused. 'I know Richard was your dad's name, but you have to think of what kids are going to call him, and you know how cruel other children can be. Do we really want our boy being called "Dick"?'

Conrad agreed. He remembered the hard time he'd had as a kid. Conman and Connie had been the names they called him. Sometimes it had made him so sad he'd cried, not that he'd told anyone it had hurt him. He hoped

Hope wouldn't want to use his name as the child's middle name. 'Right, so we're left with Dexter, unless you have another name to throw into the ring?'

'No, I like the name Dexter. It's different. Dexter Richard Adamson.' She smiled. 'Yes, I think that name has the right ring to it. Or do you want his middle name to be yours?'

Conrad shook his head. 'No, not at all. I think honouring my dad by using his name is the best way.' Conrad shuddered inside.

'One down and one to go. If you don't mind, I've already thought of the name for our little girl. I'd like to name her after my mother and your mother. Teyah Chloe Adamson.'

Conrad rolled the name around in his mind a few times. He shrugged his shoulders. 'Sounds okay to me, love. Teyah Chloe it is.' He leaned over and kissed his wife. 'Now we really are a family. Mum, Dad and two babies.' He gazed at her, stars in his eyes. 'Hope, I love you so much!'

Hope wrapped her arms around his neck, hugged and kissed him back. 'As I love you, Conrad. Why don't we go see our newly named babies, and you can meet them, now they've had a bath and look clean.'

Conrad turned to the side and slid off the bed. He found Hope's dressing gown and helped her into it. She grasped his hand in hers and led him down the corridor to meet his new family.

The nursery held more than their two babies. Two others lay in incubators. Conrad walked over. Hope followed. Two fully furred, brown tabby-coloured babies lay asleep. One had paws, the other had hands and feet.

Hope spoke softly. 'These two are the babies of the couple who came in after us last night. I don't think things went too well. The babies are very small.'

Conrad had thought so too but didn't want to say anything. 'I hope they're alright. The children are going to need each other.'

Hope looked at Conrad. 'I think we're all going to need each other.' She pulled him away from the other babies, and toward their own children. As they peered into the bassinets, two sets of bright eyes looked back. Both children mewled at the sight of their parents.

Hope reached in and picked up her son. 'Dexter, meet your daddy.' She handed him over to Conrad, who scooped him from her arms. She then picked up a little red tabby girl. 'Teyah Chloe, meet your daddy too.' Both children mewled at him.

Conrad lightly touched each of their minds. *'Hello, Dexter and Teyah. I'm so glad to meet you.'* Looking at their faces, he could have sworn they smiled. Joy and wonderment poured from their little minds.

Hope gasped in amazement. 'Conrad, I swear they just smiled at you, but surely that's not possible, is it?

Conrad smiled. 'If we think they smiled, then I'm sure they did.' Making sure Dexter was firmly snuggled into the crook of his arm, Conrad draped his other arm around his wife and hugged her and the baby close. 'We're going to have a wonderful life together.'

CHAPTER TWENTY-THREE

Four days later Conrad took his little family home. Helga and Herbert had checked the babies over thoroughly, declared them healthy and able to leave the university hospital.

Once home, the babies were placed in their cots, and Conrad insisted Hope take things easy for a few days.

'Conrad, I've been taking it easy for days.' She paced around the house. 'I've been cooped up and not been allowed to go anywhere.' She strode forcefully toward the sliding door. 'The first item on the agenda is to make sure the inmates are okay.' She pulled open the door and strode out toward the rescue centre with purpose.

Conrad had to stifle his laughter. Hope was such a go-getter, a doer. He knew she wouldn't be happy with staying in the one room or floor for days on end. After the second day, when the babies had been moved from the incubators, she'd been bugging the scientists to let her go home. She may be a good nurse, but she was a terrible patient. Eventually, not able to take the questions anymore, Helga had okayed her and the children to leave, as long as they returned weekly for checkups.

Conrad had seen the relief on their faces as he and she had walked out the door to the elevator.

Hope may think she was superwoman, but if she tried to lift the bags of dry cat food, she'd soon find out she wasn't. Conrad followed her out to the centre.

Opening the door, he found her in tears, sitting in the corner, nursing one of the kittens. He raced over to her. 'What's wrong, Hope? You seemed so happy a minute ago.'

She waved him away. 'I'm okay. I saw this little one.' She lifted the small kitten into the air toward him, 'and remembered the other two babies born the same day as our two.'

'Yes, so, why does that make you cry?'

Hope hugged the kitten to her. 'Their mother and father don't want them.' She sniffed back tears. 'Remember I told you it didn't go well?'

Yes, she'd said there had been problems when he's first visited. 'Mmm, yes, I remember.'

Conrad reached for the kitten. Hope had been so upset she'd begun hugging the kitten a little too strongly. It became scared and had begun mewling for help. Of course, Hope couldn't hear it, but Conrad could. 'Let me take the kitten from you, honey.'

Hope handed the kitten over, and Conrad placed it in the other room with the older cats. *'Sorry, my queen is distressed; she didn't mean to hurt the little one.'* A wave of understanding passed over him.

'Hope,' he held out his hand, which she grasped, and he pulled her up from the floor. 'Let's sit over here.' He walked her over, sat her down and proceeded to make a cup of tea for them both. 'So what's going to happen with the children? I did notice they were a lot smaller than ours.'

'Yes, they're a lot smaller.' Hope grew silent for a few seconds. 'Helga said she didn't know what would happen to them. The parents signed them over to Helga and Herbert.' Hope placed her face in her hands and sobbed deeply. 'The parents walked out saying they didn't want to see the monstrosities again.'

Conrad was shocked, and hurried over to Hope, enveloping her in his arms and pulled her tight against him. She cried, each sob coming from deep inside. 'How could any parent say that about babies?'

Conrad tried to comfort her, rubbing her back and kissing her neck. Usually, that calmed her down, but the hurt pouring from her now was stronger than anything he'd felt before. His beautiful wife had been holding all this in for days. He let her cry the pain out, though he instinctively knew what was coming.

Hope's sobs slowed, and she sniffled. He handed her a handkerchief, which she wiped her eyes with, then blew her nose. She sat at the table again, her face solemn and incredibly sad. 'At least the babies were born and not terminated.'

Conrad choked on the mouthful of coffee he'd just taken. 'What? Who terminated?' They'd been given a choice when they'd had the ultrasound, but there was no way they could do it.

Hope sniffed again and dabbed at her eyes with the corner of the handkerchief. 'There was another couple who'd come in. The husband had been sick with the fever as well.'

Yes, Conrad knew who she meant. He nodded, silently urging her to talk.

'Helga said the husband had freaked out at the ultrasound. His wife was screaming, "Get it out of me".'

Conrad couldn't find the words to say. The two couples had known what was going on. Hope hadn't, and even though she was mad at him, she didn't terminate the babies.

Conrad reached for Hope's hands. 'They obviously didn't want children as much as we did.' They'd discussed what they would do if the children were found to be deformed or had any sort of problem. Both of them had decided whatever happened, the child or children were theirs and deserved the same amount of love a healthy baby would. Any problems could be overcome.

Hope nodded, agreeing with him. She reached out her other hand, cupping his in both of hers. 'Conrad, I know you will think I'm foolish, but I—

'—Want to adopt the two babies left behind.' Conrad finished her sentence for her.

She gasped. 'How did you know?'

Conrad leaned in and kissed her reddened nose. 'Because, my darling, I know you. I know you wouldn't want the kids to be brought up with scientists as parents, and it's not as though the children could be fostered out like any abandoned baby, is it?'

Hope looked up, her eyes shining. 'Can we really? Can we adopt them? It'll mean more money for schools and food and anything else they'd need. They may also need extra care?'

'I know there will be problems, but I also know you won't be happy until the two of them are here with us.'

'Oh Conrad, I do love you so.' Hope threw her arms around his neck and kissed him hard.

When she finally let him go, she looked around her. Every cat sat on the floor and a couple on the table. 'What are they all doing here, and do we have a few extra?'

Conrad mentally counted them. Yes, there were three new kittens. Rufus must have brought them through. A few tiny meows told him he was right. 'Yes, I forgot I had a lady coming around with three she'd found in a shed.'

Hope glared at him. 'How could you forget that?'

Conrad shrugged his shoulders. He was happy to be in trouble for something he'd made up. 'The answer to your question is I think they were worried about you. Cats are very perceptive animals.'

One of the smaller kittens approached Hope, and put its paws on her chest. *'Unhappy queen, please don't cry. We love you for what you are doing for us.'*

'She can't hear you, furry one. One day she may learn if she is able, but for the moment, I am the only one who can speak the people's language.'

The kitten sat back and crooked its head at Conrad. 'The queen cannot understand us, or talk? Why?'

'I will explain later.'

The kitten seemed to understand and moved back to receive a pat from Hope. 'That's nice. Animals are so much better than people.' She smiled back at Conrad. 'Can we make a call to the university and ask for the babies?'

Conrad already had his phone out and was dialling the number.

****

'Thank you so much for taking on the two orphans.' Helga handed over the signed birth certificates registering the two orphans as their own biological children. She looked Hope in the eye. 'You look extremely well for someone who has given birth to quads not long ago.'

Hope smiled back. This would be a secret shared between four people.

'There's no chance the real parents could be a problem later in their lives?' asked Conrad. As far as he was concerned, these children were his and Hope's.

'Don't worry. If the real parents ask, the babies were too premature and passed away.'

Conrad looked down at the precious bundles they carried. 'They'll never know they were born to someone else.'

Hope started walking toward the door, carrying the little girl. 'Come on, Conrad. Let's get these little ones home. We have names to decide on.'

Conrad laughed. 'Like we didn't have a hard enough time with the other two.' Glancing back at the two scientists, he noticed a tear in Helga's eye. 'Hope, hold up a minute.'

Hope stopped and looked back. 'Why.'

Conrad walked back to Helga. 'You started falling in love with these two, didn't you?'

Helga dabbed the tears away from her eyes and smiled. 'Who couldn't. Look at those little faces. I've never seen myself as anything other than a scientist, but I was prepared to bring these two up. It wouldn't have been easy, but I would've done my best.' She stroked the furry forehead of the boy Conrad held.

'We need names for these two.' Hope had walked back over and stood beside him. He glanced at her, then back at Herbert and Helga. 'What do think, Hope? Would they be fitting names?'

'I think they would be. We have one of each so the names will fit well.'

Helga clasped Herbert around the arm. 'Children named after us. I love it,' Helga clasped Conrad to her and kissed him on the cheek, Herbert did the same with Hope.

Herbert cleared his throat. 'Helga, I don't know about you, but I would prefer the boy to have my middle name, Axel.'

Helga nodded. 'Yes, I understand. Our first names are a bit old-fashioned, aren't they? My middle name is Charlotte. I think that would suit this little girl quite well and they still have our names, just not the old-fashioned ones.'

Hope smiled. 'I love those names.' She glanced at the little girl in her arms. 'Yes, I think she looks like a Charlotte too.'

'It's not like we'll never see them again, there are the usual check-ups needed as they grow, and of course, if they get ill, you will have to bring them to us.'

'Of course we will.' Hope stepped forward and hooked her arm into Conrad's. 'The children will always know of both of you, and like you said, we will all see each other again.' She pulled Conrad toward the door. 'We need to go home, sweetheart. These babies need to be fed, and we have to relieve Mum and Bill from babysitting duties.'

Conrad extended his hand to Herbert and Helga. 'Thank you again for all you have done. Others may not appreciate these little miracles, but we do.' Together he and Hope turned, and a little later drove out of the car park on their way home, with two more bundles.

****

'Wanderer, don't sit so close to Teyah, please,' Hope called out to the kitten. Except she wasn't much of a kitten anymore. She was still young but larger than any cat Hope had seen.

'Hope, don't worry. Wanderer won't hurt the baby. None of the cats will hurt the babies.'

'How do you know?' Hope walked over, picked up Wanderer and cradled her as she had when the kitten had been a lot smaller.

'The cats see themselves as the protectors. Haven't you noticed when others are around, Spook, Wanderer and a couple of the other older cats hide the babies from view.'

Hope had been wondering about that very thing not long before. 'I have been wondering why they do that.' She looked down at Wanderer who lay in her arms like a baby herself. 'Do you know the children are different?' she asked her. A piercing pain shot through Hope's mind. She nearly dropped Wanderer but held herself together enough to place the cat on the floor before staggering to the couch and sitting down.

'Hope, are you okay?' Conrad asked, concerned.

'It's my head again. I don't understand it. I've never had so many headaches. It must be a hormonal thing.' She cradled her head in her hands, closing her eyes tightly. 'They started the day I found out I was pregnant, and you brought Wanderer and Spook home.'

She sat upright quickly and opened her eyes, even though the pain from doing so was horrendous. 'You don't think I'm allergic to them, do you?'

'No, you're not allergic. It's something else.'

Hope closed her eyes again, trying to close out the pain. 'What else could it be?'

Conrad took a deep breath. 'The pain could be the children, or the cats trying to talk to you.'

Hope's eyelids flew open. 'Conrad, it's not nice to make jokes. I know you think I treat the cats like babies, and I do talk to them, but come on, cats can't talk.'

Conrad took the few steps to the couch and sat at the end. 'That's where you're wrong. The cats do have a language. They think we're the dumb ones because we can't understand them. The children also tried to communicate with you, and they're still trying, that's why you're getting the headaches.'

Hope leaned on her elbow and looked at him, disbelief covering her face. 'The children are trying to talk to me?'

Conrad nodded. 'Yep, and they've been trying to get through to you for a while. Do you ever feel like you are soaking in warm water?'

Hope smiled. 'Yes, I've felt that recently. I thought it had to do with some hormonal thing.' She sat up slowly, still holding her head. 'I usually feel the warm bath thing when I'm feeding the children.'

'That's the kids trying to let you know they love you and they are contented. They can't use proper language at the moment, but they can let you know how they are feeling.'

'Can you talk to them?'

'Yes, I can.' Conrad knew she was going to be unhappy about this new revelation. He could do something and she couldn't.

'Really? How did you learn, and when did you learn?'

Uh-oh. Those drawn together eyebrows indicated only one thing. She was about to get very cranky at him. 'Rufus taught me at work.'

'When?'

Conrad gulped a nervous breath. 'Just over six months ago. When I went back to work after being sick.'

'Were you having headaches too, like I've been having?'

Conrad nodded. 'It wasn't until I concentrated on Rufus that he finally broke through.' Conrad laughed. 'He was so angry he couldn't get through to me that he was swearing.'

'Cats swear?'

'Oh yes, Rufus has some very colourful language.'

'Can you teach me to hear the cats and our children?'

That question brought Conrad up short. He hadn't thought of it at all. It would be great if Hope could speak to everyone telepathically. It would be worth a shot.

'Truly, I don't know. It took me a while to be able to concentrate enough to be able to talk back. And it hurt.' Conrad remembered the stinking headaches he'd suffered under Rufus's tutelage.

'So if you had headaches, and knew the cats were trying to talk to me, why couldn't you have said something sooner?' Hope stood up and stormed off a few steps before turning around again. 'Or do you like seeing me in pain?'

Both babies woke and began to cry. Conrad rose to quiet them. 'Hope, please settle down. You're upsetting the babies.'

'Well, you seem to have the magic spell to get them to go back to sleep or quieten down, so why don't you just talk to them.' Hope voice broke into sobs as she strode angrily to the glass patio door, threw it open and stormed outside.

Conrad could only watch. He knew she'd be upset, and he probably would feel the same if it had been her. The best he could do was to let her cool down in her own time. Hearing the children cry out again, he walked up the hallway to tend to them.

****

Why? Why was he keeping secrets from her? Her head didn't hurt as much now; at least it wasn't migraine strength. She sat down on a stump outside the centre. The valley opened up in front of her, and she realised she'd never really just sat and looked at what was around her. It was always hurry hurry hurry. Feed the cats, do the housework, tend to the garden. She'd never taken the time to sit and relax.

She chortled to herself. That wasn't going to happen now, not with four children to look after.

'You'll still have time to look if you want to.'

'No, I won't. I've always been busy; I've never stopped to take time out.'

'Then why don't you? You've seen us. We walk

around, play with leaves, and then sleep. It's not a bad life, you know.'

'Play with leaves?' Hope looked around. Only Wanderer sat near her. She held her head in her hands. She was going insane, hearing voices.

'Ha-ha-ha, you do not hear things, Hope-queen. It's me, Wanderer. I've been waiting for you to calm down enough to hear me.'

'You're talking to me.'

'You need to talk to me through your head. If you don't, you make funny squeaky sounds. I know when you call my name, I understand that without mind talk, but I can't understand anything else.' Wanderer twisted around, and raising her back leg, scratched the back of her neck.

Hope burst out laughing. Wanderer looked so comical, with her leg in the air. She reached over and scratched behind her neck. 'Is that better?'

'Remember, mind speak, not mouth speak. Yes, that is much better thank you.'

'How?'

'You must be calm. Think the words at me. If it helps, move your mouth, but do not speak. Only think.'

Hope took a deep breath. *'Can you hear me?'*

Wanderer let out a meow of joy. *'Yes, I hear you, but you speak softly. You need to speak louder.'*

Hope tried again. *'Okay, how about now?'*

'Much better, definitely louder.'

'Thank you for teaching me, Wanderer.'

'There are many things to teach you Hope-queen, but this is a good start. Are you happier now? Not sad anymore?'

Hope leaned to her side and picked up Wanderer and hugged her tight. *'I'm much happier now I can talk to you.'*

Wanderer knocked her head under Hope's chin. *'I'm happy to be able to talk to you too. I have been trying for so long. I am sorry I made your head hurt.'*

'Do not be sorry, little one. You didn't know I couldn't talk like you do.' Hope kissed her on top of the head. She revelled in the knowledge she could now speak with the cats, just as Conrad could, but as he'd kept the ability secret, she'd keep her ability secret too.

Calmed down, with still the buzz of a headache numbing her mind, Hope let the kitten onto the ground and went back inside. She'd forgive her husband, but she wouldn't tell him what she could do.

She and Wanderer had plenty of time for practice, now she'd given up her job as a nurse. With four babies to take care of, a day job wasn't an option. She could have asked Chloe to mind them when at work, but that wasn't fair to the children, her or Chloe. Hope smiled to herself. She'd be able to talk to her babies now too.

CHAPTER TWENTY-FOUR

Time passed quickly when you had four children in the house, especially when all four had the added curiosity of kittens. Spook and Wanderer had learnt to keep their tails either tucked in around them or high in the air, where grasping little hands couldn't snatch at them.

Axel and Charlotte soon matched Dexter and Teyah in height and weight. Hope's hands were full at feeding time. Sometimes she wondered if it would be easier to lie on the floor and suckle the children as a female cat did. As there was no way she could suckle all four children at the same time, they took it in turns.

One sanctuary remained hers. The Cat Rescue Centre. There she could talk with all the cats and kittens. Her language skills increased, and soon she talked freely, without any fear of headaches. The queens in the centre helped her understand the children and how to talk to them.

Three months had passed. Conrad raced into the house one afternoon after working a day shift, picked her up, and swung her around in happiness.

'The first of the other children have been born.'

Hope smoothed herself down once he placed her back on the ground. She'd been working in the garden and felt sweaty and smelly. 'What do you mean, the "other" children?'

'You know, the children of the other men in the trial, the ones who didn't get sick.'

'Oh, okay. So are the babies healthy?'

'Yes, they are healthy.' Conrad grabbed hold of Hope's hand, turning her around to face him. 'Hope, what's wrong? I thought you'd be happy for the others and their babies arriving.'

Hope took back her arm. 'I'm okay, and yes I'm happy for them. I'm wondering what the children are going to experience when they grow up.'

Conrad grew concerned. Hope had never expressed feelings like this before. 'Honey, please come and sit down. You need to tell me what has happened for you to think this way.'

Hope shook her head. 'Not now, Conrad. I'm hot, dirty and sticky. I need a shower before I do anything else and before the children wake up.' Hope walked off up the hallway and turned into their bedroom.

Conrad knew she'd be a while and didn't want to bother her, but something brewed within her. She was upset about something and needed to let it out.

Conrad rose, made himself a cup of coffee, and one for Hope. He sat it on the table as she walked back into the room. 'Feel better now?'

Hope only nodded, sat down, and turned the mug in her hands.

'Hope, please talk to me. What has upset you?' he reached across to hold her hand, hoping to give her reassurance.

She stood and walked a few steps to the back door, where she stood gazing out into the backyard. 'Someone came the other day to adopt a kitten.'

Conrad was confused. Why was she upset if someone wanted to adopt one of the animals? 'Yes. Was there something wrong with them?'

'No,' she shook her head, 'or maybe, yes there was. I was breastfeeding Axel at the time; she saw him.' Hope turned.

Conrad sat up and paid attention. Nothing had been mentioned about the early arrival and the visual appearance of the children. 'What did she say?' The general populace wasn't supposed to know. Also Axel had paws, not hands and feet. He was the most cat-like out of the four children.

'She was okay until she realised he was suckling. She laughed at me and called me weird.' Hope looked crestfallen.

'Oh honey,' Conrad rose and hugged her tight. Hope sniffed. He could tell she was close to tears.

Hope pushed herself away and looked up at Conrad. 'That's when she noticed he wasn't a cat.'

'What happened?' A growing unease began growing in Conrad's chest. 'Hope, what did you do?'

Hope pushed herself out of his arms, and he followed her out of the house and into the garden. She stopped beside the garden bed Conrad knew she'd been working on for a week. Hope glanced at Conrad, then fixed her eyes on the mound in front of her. 'She tried to grab him. Said he was an abomination.'

Conrad took a step toward her, arms outstretched, but she shrugged him off.

'He's not an abomination, he's our son. I may not have borne him, but he is our son, and I will defend him to the best of my ability.' Hope turned around, 'And I did.'

'You killed the woman? Is she buried in there?' Conrad pointed to the garden bed.

'No,' Hope shook her head, 'I didn't kill her, but I did bury her.'

'Then who killed her?' Conrad tried to clear the confusion in his mind.

'We did. She attacked one of us. No one will attack one of the people here.'

Conrad turned around until he faced the rescue centre. Every cat and kitten who could walk sat or lay outside the building. *'We could be in a lot of trouble. The two-legs you killed may have told someone she was coming here.'*

'There is no danger, Conrad-hero. No one will find her. Hope-queen called out in fear, as did the child-kitten. All has been covered over, like the leavings of a meal.'

'You didn't eat her, did you?'

'Hissss! How can you think of something like that? No, we only knocked her down when she tried to harm the kitten. Her head hit a rock. The death is regrettable, but it was an accident. Hope-queen helped us dig a hole. She is not at fault.'

'Conrad? Are you alright?'

Conrad shook his head to clear the voices he'd been hearing and looked at his wife. His dear, sweet loving wife, who had covered up a death, and buried someone in the garden. No wonder she'd been out of sorts.

'They told you, didn't they?'

Conrad was speechless. All he could do was to look at her, and wonder, could he have done the same thing?

'Conrad, please speak to me.' Hope pleaded.

'Yes, yes, I'm okay, and yes they told me.' Conrad hugged her again as hard as he could. 'How on earth did you manage to do that?'

Hope shrugged her shoulders. 'I just did. The cats protected me, and I had to protect them.'

'Hmmm. I do understand, but it does raise a point. Eventually, the world is going to find out about the children, both ours, and the ones being born now. We need to speak to Helga and Herbert about this and figure out what is going to be done.' He paused for a few seconds. 'So are you okay now you have let it out?'

Hope smiled in relief. 'Yes, I'm okay now. It's been weighing on me every day since it happened, and I haven't been able to sleep at all. I'm so tired, Conrad. I want to sleep for a month.'

'I can understand that, love. Come back inside, and we'll take care of it.' A wail came from inside the house. Conrad sighed. 'Correction, we'll take care of it as soon as the babies have been fed.' He turned her around to face him before they entered the house, bent down and kissed her on the lips. 'That's for being my brave wife, and an awesome protector of the children.'

'Hmm,' she murmured, 'Maybe I should do more of that. I liked that kiss and would love some more.'

Another wail came from within the house.

'But,' she sighed, 'it'll have to wait until later.'

****

Rufus sat at the entry door to the centre as Conrad and Hope walked toward it in the morning. He yawned as they drew closer.

'Good morning Conrad.'

'Good morning Rufus. What do we owe this visit to? Have you brought more kittens with you?'

Before answering, Rufus turned a curious look toward Hope. *'Good morning Hope-queen. I see you are well?'*

Hope didn't answer, but a smile crossed her face.

'Rufus, Hope-queen can't speak yet, and I'm not sure she will be able to.'

Rufus gave a wry smile. *'I see.'*

Hope tapped Conrad on the arm. 'While you're talking to Rufus, I'll go feed the cats, before they scream the place down.

'Okay love. I won't be long.' Conrad and Rufus watched as she closed the door behind her.

Rufus turned his gaze to Conrad. *'Your kittens are healthy and well?'*

'Yes, they are growing fast, all four of them. They are only six-months old and are already crawling.' Conrad felt proud of the children's achievements and didn't mind boasting a little.

'Conrad-hero, you are funny. My kittens are walking in two weeks, let alone six months. At that age, the young females are nearly ready to have their own litters of kittens.'

Conrad caught the chastisement. *'Yes, your kittens are quicker than mine in all things. Six months is fast for human kittens.'*

'As long as they are progressing well.' Rufus paused and took a breath. *'Conrad, I have come to say farewell. I will no longer be coming through the box to see you here. Spook and Wanderer can take over my task of bringing the kittens here. The Great Siam is getting old, as am I, and I wish to spend my remaining time with my queen. She has been patient with me taking trips and disappearing, and I feel now is the time to be with her.'*

Conrad dropped to one knee and stroked the shaggy head. They'd been through so much together. He'd miss his furry friend. *'I am sorry to hear that, but I am still able to come and see you, aren't I?*

'Of course. The work you have done on Catatopia is well appreciated by all the families. Of course, the Great Siam is upset, as he didn't know what was happening until one of the soldiers mentioned it to him.'

'Will that cause you any hardship, my friend?'

'No, no hardship at all. As I mentioned, he is getting older and prefers his subjects to come to him. He has grown weak, and will soon be deposed.'

'Do you know who is going to take the job on?'

'No, but some fool will.'

Conrad had a sneaking suspicion he knew who the 'fool' would be. *'I will miss our trips to gather pure bloods with you. We had some good adventures.'*

'Yes, the adventures were interesting. I could not have gathered the number of breeds we did without your help, Conrad, and as you say, I shall also miss our time together.'

Conrad stood. He could sense Hope had given him room to speak but expected him to not be too long. He had a few chores to do before he and Bill departed for the shift at the university.

'Will you be seeing Wanderer before you leave?'

'Yes, I will. She and Spook are in the large cave at the top of the hill?'

Conrad had to laugh at the terminology Rufus still used. Countless times he'd been told the word was 'house', but he continued to use the word 'cave' for the dwelling. *'Yes, both of them are there. They are playing with the children.'*

'Excellent. I will be pleased to see how they are. I have not seen my daughter in a long time.'

Conrad watched as his furry companion trotted up the hill. *'Keep your tail high; the boys like to pull them if they drop low.'*

Rufus stopped and looked back. *'Thank you for the warning. I shall do as you say.'*

Conrad watched him walk into the house and heard the gurgled baby words announcing his arrival. Rufus would have to be fast on his feet; the children crawled faster than he may have let on.

Conrad opened the door to the centre and walked in, making sure it closed behind him. The great majority of the cats who lived here at the moment knew how to go out and come in as they pleased. Only the Earth-born cats couldn't leave.

'Have you and Rufus finished your discussion?' Hope stood at the sink, cleaning dirty cat bowls. Cats milled around her feet or sat on the sink beside her.

'Yes. He came back for one last time to say he wouldn't be visiting anymore.'

'Remind me, where does Rufus come from? Surely he didn't walk all the way from the university.' Hope turned to face him, leaning her hands behind her on the sink. 'Or did he hide in the car when you were at work yesterday?'

Conrad knew the tone she used. It was the voice that said he'd been caught out again. He shrugged his shoulders, 'Umm, I don't know how he got here.'

Hope turned, grabbed a towel and dried her hands, before walking the step or two toward him. She reached up, placing her hands behind his neck. She sighed. 'Conrad my dear, you are a lovely man, but you are an extremely bad liar. You know exactly how Rufus got here, but you have been keeping yet another thing from me.'

Conrad shuddered. Had she guessed? How possibly could she know? The cats around them began meowing. Conrad caught the sound of feline laughter.

Hope smiled at him as the realisation crossed his face. *'You can talk to them, can't you?'*

'Yes, I can Conrad, and I heard everything Rufus said. Now,' her face grew stern, *'who is the Great Siam, and where or what is Catatopia?'*

The feline laughter continued. He'd been set up.

'Hope, my darling, you're in for a wild story. I suggest we get this lot fed, get a cup of tea and sit down, then I'll fill you in on what has been happening for at least a year.'

'Fine, I look forward to it. I also want to know how Rufus, Wanderer, and Spook appear and disappear.'

Conrad's throat grew dry, and he quickly filled a glass with water from the sink and drank. 'That may be a bit harder to believe.' He gasped hoarsely.

'I don't know, I think I'm pretty well up on believing the impossible now.'

****

'What do you mean you can't take me to Catatopia?' Hope stormed back and forth across the lounge room floor.

Conrad sat on the couch watching her. 'Why can't you just believe me, why do you have to see everything with your own eyes?'

Hope stopped and stood legs apart and hands on her hips. 'If you'd been told a fantastic story about being able to travel to another planet by stepping into a cabinet and pressing a few buttons, wouldn't you want to go?'

'Yes, but you can't just "go". Helga and Herbert can't travel there anymore. One more trip through the portal and they would be dead on the other side. Without the special gene the cats and I carry, the planet or the air you breathe there would kill you within a few years.' Conrad stood and walked to where his angry wife stood. 'Sweetheart, I don't want you to die just because you want to visit the planet.'

'Well, I want to go. Can I be tested for this gene to see whether I carry it?'

'I don't know, I suppose so. I know have it, because of the serum I stuck myself with, plus it made me able to understand and talk to the cats.'

'I can talk to the cats now too, so that means I have it as well.' Hope made to walk out the door.

Conrad knew exactly where she would head. He reached forward and grabbed her arm. 'Please Hope, no. Not until we find if you have the gene. You may only be able to talk to the cats because you carried the children.'

SILENCE!

Conrad and Hope covered their ears and dropped to their knees in pain. The shouted command had come through so loud, it was as if a lightning bolt had seared the inside of their minds.

'Good. Finally, the incessant noise has stopped.' Rufus stalked into the room and sat in front of them. *'Those in the big cave down the hill can hear you arguing. It is painful to us. It must stop. When you talk your sounds, you now also think with your mind. We can all hear you!'*

Conrad began to open his mouth, but a look from Rufus stopped him.

'You were able to open the door to the lower cave when I took you to Catatopia the first time.'

'Yes, that is true.' Conrad removed his hands from his head. His mind still buzzed from the assault, but at least it didn't hurt anymore.

'I understand you took something from the door when you moved the box here.'

What Rufus was suggesting finally dawned on him. He'd placed the diode in the cat door. If Hope could open the cat door, it would mean she had the gene and could travel off world. Conrad's face broke into a smile.

'Thank you, my friend. Your suggestion will definitely tell us whether or not Hope can travel to Catatopia.'

'Finally, you realise.' Rufus shook himself, walked to the door, then looked back. *'Are you coming?'* He looked pointedly at both Hope and Conrad.

'But the children are asleep. I can't leave now.'

Rufus huffed. *'Hope-queen, you were about to do just that. No, you cannot leave now, but you can test the door to see if it will open for you.'*

'And if it opens, I'll be able to travel to your planet, with no harm?'

'Correct.'

Conrad helped his wife to her feet, and together they trooped down the hill toward the centre. Once they entered, Rufus passed his paw over the diode. The cat flap opened, he walked through and it closed behind him.

'What do I do?' Now Hope was there, she wasn't sure she wanted to try. What if she couldn't open it?

'Stop wondering about what happens if you can't. Try it, and it may work.' Conrad urged. He waved his fingers over the diode, and the door opened. After a few seconds, it closed again. 'Now, your turn.'

Hope bent down and waved two fingers over the diode. She waited for it to open, but the door didn't budge. Her vision became blurry, and her eyes filled with tears.

'Try again,' urged Conrad.

She bent over again, this time touching the panel where the diode had been placed and held her breath. The door opened. Tears poured from her eyes, this time not in sadness, but in joy. She could follow Conrad to Catatopia. Finally, there were no more secrets between them.

Hope stood, walked back to her husband, and wrapped her arms around him. 'Finally, we can do things together.' She lifted back her head and looked up into his beautiful face. 'I feel so happy. There are no more secrets. I know what you know. It's like a light has finally opened up over us.'

Conrad dipped his head to kiss her. He too had felt the weight of untruths and lies lift from his shoulders. He rarely cried, but somehow, he couldn't stop rivulets from cascading down his cheeks.

'Oh Hope. Let's not lie or hide the truth from each other anymore. From now on, we're partners in everything we do.'

Hope could only nod and smile. She'd seen the change in Conrad and rejoiced that she had her husband back again, the one she'd lost just over a year before.

CHAPTER TWENTY-FIVE

Conrad couldn't believe his eyes when he opened the paper.

HYBRID CAT/HUMANS BORN
SCIENTIFIC ADVANCE OR FREAK SHOW

Underneath, the pictures showed two babies looking very human, except for little tips on their ears and almond-shaped eyes.

Conrad looked over the top of the paper and gazed lovingly upon his four children, each special in their own ways. Three of them were close to walking; they pulled themselves up on anything larger than them. Teyah still crawled, but it wouldn't be long until she followed the others.

Anger bubbled in Conrad's stomach. How dare they say his children were freaks? What angered him even more were the so-called comments from leading people of the community. Only one of them had anything good to say about the children. Conrad could only hope that in the next couple of years, minds would change and the hybrid children would be accepted every bit the same as a child born without the intervention of science.

'Hi love, what's new in the world?' Hope walked in after completing her chores in the rescue centre.

Conrad quickly folded the paper in half and shoved it down beside him. Crossing his arms in front of him, he shook his head. 'Nothing much. They think they've found a way to take the excess radioactivity out of the atmosphere.'

'Oh, that's marvellous. It means the farmers will be able to grow proper fruit and vegetables again. Surely if they find a way to remove it from the air, they'll be able to take it from the ground too.' She washed her hands, then sat down next to him, and grabbed the paper before he could stop her. 'Now, let's take a look at what you didn't want me to see.'

Conrad grabbed for the paper, but she turned and held it from him. 'Hope, just give it back. You know you get upset by bad news in the paper.'

'No,' she turned her head back to look at the paper and groaned. She stood and walked a couple of steps with the paper spread in front of her. 'How can they say that? My babies aren't what they are calling them here.' Conrad rose and pulled the paper out of her hands, wrapped his arms around her and held her tight.

'It's not true, Conrad, it's so not true.'

'Shhh, I know it's not true. The problem is, how do we show them it's not true? How do we show them they are children, just like any others?'

Hope pushed herself away and picked up the paper. 'Conrad, these are the human-looking babies. What would they say if they saw Axel, Dexter, and Charlotte?'

Conrad sat and placed his arms on his legs. 'I think we know the answer to that one, don't we.' He gestured toward the garden bed, which sported some very healthy petunias and calendulas.

Hope sighed. 'I suppose we do. Do you think we can change people's opinions?'

'It's going to be a while before they need to go to kindergarten or school. Surely with all the advancements they've been making in medicine, people will understand they are only children with markings on their skin, and maybe a bit of fur.'

Conrad shrugged his shoulders. 'All we can do is hope people can change, and accept difference.' Inside, he knew that was a big ask. People hadn't changed in the way they viewed the world in years. Religion, race, and colour still separated mankind. Conrad couldn't see them accepting furry children. He'd have to come up with a way to keep the children safe, and perhaps also the other children. 'I'll give Helga and Herbert a call, and ask them what's going on. I can't see them springing something like this on the people who took part in the trial.'

'It says here that the scientists were contacted, but declined to comment.' She kept reading. 'Conrad, this was put out by one of the couples on the trial. Apparently, they aren't happy that their children have markings and tips on their ears.' Hope laughed. 'Oh, the poor dear people. How sad they are not to see what they have been given.' Hope placed down the paper, folded it and threw it to the side where it landed on the couch. 'If these children have a thimble full of the intelligence of ours, their parents are going to eat their words in a few years. How can they have decided they are the best of what this race can offer?'

Conrad smiled at his wife's rant. She considered herself lucky to have the children she did. Sure, it had been a shock at the start, but the babies had proved themselves smarter than any human child of the same age. Yes, no other child could have a protector like his Hope.

Any further discussion was cut short as the phone began to ring. Hope moved to answer.

After announcing herself, she listened to the person on the other end, then motioned to Conrad to join her. 'Herbert, can you hold please, and I'll put Conrad on the line for you.'

Hope handed the phone over to Conrad and sat on the couch. She knew he'd tell her what the conversation was about. She watched as he paced back and forth across the polished floor. A lot of 'I see' and 'ahas' were said before he hung up.

Conrad walked over to the couch and calmly sat down. 'Apparently, Helga and Herbert are being sued for malpractice. They are worried the university will cut their research grants and they won't be able to continue.' Conrad smacked his fist into his hand. 'This has all come about because one of the couples decided to go on a camping trip and the wife gave birth in front of all their friends. With the way social media is, the babies photos were seen within minutes of being born. That's where the media got the photo from.' His fist smacked into a palm again. 'Herbert just wanted to assure us that it wasn't anything they'd done and they wouldn't be volunteering any information on the children to anyone.'

'That's all well and good, but you know what people are like, and what the media is like. If they don't get the real story, they'll make up their own anyway. Maybe Helga and Herbert should tell their story, the real story. It may also make it easier for people to accept the children when they get older.'

Conrad could see sense in what Hope said, but doubted the university would see it the same way. 'I'll give them a call back and mention what you've said. Who knows, it may make a difference.' Conrad picked up the phone and began dialling. After the happenings of the last six months, he could have dialled the number in his sleep.

Hope waited, leaning on the back of a chair. Conrad mentioned what she had said and suggested they give the correct details to the media, but not hand over any information of who the parents were.

Hope thought it was a good idea. Publicity could go both ways, good and bad. She didn't want the Cat Rescue Centre harmed. The centre was needed, and the children didn't need to be in the media spotlight only to be treated like they were some inhuman species. After all, the human race could do with a little variation. With changes to the serum already made, children born in the future wouldn't have the same stigma attached to them.

The sound of the phone hanging up brought Hope out of her thoughts. 'What did he say?'

'Herbert thought it was a good idea and agreed with you. The media circus would only start their own story to suit themselves. He's ringing all the people in the trial and hopes they all think the same way. He's agreed to keep names out of it, as we've signed the privacy agreement. He also said not to worry about them being sued. All the men had signed consent forms before they were injected, which means the couple have no comeback on the university at all.'

'And the cancelling of their research grant?' The human race needed people like Helga and Herbert, and the work they were doing. Without it, man would slowly die off. Sometimes, Hope thought that wouldn't be a bad idea.

'That's still to be decided,' Conrad said ominously.

****

As was usual, the media lost all interest in the hybrid children once something else caught their attention. More people had come out with the opinion that having the smartness of the feline race couldn't hurt the slow moving, apelike, Homo sapiens sapiens race. The children had been given another classification. They were to be the first Homo Feline sapiens sapiens. Time wore on, and the headlines were forgotten, as were the children, for a few years.

Until they began kindergarten at the age of three.

Children are inquisitive, but these children were more than that, they were intelligent and took in knowledge like it was a needed food or a supplement they couldn't do without.

Conrad and Hope were always being asked 'Why?' and 'How?' They couldn't keep up with the questions, so had begun a computer link-up with the scientists. It was they who suggested the children start school early. That's when problems began.

After being kept apart from other children because of the chance the media may start another witch hunt, they didn't know how to act around the other children. Ears, tails, and fur received tugs, and fights ensued. When one child fights another child, it's normal, but when one of those children sprouts retractable claws and rakes the other child's face, there's going to be trouble and consequences.

Such a fight happened between Conrad's son Dexter and another child who had been taunting Teyah. All the children had been told not to fight and to walk away if someone called them names.

When Conrad arrived at the kindergarten, he found Dexter and Teyah sitting outside, while everyone else was inside. Confused, he squatted down in front of them. 'Why are you out here?' He could see Teyah was upset; the tear marks still showing on her cheeks. Teyah looked down, and the tears began to fall again.

Dexter was the one to tell him what had happened. 'A boy was teasing Teyah, and she told him to stop, but he didn't. She walked away, but he kept following her and kept pushing her in the back. I saw what was happening and pushed him back. He got angry and said I wasn't a boy, but a cat and cats shouldn't be in kindy. He hit me, and I was so mad, I scraped him with my claws. Then the teacher saw me and saw the cuts on the other boy's face, and both Teyah and me had to sit out here.'

Conrad gathered both children in his arms. 'It's alright. I understand you were only protecting your sister.' He cuddled them, trying to soothe and calm them. Both children were upset. Teyah hadn't done anything wrong. She'd tried to walk away like she'd been told to, but the other boy was being nasty. Dexter had only done what a good brother would. It wasn't his fault he had claws instead of fingernails. The other boy should have been sent out, not them. It wasn't fair.

'I see you've turned up to claim the "children".'

Conrad looked up to see a woman with a rather snooty look upon her face. He rose, and she took a couple of steps back. 'What do you mean by "claim the children"?' Conrad's rage began boiling.

The woman took another few steps back, looking behind her to see where the door was. Conrad advanced on her. 'What do you mean?'

'I mean creatures like them should not be allowed in kindergarten. That is for human children, not "pets".' She took a couple more steps back through the doorway, then closed and locked it on her side. 'Take them away, and tell the others that your kind are not going to be admitted here, or any other school.'

Conrad's anger exploded, and he made it to the door in two steps. He grasped the handle, rattling the door. It was locked, and no amount of force would open it.

'Go away, and take those creatures you call children with you. If you don't leave, I will call the police.'

Conrad debated staying there and letting her call the police. The teacher had no right to bar his children from kindy. One look at his children dissuaded him from staying. The lost, forlorn looks grabbed at his heart and squeezed hard.

'Daddy, why don't they want us? Why are they so mean?' Dexter's face said it all.

Conrad gathered both in his arms, hoisting them up onto his hips. 'Because they are scared of what they don't understand. Because they are ignorant.'

Conrad didn't want his children subjected to any more of what had happened today. Until they reached school age, he and Hope would teach them what they needed to know.

He only hoped in a couple of years feelings would have changed. Once he had the twins in the car and buckled in, he rang Herbert.

The man answered, and Conrad spoke only one sentence. 'Herbert, we have to talk.'

CHAPTER TWENTY-SIX

The setting could have been anywhere in the country. A group of families in a park, children playing ball, climbing trees and playing on the playground equipment. Only, if the watcher looked a little harder, they would have noticed all the children were roughly around the same age, and every one of them had markings of some kind. Some were orange, others were black, grey or brown. A few sported a coat of fur.

While a couple of wives supervised the children at a picnic table not far away, a group of adults congregated, gesturing, talking, sometimes thumping the table in anger.

'I'm not sending my kids back to the kindergarten to be picked on, and to be told they aren't human, that they should be in a cage somewhere,' one angry parent spat.

'I'm with you. Did you know they made my son wait outside, because "pets aren't allowed in the classroom". I was furious. How dare they call my child an animal!' roared another infuriated parent.

Herbert and Helga sat in the centre of all this and tried to calm the parents. 'We have heard what has happened, and understand how painful this has been for you and the children. That's why we have called this meeting.'

'So what are we going to do? I don't know about the other parents, but I've decided to teach my kids myself. I know I won't go too far, but after that, I'll hire a tutor.'

A chorus of hear hear could be heard.

Herbert thumped the table. A hush fell over the group. 'I propose we set up our own school. If the education system can't cope with our children, then it falls to us to provide their education.' Herbert stood. 'Among everyone here are a range of vocations. We have trades, clerical, accountants, writers, and of course, Helga and myself who are geneticists. I think between us all, we can give the children a reasonable education.'

'Where will we teach them? Is there a place we can all go, like a classroom set-up?

A hum sounded as the adults talked together, trying to find a place.

'I suppose we could make a system up, where one family had all the children around for one week for lessons?' a man suggested.

Someone else laughed. 'I suggest you ask your wife that question before voting on it.'

Conrad stepped forward. 'Herbert, Helga, would it be possible to use a room at the university? It has computers the children will need. Not one of us have anything close to what the university can provide. You would have the chance to observe the children, and mark and measure their IQs.'

The scientists put their heads together and conferred for a minute. 'That would be desirable, Conrad, but the trouble would be getting the needed room. Did you have somewhere in mind?'

Conrad smiled to himself. He may not think himself smart, but the university was one place he knew like the back of his hand. 'There are a couple of rooms that are unused on the first floor. Desks and chairs are already there, and it would only need a tidy up. I wouldn't be surprised if other researchers at the university offered to help with the teaching.'

He waited as Herbert and Helga considered the information. 'Herbert, if you and I met with the university directors and put forward our case, I'm sure we'd be given at least one room.'

Conrad had an ace up his sleeve. During his time as a security guard, he'd seen many things he'd turned a blind eye to. Midnight rendezvous, lights being on in offices they shouldn't, and some very embarrassed faces when he'd walked in on people in the dark. The time had come to call in some favours.

Herbert stood and shook Conrad's hand. 'If you are willing to come with us and plead the children's case for education, then we accept.'

One of the mothers spoke up. 'Will this cost us a lot of money? When my husband's boss found out our babies were "different", my husband lost his job. We're surviving, but we can't pay a huge amount of money for the children's schooling.'

Hope placed her arm around the embarrassed woman's shoulders. 'I'm sure something can be worked out, and I wouldn't think the university would charge us huge sums.'

'What do you think, Conrad? Will they charge for the use of the room and facilities?'

'I don't think so, Hope. I think they'll be happy to

supply us whatever the children need.'

'Do you know something the rest of us don't?'

Conrad smiled again. *'You might say that. Let's say they'll be glad to give us whatever we need and clear their consciences.'*

Hope gave the woman's shoulder a comforting squeeze. 'I think we'll be alright, won't we, Conrad?'

Conrad winked at her. 'I'm sure the university directors will see us right.'

Hebert banged on the wooden table. 'I think that concludes this meeting. You can all help your children with their education, by teaching them to read and write. With luck, the rest will be taught by people in the appropriate fields. These are clever children who are learning fast. We need to keep their minds entertained and fulfilled. Conrad, Helga and I will make an appointment to meet with the university directors, and we will give you all a call with the result and what will happen from there on.'

Couples broke away, each going in different directions, while their children ran in circles around them.

Conrad, Hope, and the children were the last to leave. Herbert and Helga stepped up as they were about to walk away. 'Are you sure they will see us, and give us what we need?'

Conrad clapped Herbert on the shoulder. 'Herbert, I know little secrets about each one of them they wouldn't like being known about, especially by their spouses, if you know what I mean.' Conrad tapped the side of his nose with his forefinger. 'Some may call it blackmail, but I call it an "education expense".'

Herbert's mouth dropped open, shocked. It lasted only a few seconds before his mouth split into a huge grin, finally understanding what Conrad meant. Helga and Hope were already laughing.

'Conrad, I have severely underestimated you. I will call you tomorrow with the meeting details.'

'I look forward to hearing from you. Have a good night, both of you.'

Conrad called his children, placed his arm around Hope, and walked off toward their car, chuckling to himself.

****

Two days later, the directors granted the children the use of the rooms for no charge, on the proviso that their researchers could monitor the children's progress. All textbooks and education expenses would be paid by the university. The parents wouldn't have to pay a cent.

A day after that, a working bee cleaned, dusted and repainted two of the disused rooms on the first floor.

Monday of the following week, a kindergarten teacher and a couple of aides were brought in to start teaching the children.

Conrad and Hope stood outside the door to the classroom and smiled. The term 'underhanded' may have been used, but none of the children would be bullied or subjected to cruel taunts during their schooling. Hope grasped his hand, looking up at him.

'You did the right thing, Conrad. The children are happier here than they ever were at the other schools.'

Conrad agreed. The children's demeanour had picked up, and all being in one group, they didn't have the distraction of lesser minds holding them back. He wouldn't be surprised if the university had to bring in higher qualified teachers every few months.

'Pretty soon our kids are going to be smarter than us. What do we do then?'

'We'll worry about that when it happens, until then they are little children who need cuddles and discipline for at least the next few years.

CHAPTER TWENTY-SEVEN

Ten years on

Conrad sat in front of the Cat Rescue Centre looking in through the glass door. He could see the inside door to the cabinet. When had he stopped taking trips to Catatopia? He looked down at his hands, seeing the large scar that ran up his palm and disappeared between his fingers. He remembered the last time. The last house had been finished being repaired after what they had called the 'big storm'. A couple of small jobs were all that was left to be done. He'd been up the ladder, hammering a last nail in a window surround, when a searing pain cut through his calf muscle.

Crying out in shock and pain, he dropped the hammer. A cat shrieked below him, having been struck by the falling tool. Trying not to fall himself, he stepped back carefully, testing the muscle before placing his full weight on the leg. One step at a time, until he placed both feet on the floor. He bent down to examine the cat who'd been struck by the hammer. The tom leaned away from him, cautious of being hurt again. 'I won't hurt you, Siam, you know that.'

'Leave my servants alone. You have been here too long. I want you gone.'

Another slash marked his skin, this time the claw sliced through his hand. The Siamese lifted his paw for another swipe.

'Siam, what are you doing? I've been fixing the damage. No feline could do this. I am helping you.'

'You are only a two-legs, and I want you gone. I said at the start that no two-legs would ever be here again, and yet you keep coming, taking away my best kittens to populate your two-legs world.'

Conrad stood and picked up the hammer. 'I don't understand what is happening, but if you don't want me here, I will leave.' Conrad walked out of the house, down the street, and entered the building that housed the portal cabinet back to Earth. He removed his handkerchief from his pocket and wrapped it around his bloody hand, entered the portal and a minute later, walked out of the cabinet Earth-side.

He shook his head to clear the memory. He hadn't been back since, but the time fast approached when he'd have to. Problems had arisen with the children. Children may be the wrong word to use. Even those who didn't have fur displayed the same high IQ as the furred ones. They were adults in all but age. Unable to teach them further, Herbert and Helga had them working in the laboratory, assisting the scientists.

The old media reports surfaced, with some of the agencies doing a 'what happened to …' series on them.

Suspicion grew, and a couple of them had been attacked in the street. To save them and let them live a life away from harm and ridicule, they'd have to leave.

They couldn't go to another country, they'd get the same treatment as they had here.

Conrad looked up again at the doorway to the only future they had. Rising, he sighed deeply, entered the centre, opened the door to the portal, stepped inside the cabinet and pushed the button. The familiar whine began.

****

Stepping out of the cabinet on the other side, Conrad walked into the office and began rummaging through the cabinets. Herbert had mentioned maps of the area and of the entire planet should be there—somewhere.

He'd kept the place reasonably tidy when he'd been through before, but again, the dust lay thick on the cabinets, and the windows only showed a blurred semblance of the outside scenery. They'd need cleaning again. Conrad shuddered. Why think that way? It wasn't as though anyone remotely human would be ever using them again. He stopped and thought. Why couldn't they use the place again?

If the lot of them were to maybe call this place home, was it possible they could use a few of the houses as a layover, or as a place for the others to acclimatise? Conrad thought it was definitely a possibility. He kept digging through the filing cabinets. When he closed the last one, without finding what he was after, he put his mind into action.

If he was the person who'd left the maps behind, never thinking anyone would want to use them again, where would he put them? The person would possibly have been in a clerical position.

Conrad groaned. They'd be in the council offices. The same place the Siam was. He'd have to brave the bully. Conrad never thought he'd be afraid of a cat, but the Siamese was mentally unstable, and Conrad sported the scars to prove it.

Stepping outside, he looked around. Apart from a few boards lying on the ground, all looked okay. He walked down the street, remembering the repairs he'd made what seemed a lifetime ago. As he turned the corner, he could hear the conversations coming from the houses. They were still here. Eyes followed him, he could feel the owners' gazes. Most of these cats had never seen a human, or two-legs as he remembered being called. A couple of brave young souls even ventured out and sat partway up the pathway, watching as he walked past. Conversations ceased as they watched the 'monster' walk down the street.

Conrad stopped when he reached the council building. A few of the letters had fallen from the sign, the words left making no sense. He stepped forward, and a silver tabby blocked his way, snarling, and hissing.

'I'm here to see the Great Siam, if he's still around.'

The tabby ceased his hissing and sat looking perplexed. 'You speak like people, and yet I have never seen such as you.' The cat walked forward and placed his paw on Conrad's shoes. 'What manner of people are you?'

'I'm what your stories call a two-legs. I am the special two-legs who put the caves back together after a big storm wrecked them. Have you been told that story?'

'You are Conrad-hero? Oh, my Bast.' The cat bowed to Conrad and backed up, still bowing. 'Please go in, Conrad-hero. You do not need an invitation to see the Great One.'

'The Great One, huh. Not the Great Siam?'

'No, Conrad-hero, the Great Siam does not rule anymore. Not since he was banished from Catatopia.'

Conrad recognised the voice, one he hadn't heard for a long time. 'Rufus, you're still here, still alive!'

'Of course I'm still alive, two-legs, it hasn't been that long, has it?'

Conrad strode quickly into what had been the administration office. Rufus sat on the CEO's leather chair. As he stepped forward into the room, Rufus leapt onto the table, then sprang at Conrad. He put his arms out and caught the old cat, cuddling him close. He'd missed his old friend, telling him of the problems he'd had. Wanderer and Spook were great companions, but Rufus was special to Conrad, and he liked to think the two of them had shared a bond.

Rufus purred loudly in Conrad's ear, his thick fur and whiskers tickling a cheek. 'I have missed you, my old friend. I thought never to see you again.' Conrad gave the cat a final hug and sat him back on the desk, where Rufus promptly began washing and straightening his fur.

Once he'd finished, Rufus looked up. 'What brings you back to Catatopia?'

Conrad found a chair, pulled it over, and sat down. 'Remember the children, Rufus?'

'Yes, I remember them, the ones made with my essence.'

Conrad knew it was a sore point with him and grimaced. 'Yes, the ones you helped give life to. In a way, they are all your kittens as well.' He hoped that wasn't pushing it.

'What about them, Conrad? Is there something wrong with them?'

'No, there isn't anything wrong with the children. They are all extremely clever, but the two-legs will not trust them and harry them in the streets.' Conrad took a deep breath. 'We need to find them another place to live, Rufus.'

Conrad watched the cat's eyes grow large with understanding. 'You want them to move to Catatopia? Do you not remember what you were told when you first came here?' Rufus jumped from the desk, back onto the plush leather chair.

'Rufus, I was hoping with the Siam gone we could come to an understanding. Surely there aren't too many cats still here who remember the time of when the two-legs walked the streets?'

Rufus hissed his anger. 'Regardless of who is left, that is our law, and as the leader at the moment, I must follow that law. Two-legs cannot live here in our caves.'

Conrad caught a bit of a message in what Rufus had said. 'So two-legs, even the children who have your essence running in their bodies, cannot live in your caves here. Can they live in other caves, somewhere else?'

Rufus became quiet and began cleaning himself, especially his paws. Conrad recognised the sign, and let him clean. Rufus always washed his paws when he thought.

'You are correct. They can live in other caves.'

'Rufus, are there other caves I wasn't shown before?'

It would make sense. Sure, Conrad had seen the town and a few offices, but surely there were more buildings elsewhere.

'There are, but we do not want two-legs coming to our caves.'

'We will need to use the portal to come here. That building is away from your caves here. Is that good enough?'

'For the moment, it will have to be. The children cannot be harmed. The children can come.'

'Their parents will want to join them. Even though they are smart, they are still what the two-legs consider children, and will want to stay with them.'

'You push my patience, Conrad, but we owe you a great deal. The children may visit here, but the human two-legs, apart from you, cannot. I will show you where the other caves are, but they are to stay away from here unless invited.'

'I understand, Rufus. Can we look now? Is it far to walk?'

'It is far away, at least a one morning's walk. I would sometimes go there when I wanted to be alone.'

'If we take the cart I used when I mended the caves, would that make it faster?'

Rufus licked his mane. 'Yes, I think it would.'

'Great.' Conrad stood. 'I'll get the vehicle and meet you out the front.' Conrad turned and stopped. He turned back. 'Rufus, thank you. You didn't have to help, but you know I wouldn't ask unless I really had to, don't you?'

Rufus looked at him. 'I do, Conrad, and I'm sorry you had to ask.'

Conrad nodded sadly and left the room and the building. He returned within minutes to see Rufus sitting out the front. He hadn't come to a complete stop when Rufus leapt onto the cart and sat beside him.

'Back to the portal, Conrad, and then follow my directions.'

****

Conrad drove for what seemed only a few minutes. In the distance low roofs appeared. As they drew closer, the buildings looked more industrial than residential. His suspicions of having the working areas and the living areas separated had proved right.

'You are worried about the caves?' Rufus asked.

'No, not especially. I thought there might be an industrial area. With only the large office at Catatopia, I knew there had to be other buildings.'

They drove down the road and entered the sector. Conrad stopped and alighted from the vehicle. 'Let's go for a walk and see what's available.'

'You realise this would be only for a short time, don't you?'

Conrad looked down at his furry companion. 'Rufus, I know you don't like the two-legs so near, and I understand why you don't want them around, but these children have nowhere else to go.'

Conrad looked through the windows and tried the doors on a few of the buildings. Although they were set up as labs and clerical areas, the building held rooms that could be easily converted into bedrooms and living areas. All they needed was a good cleaning, and maybe some walls moving around.

'Yes, I think these will work well. Now to find out if everyone has the gene to be able to survive here.'

'Gene? What do you mean, Conrad?'

'Humans need the gene you have. When the humans became ill and had to leave, it was because they didn't have the gene to survive in this world. When they took your essence, it was passed onto the males, but we don't know whether the females have it. As you pointed out long ago, we have the gene to use the portal, but does the same gene allow us to survive here?'

'So, without using my essence, two-legs would not be able to live here?'

'That's right. From what I have been told, the same gene allowed me to be a father.'

'Hmm, so my essence proved good for you but bad for my kind.'

Conrad stopped and squatted down to be nearer the distraught feline. 'Why is it bad for your kind?'

Rufus looked up. 'Have you noticed what your world looks like? Tall caves, where many live, the metal monsters that have no care as to where they go or who they kill. Air so bad to breathe, you choke?

'I do not want that for my world. If two-legs come here, whether they live here or in another place, they will bring these bad things too. What will happen to our food machines when the air changes? What will we do?'

Conrad remembered stomping around the floor many years ago when Herbert had mentioned the possibility of colonising the planet. He'd been so angry at the thought of the pure air being polluted, he'd said no to Herbert taking his blood. Anyone who made this world their home would have to accept living close to nature so as not to disturb the ecosystem. Could the children live like that? Could he and the other humans live like that? They'd have to turn back time. No machinery, everything would need to be man-powered. That would take some doing. They did, however, have some machinery already on the planet in the New Earth complex.

'We will work something out before we arrive, Rufus. I wouldn't like to see this beautiful world damaged either. We may need to have someone in this complex all the time.'

'Why? We have done well without two-legs here.'

'Have you forgotten the great storm, Rufus? Many would have died, and many of your caves had to be rebuilt. Your people can do small things, but you wouldn't have been able to fix the caves like I did. You need two-legs here, just in case.'

'Two-legs would want to rule us, and we don't want that. We want to live on our own.'

Conrad thought for a minute. There had to be a way around this. 'When countries back on Earth make decisions, involving another race or country, they make rules. We could do the same, lay down rules about what can and can't be done on Catatopia. You will tell me what you want and don't want to happen, and I will tell you what the two-legs will need. When we agree, we write it down, and everyone must live by those rules. Does that sound okay to you?'

'I cannot read two-legs marks, and we Catatopians don't "write". How will I know if what I agree to is written down?'

'Don't you trust me, Rufus?' Conrad's chest tightened. Rufus didn't trust him. He thought they were friends …

'Of course, I trust YOU, Conrad, I don't trust other two-legs, like the one who caught me to take my essence.'

Conrad supposed he could understand Rufus's view. The cat had been badly treated by the scientists. 'Rufus,

I'm sure if Herbert had known you were from Catatopia, he wouldn't have used you like he did. Don't forget, he and Helga were the ones who invented your food and toilet machines so you wouldn't starve or live in a stinky cave. Do you think you would all be here if they hadn't left that behind for you?'

'Maybe, maybe not, but it has been a rule for us that no two-legs would ever live in Catatopia again.'

Conrad caught the one word that may work in his favour. 'So if no two-legs lived in Catatopia, that would be alright? This settlement isn't "in" Catatopia so it would be okay to live here for our two-legs kittens.'

Rufus issued a small growl. 'You play with words, Conrad, but yes, as I said before, for a small time it would be okay.'

Conrad kept moving, looking in windows and trying doors. The settlement appeared larger than he first thought. He was about to pass another nondescript looking building when he noticed a door inside with a sign, saying 'Transmission Room'.

He tried the door handle on the outside door, and it opened. Walking through, he entered the transmission room. Tables and older-style computers ringed the walls. A large mainframe cabinet, filled with some kind of digital computer machinery, sat in the middle of the room. To the side sat a platform reminiscent of the multicoloured disco floors from the previous century. Conrad walked over to what appeared to be a control booth. Switches and dials dotted the board set into the desk.

'Do you know what this is, Rufus?'

Rufus jumped onto the desk and sniffed the dials. 'Sorry, Conrad, I have no idea. I have never been inside any of these caves. None of them have an opening I could use.'

Conrad located a pen and some paper not far away, and drew a crude map of the streets, indicating where certain buildings stood. He'd be able to ask Herbert when he went back to Earth. As he turned, his arm knocked a folder onto the floor. It fell open to reveal maps. Conrad picked it up and was about to place it back when he noticed one place of a map a few pages in was called "Terra". Beside it, an X had been placed, and the word "settlement".

Was this an early map of New Earth, and the place they had chosen for the settlement or was this another settlement? Only Herbert and Helga could tell him. He tucked the folder, along with his mud map, under his arm.

'I think I have seen enough, Rufus, let's go back.'

CHAPTER TWENTY-EIGHT

Back home, Conrad took one step out of the portal room and his phone jingled. A message flashed on the screen. **Axel injured badly. Come to hospital. Hope.**

Conrad dropped the folder on the table as he ran out the door, jumped into his car and sped off. He thanked the car manufacturers this car needed no keys to start it.

If traffic had been any heavier, he might have been involved in an accident. He had a few near misses, and as he drew closer to the hospital, common sense took over and he slowed down. Getting himself killed wouldn't help Axel or anyone else.

Abandoning the vehicle in the car park, Conrad raced inside. Hope had sent him the room number. He made it to the right floor and saw Hope waiting outside a door as soon as he rounded the corner. He ran up the hall, gaining disapproving looks from the nurses on duty.

'Hope, what happened? Where is he?' Conrad looked into the room but didn't see anyone.

'Oh Conrad, poor Axel. This time they really did a job on him. He's been beaten badly, and to add to the insult, they held him down and shaved him.' Hope broke into tears and buried her head in his chest.

'How on earth did they shave him? He wears the same clothes as the other boys. Did they strip him first?' If they had, Axel would have been mortified. He was the only one with four paws, and though they had the dexterity of human hands, he'd had a harder time than the others growing up.

Hope nodded. 'He said two roughs chased him, and though he easily outran them, he didn't know about the ambush. Conrad, there must have been a few attackers, he's in a bad way.'

'Okay, all of that can be fixed. Where is he? There's no one in the bed.'

'He's in there, but he didn't want me to see him. He only wants you in there. He says he too embarrassed to let me see him.' Hope burst out crying again.

'Hush love,' Conrad kissed her forehead. 'I'll have a talk to him and see if I can talk him around.'

Hope tried to sniff back her tears, but no amount of snuffling could halt the torrent that poured from her eyes. Conrad took a last look at her and tried to reassure her with a half-hearted smile. She looked at him, and the tears continued. He walked inside and looked around. The room was a normal hospital room. Bed, cabinet to the side, cupboard in the corner. Axel was not in bed, so that left only one place to look.

'Axel, come out of the cupboard, please. It's your dad.'

'Is Mum with you?'

'No, she's not. She's sitting outside crying because you won't let her come in. She needs to see you, son.'

'I can't let her see me like this.'

Damn, what had they done to the boy? 'Axel, please come out, it's never as bad as you think.'

The cupboard rocked; the door creaked open. Conrad had to gag himself with his hand when he saw what the roughs had done to his son.

'See, Dad, it is as bad as I think.' Axel stepped all the way out and turned around. Hope said they'd shaved him. They sure had, all over. They'd left some patches of fur, but the poor boy looked like he suffered from a bad case of mange. On top of the defurring, he noticed cuts, scratches, and some butcher had attempted to remove his ears. Conrad could see the stitches where the doctors had sewn up the cuts. He also had a plaster cast on his leg.

'Being shaved isn't that bad, Axel. I do it every morning.' Conrad tried to make light of what had happened, but the internal wound to his self-esteem could be seen in his son's eyes.

Axel turned his head to the wall. 'It's not funny, Dad.'

Conrad walked over, placed an arm around his not-so-furry son, and hugged him. 'Your fur will grow back. You know it always has.' When they had been younger, Teyah had decided Axel needed a haircut. Hope or he usually stopped her before she'd gone too far, but he'd lost a bit of fur to his sister many times.

Conrad held his son at arm's length and looked at the boy. Out of all of them, Axel had the closest resemblance to Rufus. 'You know,' he turned the boy back and forth, 'it doesn't actually look too bad.'

'Don't joke, Dad, please.'

'Okay, I won't. Did they hurt you much in any other way, apart from your ears?'

'Dad, they had knives. I'm sure they wanted to kill me. They kept saying they were going to skin me and hang my pelt in the university foyer.'

Conrad shivered. He could only imagine the terror Axel must have felt. 'Do you know who they were?'

Anger filled the boy's eyes, the slitted pupils growing thin. 'Yes, I know who a few of them were. I'd seen them at school, and they always shouted out horrible things, about what they were going to do to me.' He shrugged. 'Looks like they finally carried out their threats.

'So let me get this right, they were adults?'

Axel hung his head. 'Yes, Dad. From the university.'

Conrad sat his son on the hospital bed, and paced angrily across the floor and back again. 'Did you manage to inflict any injuries on them?'

Axel's demeanour brightened, and he smiled victoriously. 'Oh yes, I managed to scratch them quite well, and some of the swipes were quite deep. They'll need medical attention.'

Conrad slapped his son on the back lightly. 'Good boy. That should make it easy to find them.' Conrad wanted to do nothing more than to drive to the university, find these men, and give them a taste of their own medicine. Fighting was one thing, but doing what they'd done to Axel was unforgivable, especially to a young boy.

'Axel, please let your mother in. She really needs to see you.'

Axel looked at him, tears in his eyes. 'I know, Dad, but Mum has always liked me because of the fur. Now I don't have the fur anymore, I'm just like Teyah, with tufts.'

'Come on, Axel, you know that's not true. Your mum loves all of you just the same. Fur or no fur, you are all her babies.' Hope loved stroking Axel's fur, and when he moulted, she enjoyed brushing the loose fur away.

Hope rushed in, taking them both by surprise. She took one look at her son, cried out in grief, and hugged him to her. 'I don't care if you have no fur, Axel, you will always be my baby boy. Besides,' Hope pulled back and looked him in the eyes, 'as your father said, it'll grow back.'

Hope stroked his back, just as she'd done when he was a baby and wouldn't settle, or when he was upset because he couldn't understand why he had paws and everyone else had hands. 'I'm more worried there are people out there who could do something like this to a child. I'm also worried about your ears and your leg. The doctors say you'll be okay, but I know how sensitive your ears are.'

Hope stood and carefully examined the stitches, then changed her attention to Conrad. 'I want these men, Conrad, and something needs to be done to protect the other children from so-called people like that.'

'Don't worry, I have that under control. I need to make a phone call, but I'll be back.'

'Dad, please don't be long. I don't want to stay in this hospital. People keep peeking in and giving me strange looks.'

Conrad turned his head quickly to look at the door, catching two young nurses pointing and laughing. 'Don't worry. I'm sure Helga and Herbert won't mind having you for a few nights.' Conrad walked a step or two closer. 'We may even have a little bit of fun while we're

there. A little bit of payback, if you know what I mean.'
Conrad gave his son a cunning smile.

Axel smiled back. 'Sure, Dad, would love to.'

Conrad drew his phone out of his pocket as he
walked through the door. He paused in the doorway. 'Get
everything you have together. Once I've made the call,
we're leaving. Hope, can you find a doctor, and tell him
or her that we're taking our son out of here.'

'Will do, Conrad.'

He stepped out and walked toward the common
room where he could make the call. On the way he
overheard some disturbing conversations regarding Axel,
and what type of 'creature' he was. Making a detour, he
followed the voices and found a few nurses gathered
around a desk. 'Excuse me, my son is NOT an animal,
nor is he deformed. He has the same genes as you, except
he has one extra. I'll also have you know that the child
you are talking about has accumulated more knowledge
in his fifteen years than you could ever hope to achieve in
your whole life. He graduated from university when he
was twelve years old. He may look feline, but I can
assure you, he is one hundred per cent all human boy.'

Conrad had to walk away. He'd grown so angry, he
was afraid he might strike out. If he found the men who
had attacked his boy, he wouldn't be holding back. When
he reached the common room, he made himself drink a
cup of tea in a small paper cup. Once he'd finished
drinking, he was calm enough to make the call and
inform Herbert they were coming in, and what had
happened.

****

With Axel safe at the university hospital behind locked doors, Conrad took Hope home to be with the other children, who were extremely concerned about their brother. Conrad took Dexter to the side. 'Do you know these people who attacked Axel today, or know who they are?'

'I know some of them, Dad. I mean, I don't know who did it to him, but I do know the ones who have been giving him a hard time. They've done it to me too, but I had a go at them, and they left me alone. I've only found out recently they've been giving it to Axel, and that was through someone else. He's always so secretive about things.'

'Can you come with me tomorrow and point them out? Do you know what department they are in?'

'Sure, Dad, I'll point them out. What are you going to do?'

Conrad smiled. He had plans for those men. He clapped Dexter on the back with his hand. 'Leave that to me, son. I only need to know who they are.'

Dexter began to walk back to the others, but he turned. 'Dad, hurt them, and hurt them bad please.' He turned again and continued his walk.

Conrad shook his head. All the kids were peace loving, and apart from the fights with each other, he'd never had a problem with them fighting others. They preferred to learn rather than fight. To hear his son asking him to hurt someone made his heart bleed. The statement only reinforced his intention to get all the hybrid children off this planet, and onto the other one. He'd talk with Herbert the next day, and this time he'd have the book of maps with him.

The next morning, accompanied by Dexter, he drove to the university. Both entered the building, and Conrad followed where his son led. Four floors up, Dexter stopped at a glass door and pointed out a group of men in the engineering department.

'Thanks, Dexter. Go back to the research room and check on your brother, please.'

'What are you going to do, Dad?' Dexter sounded worried.

'I'll be alright, son. Run along and stay with your brother. I'll be down soon.'

'Okay Dad, but be careful.' Dexter turned, pressed the button for the elevator and stepped in when it arrived. Conrad waited until the doors closed before he pulled a balaclava from his pocket and pulled it over his head, covering his face. *Let's see how brave you fellows are.*

Conrad opened the door, walked through and locked it behind him. He placed a plastic lock strip around the door handles so no one could enter or leave. Under the mask, Conrad smiled. Payback time, boys.

Pulling a pistol from the back of his pants, he walked through the floor. The young men Dexter had pointed out seemed oblivious to anyone else but each other, slapping each other on the back and mimicking Axel as he lay on the ground. Conrad ground his teeth together. *They thought it was funny, did they? Let's see how funny they thought this was.*

'Hey, you guys. Heads up.' Conrad kicked the cabinet standing in the skinny walk space between the cubicles. It fell on its side against a desk, slipping to the floor. Sounds like glass breaking came from inside, and liquid poured from one of the drawers. Booze? Hopefully it wasn't expensive. Conrad brought the pistol up to chest height and pointed it at the group.

'Hey man, what do you think you're doing?'

'I think I'm pointing a pistol at your chest, and I think I'm slowly squeezing the trigger.' Conrad's rage continued to grow, coiling tighter within his chest. He noticed their faces change from laughter to alarm. 'So now you're worried, are you?' Conrad motioned with the firearm for the group to move into one of the offices. 'Move, or my finger may spasm and put a hole in one of you.'

The group moved as one through the open office door. Conrad stood within the doorway and uttered one word. 'Strip.'

One of the men laughed. Conrad pointed the pistol at him and squeezed the trigger. The sound of the shot reverberated within the room and the youth fell screaming to the floor, holding his leg. Blood flowed through his fingers and over his hands.

'Think it's a laughing matter, do you?' Conrad cocked the gun so the slightest pressure would cause another shot to be fired. From the terrified look on the men's faces, they realised it. 'I said strip.'

The men began removing their clothes. Conrad drew a camera out of his pocket and set it up on a nearby table. 'You seem to think it's funny to bully and terrify people. People who you know won't fight back.'

The men stood in their singlets and underpants, their hands covering their private parts. 'Did I tell you to stop? I told you to strip, and I mean everything. Drop those boxers, boys.'

'Come on, mister, you can't mean that, and why are you taking photos? Going to watch it later to get your jollies?' The idiot who spoke stepped forward and waggled his tackle at Conrad.

Conrad laughed, a deep, dangerous, sound. The offender realised the foolhardiness of his action and stepped back in line. 'I won't be watching this, but once it's up on the web to see, I'm hoping it'll go viral.'

The man on the ground with the hole in his leg was still screaming, which rattled Conrad's nerves. He swung around, again pointing the gun at him. 'I suggest you shut up before I do it for you.' The man whimpered in terror, but did stop screaming.

'Right, kick all your clothes over to me.'

The men looked at him. 'What are you going to do with them?'

Conrad growled. He pointed the gun at the fellow he thought may be the leader. 'I said, kick all your clothes over to me.' Conrad took a couple of steps forward, pointing the pistol at the man's groin. The man blanched, and Conrad watched as he wet himself in fear. 'Thank you, that's a nice little addition to the film I didn't count on.'

As the clothes piled around his feet, he kicked them out the door. He stepped over to the camera, which was still recording, and picked it up. 'I am going to put this in front of your faces. You are going to say your name, and what part you played in the assault of the young hybrid boy yesterday. I also want to know who shaved his fur.'

'No man, I'm not going to say anything about it, and you can't make me. We'll lose our jobs here. Anyway, the little half breed deserved it. Walking around like he's something special. They all do. They're nothing but animals that should be in a cage.'

As he spoke, his friends looked aghast at him, and stepped away, as if to distance themselves from the comments he made.

Conrad growled, and it was audible. He brought up the pistol. He wanted to kill this man, his rage was so strong, but he held back. His idea was to embarrass and open these people to ridicule, not to murder them. 'They're more human than you are. You are the animals, not them.' Conrad laughed again, and he saw the others cringe. 'Actually, "animal" is too good a name to call you. You are slugs, slimy slugs, that feed off dirt. Get on the floor, all of you.' He stepped back. None of them moved. Conrad raised his voice, 'I said, get on the floor. NOW!'

The one who'd spoken stayed standing. The others crouched on the ground. The one standing stuck his chin out. Conrad snapped. He took a step forward and swung the pistol round, slamming it into the cheek of the idiot, who fell backward, hitting his head on the carpeted floor. He groaned, his head falling to the side.

Conrad stood over the motionless man. His chest still rose and fell. Good, he wasn't dead, but he'd have a broken jaw for his stupidity. 'Right, now. I will start.' He walked to the first man in line. 'Stand up, say who you are, and what you did.' He held the camera; each man stood, said his piece, and then lay back on the ground. Once he had made his way down the line of six men, he pointed to the unconscious one. 'Who is he, and what part did he play?' The one next in line answered his question. Conrad had been right. The jerk was the ringleader.

Conrad stepped backward until he reached the door. 'You will all stay here. I am going to lock this door, and you can think about what you did to a poor boy, who never did you any harm.' Conrad stepped back one step, closed the door and locked it. The men's clothes lay at the bottom of the door. He bundled them up, placed them under his arm and walked away.

He cut the ties holding the door together, opened the door and walked out, dropping the bundled clothes into the incinerator chute as he passed. He looked back at them, all huddled against the window watching what he did. He laughed at the look of dismay as they watched their clothes drop into the chute. Walking down the hallway, he pressed the button for the elevator and stepped inside, removing the balaclava as the doors closed. He'd been lucky no one had walked down the hall or had been in the elevator.

Conrad pressed the button to stop the lift and leaned his head against the cool metal walls. He shook bodily, aware of what he'd done. He hadn't meant it to go so far, but he wanted them to pay for the hurt they caused Axel, and probably the other hybrid children as well. They'd pay alright. He'd load the video onto the web at a library a few suburbs away. They wouldn't be able to trace him. He hoped it went viral. He hoped they'd be as embarrassed as his son had been.

Once the tremors had stopped, he wiped his brow and pushed the button to continue his trip to the ground floor.

****

Conrad wasn't proud of what he'd done, but it was payback. What kind of people pick on children to hurt and humiliate them? He'd show them up for the cowards they were. He'd made a fake email address, attached a copy of the video to it and sent it to the directors at the university. The attack had made his mind up. It was time to start being tested. He waited in his car in the car park opposite the university, trying to gather his thoughts. Herbert and Helga would ask questions, and he wanted to be ready with the answers.

Taking his courage in hand, he alighted from the vehicle, locked the car and crossed the road. Standing outside the buildings he'd been walking around for nearly nineteen years, he shook his head. They'd all have to let everything go, leave jobs, homes, security and extended family behind.

Conrad clasped the folder with the maps to his chest, entered the door, signed in, and made his way to the research unit. When he'd reached the floor, he pushed open the door and strode in, hoping he looked confident, because he sure didn't feel it inside.

'Hello, Conrad. What can we do for you today, or have you come to see Axel?'

'I have some things I'd like to discuss with you and Helga, but I think I'll see my son first.' Conrad noticed Herbert eyeing the folder he carried. 'This,' he tapped the folder, 'has something to do with it.'

Herbert nodded. 'Okay, later then. Go see your son, he's been asking for you.'

Herbert walked away, but turned back once, again looking at the folder. Conrad waited until he was out of sight before walking into the hospital room to visit his son. When he entered the room, Conrad could see the relief on Axel's face. Being a fifteen-year-old in a research facility can't be easy, even if you had been working there.

'Dad, I'm so glad you're here. I want to go home.'

Conrad had been expecting that. 'What does Herbert say?'

Axel shrugged. 'It doesn't matter what he or other doctors say, I want to come home. I don't want people coming in just to look at me and laugh.'

'Who has been coming in and laughing at you?' Conrad's back was up again. He'd trusted them to provide a safe and secure place for Axel, but if people have been coming in just to gawk and laugh …?

'Just other university researchers, you know, the ones who work on the floor. What hurts is that I work with them, and now they're laughing at me.'

Conrad sympathised. He couldn't do anything if the people worked on the floor. They had to have access to do their own work. 'Are you sure they're laughing at you? They haven't been coming in to see if you're okay?' He pulled the chair in the corner of the room over and sat down.

'Maybe, I don't know. Some just stick their heads in the door, say hi and then walk off with a huge smile on their face. Others come in, have a short conversation and laugh.' Axel pushed himself further up the bed. 'Why do they do that, Dad? Why? I thought they were my friends.'

Conrad could see the tears starting to well up. He'd been hurt and upset. Conrad was sure he had hold of the wrong end of the stick. 'Axel, I don't think they're laughing at you. I think they don't know what to say.' Conrad pulled his chair closer to the bed and held his son's hand. 'People, especially academics like the people who work here, aren't the best at talking with others, unless it's about a subject they know. You're hurt and upset, and they don't know how to deal with that. It scares them. I'm sure they want to help, but they don't know how.'

'Are sure, Dad? They aren't laughing at me, really?'

'I'm sure.' Conrad rubbed his son's hand, then stood and hugged him. 'I'll show you.' Conrad turned and walked out the door. Seconds later he returned, leading a young hybrid girl he knew Axel liked. Glancing up at the bed, he saw Axel blush red. He laughed inside. With all his fur, Conrad never knew the boy could do that.

He sat the young girl down. 'April, Axel thinks you've been laughing at him, because of what happened. Now that isn't true, is it?'

April looked aghast. She grabbed Axel's hand tightly. 'No, no. No one's laughing at you, Axel. It's just you looked so helpless. We tried to make jokes, but you've been so depressed. When you didn't laugh back like you usually do, we didn't know what else to do, so we left. We haven't been laughing at you, really. We wouldn't do that.' She slapped him lightly on the arm. 'How can you think that of us?'

'Really? I'm sorry. I thought you were laughing because I don't have much fur anymore.'

'What? Axel, I don't have any fur. Why would you think that?'

Conrad stood back listening to the two kids talking. That was interesting. Axel seemed to think he wasn't good enough without his fur. He took a step forward and interrupted. 'Axel, you are more than just your fur. You have a wonderful mind and a great personality. People may like your silky fur, but that does not make you who you are. I'm surprised at your vanity. First you say your mother won't want you because your fur was shaved, and then your friends are laughing at you because of your unfurriness.' Conrad crossed his arms, and the look on Axel's face said it all. The boy knew he'd disappointed his father.

'Dad, I'm sorry. I know I shouldn't think that.' He grasped April's hand in his paw. 'I'm sorry, April. I didn't mean to upset everyone,' he dropped his head and mumbled, 'especially you.'

April laughed. 'What was that you said? I couldn't hear that last part.' She leaned in toward him.

Axel looked up and found himself looking straight into April's eyes. He kissed her gently on the lips. 'I said I'm sorry I upset everyone, especially you.'

Conrad hid a smirk. His little boy was growing up. 'I'll leave you two alone. Herbert and I have things to discuss. April, thank you for helping me find out what the problem was.'

'No worries, Mr Adamson.' She didn't take her eyes off Axel.

Conrad continued to hold the chuckle building inside him as he left the room. His son's first young love. He was glad it was one of the hybrid girls. If the plans came together, human girls wouldn't be able to accompany them, not without medical intervention.

He caught Helga as he made his way through the research lab. 'Helga, I need to go over some maps I found on New Earth, and I also have to discuss an urgent matter with you and Herbert. Is now a good time?'

Helga looked around. 'Are you sure it's urgent, as in has to be done now?'

'No, it's not that urgent, but I would like to speak with both of you today and soon. I can wait if some experiment needs to be done.'

Helga stood on her tiptoes and waved her hand in the air. 'I'm rather busy, but Herbert isn't. Do you need me to be there as well, or will just one of us do?'

Conrad had the distinct impression that Helga would suggest anything to get out of speaking with him. 'Sure, Herbert and I can talk alone if you don't want to hear what I want to talk about.' As Conrad watched Herbert walk over, Helga turned away. 'I'm sure Herbert can take care of all you need.'

'Yep, what's up, Conrad?'

Conrad still stared after Helga. 'What's wrong with her? She plainly did not want to talk to me.'

'Did you happen to mention anything about New Earth?'

Conrad turned back the Herbert. 'Yes I did.' He pointed to the folder he held. 'I mentioned that I needed some help with these maps, and she turned cold on me.'

'Hmm, I see. Conrad,' Herbert grasped him by the crook of the arm, 'it's about time you knew about some of the things that happened on New Earth toward the end of our stay.'

Herbert guided him through the lab, then indicated he enter a room. Conrad walked in and sat, laying the folder of maps on the table. 'I'll only be a minute. I need a cup of coffee, and I'll get you one too.'

Conrad opened his mouth to say how he liked his coffee, but Herbert held up a finger. 'Don't worry. I know how you take it. I should after all this time.'

Conrad waited, puzzled by Helga's cold shoulder, and that he didn't know the whole story of what had happened on New Earth all those years ago. He opened the folder and flipped through the maps, looking for the settlement he'd seen on the map, in the land called 'Terra'. So absorbed was he, he didn't notice Herbert walking back in until a mug of coffee landed with a thunk on the table in front of him.

'Watch out, it's hot.' Herbert sat in the chair on the other corner, sipping his own.

Conrad looked up, reached for his drink, and felt the mug. Yes, definitely too hot to drink. Leaving the map for the minute, he waited for Herbert to continue the story.

Herbert took a mouthful, placed the cup gently on the table and sighed out deeply. 'Helga doesn't want to hear anything about New Earth because she lost the love of her life there.'

'Helga was married?'

'No, she and one of the engineers had something going. It was serious. His field was the new one of Transportation Mechanics. He'd perfected, or rather thought he'd perfected the ability and the machinery to be able to teleport or transport machinery and people through the ether, to arrive on the other side of the planet.'

Conrad had picked up on the 'or thought he'd perfected,' part of the sentence. 'Oh hell, it didn't work?'

Herbert hung his head for a few seconds, then looked up again. 'No, it didn't work. Helga pleaded with him to send someone else, or an animal or something first, but Auron was as stubborn as a mule. It was his project, and he was going to be the first person to teleport anywhere.'

Conrad gulped, trying to moisten the dry lump in his throat. 'What happened?'

'The procedure started well enough. The platform worked. Everything glowed, and Auron began to shimmer. Then a fuse blew, and the shimmering grew weaker, then stronger. Helga watched as the man of her dreams was torn apart, molecule by molecule until eventually, there wasn't anything left.'

'Why didn't they turn it off when it started going haywire?'

They tried. The machine wouldn't turn off. The personnel there could hear him screaming until the end.' Herbert flicked the folder of maps. 'Those maps were his.'

Conrad blanched and felt ill. 'Herbert, was the transporter ever fixed?' If it wasn't, the new settlers were going to have a hard time getting to the other landmass.

Herbert took another mouthful of coffee and nodded his head. 'Mmm. Yes, the transporter was fixed—eventually. People were so scared of it. The machinery was left alone for a long time until Helga tried fixing it.'

Conrad was confused. He looked out the office window in the direction of where Helga was working. She looked around, maybe sensing someone had looked at her, and Conrad was sure he could see where tears had run down her cheeks. 'She still grieves for him, even after all this time, doesn't she?'

Herbert sighed. 'Yes, to this day, she still grieves for what may have been.'

Conrad was sure he knew how she felt. If he lost Hope, he knew he'd still be grieving for many years to come. Snapping himself out of the maudlin thoughts, he chased his mind back to the last thing Herbert had said, how Helga had tried to fix the transporter. 'Hang on, Helga is a geneticist, not an engineer.'

'Very true, but Auron had taught her enough for her to think she could fix it. She let her work go and concentrated only on that infernal machine. One day, someone went in to get her, and she had disappeared.'

'Where was she? Where did she go?' Conrad leaned forward, grabbed his now cooling coffee, and took a quick sip. Please let her have fixed it. Please!

Herbert reached for the book of maps, opened it and flicked through the pages. He found the map he was looking for, pulled it out of its sleeve and pointed to where an X was marked.

'This is where she went. Right here.'

Conrad looked down. The X marked the place he'd been looking. The settlement town of Terra. He looked back through the window. Helga had her head down, eyes pressed to a microscope. 'How long was she gone?'

'A few days. She wouldn't tell us what she'd done, or why she'd stayed away and not come straight back. She clammed up and never spoke of it again.'

'Was the transporter used again?' Conrad wasn't sure if they'd be able to use it now. Surely she'd come back using it, but could it be trusted after all this time?

Herbert flipped his hand in the air. 'Oh, yes. We used it to build the town. If you've got these maps, then you must have seen the platform. The maps were right next to it.'

Conrad snorted with laughter. 'Do you mean the disco floor? That's the platform?'

'Yes, the so-called "disco floor" is the platform.'

Good, the transportation system worked. They'd be able to transfer straight over. Only one problem remained. 'If we need to use the transporter, how to we work it?'

Herbert looked at him, apparently confused. 'Why would you want to use the transporter?'

It was Conrad's turn to take a deep breath. 'We'll need it when we move to Terra. The children can't stay here. They are being attacked, and the abuse has only become harsher as they have grown older.'

'No, you can't take them there. They won't survive.'

Conrad reached forward and placed his hand over Herbert's. 'We have to go, and yes, we will survive. We understand you can't use the portal anymore because you'll die. Herbert, there is another world waiting for these children. The trial that created them has been perfected, and they have served their purpose. Children being born now from the new treatment aren't cat-like, unlike our children. Our kids stick out too much, and because they're so different, they'll always be bullied or persecuted in some way.'

Herbert had been mumbling, 'no no no,' all the time Conrad had been talking. He now looked up. 'No, you don't understand. There's something in the air that kills humans.'

Conrad smiled. 'Yes, I know. Rufus told me.'

'Rufus, the cat? He told you?' Herbert paused, puzzled by the news. 'How?'

'We talk, Herbert. I thought you knew that.'

'I thought you were joking, you know, pulling my leg. You seriously talked to the cats there?'

'Yes. I know about the gene needed to be able to exist on the planet. It also happens to be the gene that reversed the infertility. All the men will have it because they received it in the shot.'

Herbert remained quiet. Conrad hoped it was because he had been overwhelmed with the news. 'This is the other problem. We assume the children also carry the gene, but we need you to test them all for it. We also need all the mothers tested as well.'

Herbert slowly nodded his head, as though a glimmer of something revealed itself to him. 'That would make sense. We tried many cats, but it was only that one stray tom we caught who had the gene to counteract the virus. No other cat had it.'

Herbert looked almost beaten. He looked up with tired, sad eyes. 'Is leaving Earth the only way you can see around this?'

Conrad nodded. 'I'm afraid it is, Herbert. I'm sorry.'

'So am I, Conrad.' He stood up. 'I'll give all the departments a call and have the children come in for the tests.' Hebert began to walk off.

'Herbert, do you want me to get the mothers to come in to be tested?'

Herbert nodded, but he kept walking. Conrad could hear him muttering to himself. 'What a pity, what a damn shame. We could have accomplished so much.'

Conrad picked up the folder of maps and followed the scientist out. It was a pity this had to happen. The children had already made their mark in many areas. All had invented or improved many areas of human lifestyle. They'd also perfected a zero pollution organic fuel. At fifteen years of age, their IQ was higher than any tutor available, and he'd heard Helga remarking how the children were so much more intelligent than anyone she knew, including herself and her staff. Yes, it was a damn shame they had to leave. Hopefully, the knowledge they gained and the advancements they were making would help them later on.

****

'We have to leave Earth? What the hell are you saying, Conrad?' Hope stormed about the room. 'When did you decide all this? Why did you decide the only way to protect the children was to leave?'

'Hope, calm down. Nothing is set in concrete yet.'

'Conrad Richard Adamson, what in the world made you think I, or the children, would go ahead with this mad plan of yours?'

Conrad winced. The use of all three of his names told him how upset she was. He'd be sleeping on the couch again tonight. He could keep trying to reason with her. 'Hope, the kids are being attacked. Look at what happened to Axel. Nothing like that would occur if we lived on the other planet. Why don't we ask the kids, and find out what they think?'

Hope walked up to him, her blonde hair bouncing under her chin. She looked up and poked him in the chest with her finger. 'And what do you think the kids will say. Huh?' She paused. Conrad opened his mouth to reply but was too slow. 'They say yes, they want to go. Of course they will.' Hope turned and walked away a few steps before returning and poked him in the chest again, emphasising each word she spoke with a poke. 'They. Are. Children. Curious. Children. Do. You. Understand?'

Conrad rubbed his sternum with his hand. Oh yes, she was as mad as could be.

'Did you think about asking me, or any of the others before you made enquiries? No, you jumped straight in, like you do with everything, assuming everyone would go along with you.' Hope stormed away, throwing herself onto the couch and sat there fuming, her arms crossed on her chest.

Conrad knew he paddled in dangerous waters at the moment. 'Hope, sweetheart, just think about it? A new planet would mean a new life, plus you've got access to every type of cat breed you could ever want.' Okay, even that last remark sounded lame to him. She loved cats, but would she want a whole town of them?

'Why do I want a new life? Isn't this one good enough for you?' Hope hadn't looked at him, still having her arms crossed on her chest. She'd spoken so low, without his enhanced hearing he doubted he would have heard her. He walked around the couch and sat down next to her. 'No, love, I do love this life. I don't deny there will be things and people we will miss, but I'm thinking of all the children, not just ours.'

'Your mother and Bill won't be happy. They enjoy having the kids around, and they are getting older. Both of them are going to need help soon.'

Conrad collapsed in upon himself. Why couldn't anyone see what he'd seen? 'So am I wrong to worry about the children being bullied? Am I wrong to want to move them to a place where that doesn't happen?'

'No, you're not wrong about wanting them to be safe, but this happens to virtually every child. Are you going to tell me you were never bullied or teased?'

Conrad's mind raced back to when he was small. Patrick Smythe was his enemy. He was bigger, heavier, and two years older, and he delighted in causing Conrad pain. He'd once been thrown into a cactus by the older boy, and Conrad remembered walking home in pain, each step creating a further hell. It didn't help he'd had to ask his mum to pull out the cactus needles he couldn't reach. Yes, he could remember being bullied and would have loved to run away to a place so it would never happen again.

'Yes, I remember being bullied.'

'Did you get over it?'

'Well, yes, because the bully left to go to another school, where he probably began tormenting someone else.'

'That's not the point. What I'm trying to make you see is that you can't run away. Sometimes you have to stay and stand your ground. I understand the directors of the university found out who assaulted Axel and have kicked them off the campus, and they are facing battery charges. That's another reason we have to stay. Axel will have to give evidence.'

Conrad doubted that would happen; after all, they had been filmed giving confessions of what they'd done. That hadn't been mentioned, though, so Conrad decided not to volunteer that information.

'Will you at least get tested, Hope. Please.' Conrad couldn't say why, but somehow he felt everything had to be in place. The violence had escalated against the hybrid children, and he felt in his soul that something was going to happen. If he couldn't save all of them, he'd definitely try to save his family. He'd miss his mother, and Bill, but his kids and Hope came first.

Hope sighed loudly. 'Alright, if it will get you off my back, I'll get tested. I'll see Helga tomorrow.'

Conrad leaned sideways and hugged her. 'That's all I ask. Thank you, love.'

Hope turned to him. 'When the children arrive home, I don't want to hear you say a word about this running away to the other planet.'

Conrad leaned back, licked his fingers and made a cross over his heart. 'Cross my heart, I promise not to say a word.'

'Promise to not say a word about what, Dad?'
Charlotte walked in the door, reached over the back of
the couch, and hugged them both.

Hope glared at Conrad.

'Nothing love, just something Mum and I were
talking about. Nothing that concerns you.'

'Right. Sure.' Charlotte took a few steps toward her
room down the hallway, then stopped and called back
over her shoulder. 'The others were stopping in to see
Axel before they come home. They may be a little late.'

The warning buzz in the back of Conrad's mind
grew stronger.

CHAPTER TWENTY-NINE

Life was good.

Axel had healed, his fur had nearly regrown, and was back at work. All the hybrid children were now full time employees of the university, no longer students. They wouldn't have been able to gain employment anywhere else, except with drug companies, and the one hybrid who attempted to leave found out that the drug companies only wanted them for one reason, to run tests on them. She had run back to the university the next day. Helga and Herbert were happy Conrad's intentions of taking the children off planet had come to nothing. Their research leapt ahead with the help of the hybrids. Connections in medicine never thought possible had been made. Mankind had been saved; humankind's fertility had been restored. No further mutations had occurred after the serum was re-engineered.

Hope leaned back in her seat in the garden and watched the kittens playing in the garden beds, frolicking in and out of the colourful paper-like Californian poppies. 'Hope, where are you?' Chloe called.

'In the garden, Mum, on kitten duty. They're playing in the flower bed.' Hope put down her book, and stood, spying her making her way up the hill. Chloe breathed heavily once she reached the top. Hope made her sit down and relax for a little while.

'Has Bill gone into work, or is he asleep in the chair again?' Hope gazed down the grass-covered hill at the small cottage nestled at the bottom.

'You know him too well, Hope. Yes, he's asleep in his chair again. I don't think he'll be working for much longer. We don't need for anything, and the house was paid off long ago.' Chloe leaned back in the wooden seat. 'He told me that he's giving his notice today. Since Conrad was put on a different shift, he's lost all interest in the job. He doesn't like the new man he's been partnered with, and only wants to stay at home these days.'

'Well, you can't really blame him, Mum, he's getting older, and I think Conrad was doing more of the running around and leaving him in the security room. If you don't need the money, then I think he's due for retirement.'

Chloe sighed. 'Time isn't kind to anyone, is it?' She paused, watching the antics of the kittens. 'You know, I never told you this, but when you had the children, I wasn't sure how to take them. They were so strange, but then they were my grandchildren too.'

Hope laughed lightly. 'You put up a good front, Mum. I would never have guessed. The children loved you, and you always volunteered for babysitting duty.'

'I know, and any misgivings I felt vanished quickly. I mean, how could anyone not love a face like this.' She bent down and picked up a small kitten who had decided to hide under the chair. A small furry face gazed at up her, and the softest meow came from its little body. She cuddled it to her chest before releasing it back onto the ground, where it scampered off to rejoin its companions. 'Hope, have you thought about what will happen when the children find their own mates, the ones they want to be with?'

Hope had thought of little else for the last few weeks. Axel had begun spending time with one of the other hybrid girls, April, and the relationship appeared to be going well. 'I have thought about it, and I'll cross that bridge when it happens. They're still too young to get serious about each other, and I think they know that a normal relationship isn't available to them. I know some of the other boys have tried having girlfriends with non-hybrid girls, and it just hasn't worked. The girls were okay, the parents broke them apart.'

'Yes, parents are very protective, regardless. I can understand it though.'

The sound of crunching gravel interrupted their conversation. Two cars pulled into the rescue centre's car park.

Hope and Chloe looked at each other. 'Are you expecting any cats, Hope?'

'No, and I'm not expecting visitors either. I wonder who they are?'

Four men emerged from the cars and made their way over. One of them pulled his wallet from his pocket and flipped it open. A police badge sparkled in the sun.

'Mrs Hope Adamson?'

Hope stepped forward. 'Yes, that's me. What can I help you with,' Hope peered at the name on the card, 'Sergeant Williams?'

The policeman returned the wallet to his pocket. 'We're following up on a missing person case from a number of years ago.' He paused for a few seconds as he pulled a notebook from his top shirt pocket, and flipped the top back. 'A Miss Dorothy Brown was reported missing approximately sixteen years ago, and we have recently been informed the last place she was seen was entering your property.'

'Really? Sixteen years ago? That's a long time to remember back.' Hope paused, feigning, she hoped, a thoughtful look on her face. Inside, she shook. Dorothy Brown was the name of the woman who lay at the bottom of the garden bed they stood in front of. 'I can't recall the name. Back then we hadn't long set up the rescue centre, and we had so many people come to hand in cats or adopt one. Can you give me any other information about her?'

Sergeant Williams glanced back at his notebook. 'She was Caucasian, brown hair, brown eyes, and approximately 172 centimetres in height.'

Chloe stepped forward. 'I'm Hope's mother-in-law, Chloe Wright. That's a pretty generic description, Sergeant. Is there anything else about her that may jog our memories?'

'You were here at the same time, Mrs Wright?'

'My husband and I live in the smaller house down the hill.' She pointed to the house. 'We've been here as long as my son and Hope have been in the house.'

The sergeant again consulted his notebook and flipped a couple of pages, until he found what he'd been looking for. 'It's believed she came here to adopt some cats to breed from.' He flipped another page over. 'Yes, she was a breeder. She was reported missing after an animal inspection team had been alerted to a complaint of a lot of cats, caged and starving, found by a prospective client.'

Hope sputtered, nearly choking. 'You mean she was a backyard breeder? She ran a kitten farm?'

'Yes, I believe that is the common name for the type of enterprise she was running.'

'Sounds to me the type of person who ought to be missing.' Chloe retorted in disgust.

'Regardless, it has been reported to us that she came here to procure some stock for her "farm".'

'Sergeant, I never have, and would never, have sold any of my rescues to a person like that. All the animals here have been adopted by loving caring forever families. I personally inspect every home my rescues go to, and I have never been to such a place as you describe.' Hope's voice was close to breaking, with anger, disgust, and fear.

'Please calm down, Mrs Adamson. I do understand your anger. I'm a cat lover myself. All I want to know is if you remember her coming to see you. She may not have mentioned what her business was.'

Hope stepped back and leaned against the back of a chair. 'Sergeant, I cannot remember her at all. There have been so many people over the last sixteen years. It's just too long ago.' Tears had begun coursing down her cheeks. She hid her face in her hands and sobbed.

Chloe placed her arm around Hope's shoulder. 'Shhh, don't get so upset. He isn't saying you've done something, are you, Sergeant?'

He stepped forward. 'No, not at all, and I'm sorry for having caused you so much anguish. We realise it was a long time ago and hoped you could remember if she turned up here. I was going to ask you if we could have a look around, but I don't think we need to.' Turning around, he took a few steps back toward the car park, before bending down and picking up a kitten, which had previously been playing in the garden bed. 'Mrs Adamson, Hope, I hope you don't mind if I come back soon. My children have been asking for a kitten for a while, and I think this little fellow may be just what they want. I am happy to have you come to me to make sure my family would be a fit forever family.' He placed the kitten back on the ground, took a card from his other shirt pocket, and wrote on the back. He walked back to Hope, offering her the card. 'That's my address and home phone number. Please call me when you are able to visit.'

Hope glanced at the card, sniffed some tears back, and placed it in her pocket. 'Thank you, Sergeant. I'll give you a call when I'm next in town.'

'I'll look forward to it.' Calling to the other policemen to put down the kittens they had been holding and playing with, they walked to the car park, got into the cars, and waved goodbye as the cars drove down the hill and out onto the road.

Hope held her breath until the cars were out of sight, before exhaling all at once.

'I wonder what happened to the poor woman?' Chloe said.

'Hopefully something horrible, much like what she'd been doing to those poor cats she had,' Hope replied.

'Surely you don't mean that, Hope? After all, she's still a human being.'

'Oh, yes I do, Mum. There are some human beings who don't deserve to live.' Hope walked to the garden bed and smiled to herself. Yes, she got exactly what she deserved, and continued on her way into the house. Chloe followed behind, unaware of why Hope had acted as she did.

****

A car sped down the road, and up the track, now well worn, toward the house. Hope sat up on the couch where she and Chloe sat drinking coffee. 'That's Conrad's car. He's supposed to be at work.' Fear coiled in Hope's stomach. Something bad must have happened for Conrad to be driving like he was, and for him to be coming home earlier than he was supposed to. The two women raced outside to meet Conrad at the rescue centre building.

The car pulled up outside the centre, and Hope watched as Conrad and all four children bailed out of the car. Hope clung to Chloe as Conrad ran over.

'Hope, grab a bag and fill it with food and clothes for a few days. We have to leave now.'

'Why, what's happened? Conrad, you're scaring me.'

Conrad grabbed her, hugging her tight. 'Someone sent a private militia force to the university to take the children. We think one of the drug companies is behind it.'

'Were only our children targeted? What about the others?'

'Not just ours, the others are following. I got them out fast as soon as I saw what was happening. Their parents are on the way over too.'

Chloe grabbed onto Conrad. 'Where will you go?'

Conrad held his mother and kissed her cheek. 'Mum, where we're going, you can't follow. You need to stay here. I don't think they'll hurt you if they come here. I hope they don't. If they do, just say I wouldn't tell you.'

He glanced at Hope. 'Please Hope, make it fast. I've told the children what's happening, and where they will be going.'

Hope heard more cars speeding down the dirt road out the front of their property. She ran to the house.

'Conrad,' Chloe stroked her only son's face. 'Please take care and be sensible. I would like to see you again one day.'

'Mum,' tears streamed from Conrad's eyes, 'hopefully I'll be back in a few days. You're a clever woman, and I think you know where we're going. If you can, after we've left, I need you to let us know what's going on. If something is draped across the portal door, I'll know there are people still here. If nothing is across the door, I'll know it's clear.' He looked around, then looked back. The noise of cars engines arriving close to them made him raise his voice. 'Mum, I love you, don't forget that. Take care of Bill.'

Conrad turned and ran into the house to help Hope.

'Hope, do you need help?' Conrad called out as he entered the house.

Teyah sped past, knapsack in hand, attacking the food cupboards, and piling whatever she could lay her hands on into the bag. When that one was full, she pulled shopping bags from a kitchen drawer and began filling them. 'Dad, if you want to help, take these to the portal.'

Conrad hurried over, grabbed as many bags as he could, and ran out to the waiting crowd gathering outside the centre. 'Out of my way, coming through.' People stepped to the side as he made his way to the door, unlocked it and led everyone inside.

'Where are we going? What's happening?' One of the fathers grabbed his arm. Conrad shook him off, placed the groceries on the ground near the portal, stood on a chair and clapped his hands together. 'People, please. Quiet.' The chaos calmed, and Conrad cleared his throat. 'I know my phone calls were hurried, and I'm glad you responded so quickly.' He waited a second. 'The children were about to be stolen—kidnapped—by a private militia force.'

Clamour broke out again in the group, everyone firing questions at him, all at once. He held his hands up in the air, requesting silence. He gazed down into the small group, reading the fear and uncertainty in every face before him. 'I don't know who is behind it, but April said she recognised some of the men from the short day she worked for ANPTAS, the drug company.'

'Why did we need to come here? What can you do that we can't?'

Conrad placed his hands on his hips. The man asking was one of the problem parents, always finding a reason to argue about anything. 'Can you take your children and wife off world, so no one can find them?

The hush that followed was deafening.

'Off—world? What do you mean? How can we leave the planet?' Someone in the group said.

The big mouth opened his yap again and laughed. 'What, got a space ship back there, have you? He barged forward, nearly knocking Conrad from the chair. He was stopped by more than twenty cats, advancing down the small corridor. 'What's this? You've got an army of cats under your control, have you?'

Conrad smiled. 'You might say that, Duncan. Why don't you go stand beside your wife and behave—and shut your damn mouth! I'm trying to save your lives, and the life of your son.'

Duncan did as told, awed by the advancement of the cats, and his wife dragged him back beside her.

'Thanks, Enid. Much obliged to you.' He turned to the cats. *'Thank you for your help. Are you able to stay, please? I may need your help again.'*

'We will stay Conrad-Hero. We understand the problem and are here to help.'

Conrad cleared his throat again. 'As to the question of having a spaceship back there,' he looked over his shoulder toward the portal room, 'the answer is yes, in a way.'

A few nervous laughs scattered through the room. 'I am going to send you through the portal here,' he swung his hand around in the direction of the room, 'with one of my children. They have been trained in how to use it. You are to pay attention to them and do exactly as they say. More importantly, do not touch anything.'

Conrad looked pointedly at Duncan, who promptly found his own shoes very interesting.

'The place you are going looks different to what you know here on Earth. Everything is comprised of shades of red and brown.' He waited for the news to sink in. 'There isn't much time to do this, so if you have brought clothing, food or anything else with you, please go and retrieve it now.'

Conrad stepped off the chair, made his way out, grabbing his children on the way through, and pulled them to the side. 'Kids, I'm counting on you to get everyone and their luggage away from the portal once you're through.' He turned to Axel and Charlotte. 'Axel, you will take the first two, Charlotte will also come with you.'

Axel stepped forward. 'I suggest we take Duncan first, Dad. He's the one who's going to be the biggest problem.'

Conrad nodded in agreement and clapped his son on the shoulder. 'Good thinking. I want you to stay there and send Charlotte back. Take Duncan to one of the rooms in the building, but keep him away from anything that has dials. There is a tea room a few doors down. Take them there. Make sure no one leaves the building.'

'Okay, Dad. I'll do that.'

Conrad turned to Charlotte. 'Honey, I want you to come back. We can't send the next lot over until we know you have cleared the portal.' He grimaced. 'I'm afraid you're going to be making a few trips. I'm only going to send two adults at a time, so that means three of you in the cabinet. It may get a little squeezy, but the trip doesn't take long, luckily.'

'Don't worry, Dad. I'm okay with that.'

Conrad looked at the other two. 'Dexter, I need you to keep the others under control and get the other kids to help. I'm hoping this won't take long. Teyah, can you go back to the house and make sure your mother isn't trying to bring everything with her? You know what she's like when she packs for a weekend away.'

Teyah giggled. 'Sure, Dad. I know what you mean. I'll try to keep the mountain of bags down.'

Conrad watched as she sprinted up the hill. Damn those kids could move. He felt a tug at his sleeve. Axel stood in front of him.

'Dad, what are we going to do with all the cars? I know you're thinking the militia will come here looking for us. If they see all the cars, they'll know something is up. Can they follow us?'

Conrad shook his head. Damn, he hadn't thought about the vehicles. There were nine cars out there. If they saw them, Bill and his mum would be questioned, and if the militia were prepared to take the children by force, he didn't want to think of what they'd do to his mother and Bill. 'Okay. Once we've sent Duncan over, I'll take the other men, and we'll hide the cars somewhere. Dexter, you'll have to co-ordinate the departure of the others. Remember, wait until your sister is back before the next lot go. No more than three in the room at a time.'

'Sure, Dad, I can handle that.'

'Thanks, son.' He looked at all his children. They were handling everything better than could. 'I love you all so much.' He leaned forward and enveloped the three in his arms. 'Once you have everyone over, I mean the mothers and kids, including your mum, I want you to go over as well. I'll ferry the men over once we get back from dumping the cars.'

Conrad knew exactly where to take the cars where they wouldn't be found. He also needed his mum and Bill in on the next part.

The people began to come back in, some loaded with luggage, others only carrying a backpack and a couple of bags in each hand. Duncan, of course, was loaded to the hilt, as was his wife and children.

'I want to go over first,' Duncan demanded.

Conrad smiled. 'That's okay, Duncan, we'd already decided you would be going first.'

'Oh, did you. Why?'

Enid, his wife, elbowed him in the ribs. 'Shut up, you idiot. You're going first, be happy with that.'

Conrad smiled. 'Again, thank you, Enid.' Conrad walked to the room and opened the door. Axel and Charlotte entered, and Conrad waved Duncan in. As his wife stepped forward to enter, Conrad stopped her. 'I'll send you next, Enid, we can only send three at time.'

A smile lit her face. 'Thank you, Conrad. I don't mind waiting a little.'

Duncan's face, however, wasn't as happy. 'No, I demand she comes with me. I'm not going to some strange place on my own.'

Conrad scowled at him. 'Duncan, you will go by yourself, and you will pay attention and do what my son tells you to do on the other side. Enid will follow you soon.'

Duncan shut up. Conrad expected it. Just like all bullies and loudmouths, if you stood up to them, they usually backed down. 'Okay, Axel, ready to go?'

'Ready, Dad. Closing the door.'

Conrad heard a bit of shuffling, and the door closed. The whine sounded, and he saw the flash of light from under the door. Good, the first problem had been taken care of. He turned to face the others. 'Now that Duncan's gone, there has been a slight change of plan.'

'What, we're going to go to a different planet, and leave him on his own?' Many laughed, even Enid. Conrad did too. 'As much as that would be ideal, no, that's not the change. We need to move the cars. I have the place to put them, and if you leave your name and address in your car, I will have them ferried back to your houses, so it looks like you've only gone for a few days.'

A hand raised at the back of the group. 'Good idea, but won't we need them when we come back?'

Conrad glanced around at the children, then looked back. 'Folks, We—

'—Won't be coming back.' Hope walked in behind them. 'This is a one-way trip. Face it, if they are chasing the children now, do you think any of us are safe? We bear the genes of the first trial. We were the ones who gave birth to the "special" hybrid children. I'm sure you realise one of the "special" things about them, apart from their looks, is how smart they are. As their parents, we would be forced to reproduce many, many, more children, the same as we have now.' She looked at them, as they'd all turned around when she began talking. 'How many of you want to be forced into breeding, like an animal in a backyard breeding set-up?'

Conrad had to admit, Hope had put everything into that one spiel. He could see the heads nodding as the realisation of what she had said sunk in. He clapped his hands again, gaining their attention. 'Ladies, I'm sorry to leave you like this, but I'm going to need the men to move the cars. Meanwhile, the children know what to do. If you follow their directions, everything will continue to go smoothly. Remember, only three at a time.'

'Don't worry love, everything will go smoothly, won't it, ladies?' Sounds of acknowledgment hummed around the room. 'Take care, Conrad, I don't want to start this new life without you.' Hope lifted her head, met Conrad's kiss and held it for a few seconds.

'Mum, we don't have time for that. Let Dad go.'

Nervous laughter came from the women and teenagers.

Hope shook her head, tsking under her breath, but smiling. 'Why is it all children don't like seeing their parents kiss?'

'Because it's gross, Mum, now let the men go.'

The door to the portal opened, and Charlotte stepped out. 'Next please.'

Enid stepped up. 'I hope Duncan wasn't too much to handle on the other side?'

'Actually, no. He's pretty good about it. He was too busy looking around to give us any cheek.'

Enid sighed. 'Oh, I wish I'd seen that.' She stepped forward with her bags.

'Here, Mum, let me help you with that.' Her son stepped forward, grabbing a few of the heavier bags. He looked at Charlotte. 'Is it okay if I go with her?'

Charlotte looked for guidance from her father, who held up his thumb in a 'she'll be right' way. 'No problem, Cyrus.' She blushed, as did he. They both stepped into the room, as before, closed the door, and everyone watched the light flashed from under the door.

'Okay men, time to leave. Kiss your wives, but it won't be long until you're all back here.'

After the goodbyes had been said, and hugs given to the children, the men trooped out and stood by their cars.

'I have to stop in and get my mother and Bill. Everyone, please meet me down the bottom of the hill, then follow me to where we will leave the cars.'

They jumped into their cars and waved goodbye to the women waiting in the Cat Rescue Centre. As one, they began rolling down the hill.

Conrad stopped his car but left it running. Chloe and Bill stood in the doorway. He walked up to them, explained he needed them to follow, so when it came time to ferry the cars back, they would know where to find them. Also, the men needed a lift back.

Bill and Chloe agreed the plan was a good one. Chloe closed the front door; two cars started up, and moved in behind Conrad's. The conga line moved out onto the road, picked up speed and moved away, out of sight, and away from the house.

****

Back at the Cat Rescue Centre, there wasn't anything to do except wait. The women were full of questions about where they were headed. Hope held up her hands, ceasing the questions. 'I can't answer anything because I don't know anything. I've never been there myself. The children have, though. They may be able to answer your questions.'

All eyes turned toward Dexter and Teyah. 'Gee, thanks, Mum.'

'Sorry, but even I'm a little curious. Your dad has spoken about what it's like, but I'm not sure I can visualise it. You've been there and seen things. Come on, tell us what it's like.'

The women settled down, Hope brought out as many seats as she could find, and while Dexter and Teyah regaled the women on the delights and strangeness of Catatopia, Hope made cups of tea.

When Charlotte stepped out of the room, the next lot of two people were ready to go. They all decided one child and one adult should go each time. That way, when the men returned, there would still be people left. It wasn't any use transferring all the children, and then the adults, because as someone had suggested, god forbid, if something happened, the children would need more than two adults there to help them. Enid was okay, but no one wanted Duncan to be the only other adult. The transfers took between ten and fifteen minutes. The time difference depended on the amount of luggage going with each person. Food would be needed, as would clothing. Anything unnecessary, like mobile phones and electronic items, would be left behind.

As usual, the women had everything arranged. The transfers continued to go smoothly, and the women took everything in their stride. Hope checked her watch constantly. She hadn't asked Conrad where he would be leaving the cars. They'd already been gone an hour and a half. She was getting worried. All she could do was to keep checking out the window and keep the ladies topped up with tea.

As she looked at her watch for what seemed the fiftieth time, she heard the crunch of tyres on stony ground. A vehicle, no, two vehicles, drove up to the centre and disgorged their load. Nine men alighted, plus Bill and Chloe. Hope let go a deep sigh, and her blood pressure returned to one resembling a normal rate.

The men walked in the door and were immediately mobbed by wives and children, at least those who hadn't left yet. Hope grabbed Conrad and didn't want to let him go.

'Conrad, I was so worried. What took you so long?'
'We had a bit of a problem.'

If Conrad was using telepathy, something bad must have happened. 'Tell me.'

'We were spotted when we had to cross one of the busier main roads. A militia car was sitting at the lights and recognised some of the men as they passed. He tagged on behind us. Luckily, Derek saw him, and we tried to lose him. He forced Gavin's car off the road and was about to take him. The rest of us stopped him.'

Conrad sent through a mental picture of what had happened. Hope squirmed. It was another 'accident' like the one she'd had with Mrs Brown. 'Do you think it'll be long before they find him?'

'We hid his car behind an abandoned building. Not many go out there. The other cars are hidden miles away.'

Hope looked at Chloe and Bill. They hadn't alighted from the car but sat there talking. 'Conrad, did your mum see what happened?'

Conrad looked back over his shoulder. 'I think she might have. We tried to shield her from it, but she didn't say a word on the way home.'

'Maybe you should have a word with her, just quietly.' Hope couldn't believe what they'd both done to protect the children. When all this had started, neither of them would have killed a mouse, let alone a human being. The instinctive need to protect had taken a toll on both of them. Hope knew she wasn't the same person she'd been years ago. Hopefully Chloe would understand no matter how distasteful the action, it was all for the good of the children.

She watched as he walked out of the building, and squatted next to the car door. She couldn't see what he was saying, but the downturned look on his face told her he wasn't happy. Charlotte appeared again, and this time one of the men and his wife took their turn. From the whispers Hope observed, the men had passed on what had happened. The joyous, happy mood disappeared;

they were all strangers again, waiting for some kind of public transport to take them away.

Finally, Chloe and Bill left the car and walked into the building. Chloe walked up to Hope, looked her in the eyes, grasped both of her hands and said, 'Make this all worthwhile. So much bad karma surrounds this group.'

'I'll do my best, Mum.'

'I know you will. Also, please come back one day. I'll miss our talks.'

Hope squeezed her hand. They'd become close friends. 'Mum, it'll be up to you to run the rescue centre now. Make sure they all go to good homes and take care of Spook and Wanderer. They're old now, and I think they should stay here.'

'They're already sleeping down at our cottage, but I'll tell them goodbye for you.' Chloe's eyes glistened, and Hope knew she wasn't far off crying. Goodbyes were so hard. Maybe they would come back, and maybe they wouldn't. This new world was a total unknown.

'Please snuggle them for me. Chloe, I think you need to go now. If you wait any longer, it'll hurt too much.' The tears streamed from Hope's eyes, and there wasn't a thing she could do about it.

****

Chloe placed the curtain across the doorway and sniffed back her tears. 'They're all gone now, Bill. The place is going to be pretty empty without them, and no children running around.'

Bill placed his arm around his wife's shoulders and hugged her tight to his side. 'Don't worry, love. Conrad will keep checking to see if the coast is clear. They're going to need supplies for a little while until they can get their own food going. He said he'd check back every couple of days.'

'I know, but this is the beginning of them being gone for good. I was hoping I'd be a great-grandmother, and have kittens to sit on my lap. I'll miss Axel and Dexter's fur. They were so nice to hold and stroke, especially when they were little.'

Bill guffawed, and Chloe looked aghast at him. 'Bill, how can you laugh at a time like this?'

'You silly girl, you've got plenty of fur to stroke. Look at all the cats waiting for your attention.' Chloe looked to the side, and sure enough, twenty pairs of eyes looked up at her, as if to say, 'We're here. Love us.'

'Yes, I do have a lot of mouths to feed and coats to brush.'

Bill laughed again. 'I think you're going to need my help as well. Looks like we're Mummy and Daddy to a whole bunch of new kittens.'

Later that night, Chloe woke to lights flashing in the windows and the crunching of gravel under boots. Someone knocked at the door. Then knocked harder.

'Okay, okay. Hang onto your horses. We're coming.' Both Bill and Chloe climbed out of bed, covered themselves with dressing gowns and peeked through the window.

'Bastards. It's the militia,' Bill growled.

'Bill, be civil to them. We don't know what they're capable of,' Chloe suggested worriedly.

'Yeah, yeah, I'll be nice to the …' Bill opened the door. 'What do you want? It's two a-bloody-clock in the morning. This had better be good.'

A light flashed in his face, and he brought up his hand to shade his eyes. 'Get that damn thing out of my eyes or someone's going to be walking funny.' The light dropped down, now shining on his chest.

A man walked up to him. 'Where are Conrad Adamson and his family?'

'Why? Who wants to know?' Bill retorted.

'He's wanted by the police.'

'That's utter rubbish. You guys are the militia, and you want the kids. Well, they've gone.' Bill blurted.

'Where have they gone?'

'Don't know. It was better that way. Conrad knew you'd be round, so he just took Hope and the kids, and left.'

A rifle poked Bill's chest. He swallowed a lump of fear. 'You won't use that. I don't need any help remembering either. I'm telling you the truth. We don't know where they've gone.'

'You won't mind if we have a look around then, will you.'

'Yes, I bloody well do mind if you look around.' Bill stepped forward onto his porch. 'If you aren't off this property in one minute, I am calling the police, and I know you guys don't like each other that much.'

'We'll be keeping an eye on you.'

'Bugger off. I'll give you until the count of ten, and then I'm going to start shooting you. Ten, nine, eight ...' Bill heard the scrabbling of feet and tyres as they left the yard. He waited until he heard them speeding off down the road before he closed the door.

'That was you being nice?' asked Chloe.

'Yeah, you should see me when I'm really upset.' Bill was sure his heart rate had hit three hundred beats a minute when the rifle nudged his sternum. He knew they would be watching the place for a few days. Getting supplies to Conrad and the kids would be hard. They'd have to get sneaky.

CHAPTER THIRTY

On Catatopia
The first night was spent sleeping on the floor in the portal building. Conrad had given instructions no one was allowed into the cat's town for any reason.

He sat up, waiting for everyone to fall asleep. Once he was certain all were out for the count, he slipped out of the building and walked in the pink moonlight. The air had a pleasing odour, not rose-scented, but close. His mum smelled similar, and it calmed him. Reaching the fork in the road, he saw a familiar figure. Rufus.

'You came out to meet me, my friend. How did you know we'd arrived?'

'One of my lookouts alerted me that many two-legs were arriving through the travel box. Has there been trouble for you to bring so many?'

Conrad sat in the middle of the road. 'Yes. There has been. We escaped, no one else can follow.'

'I am sorry to hear this, Conrad. Have you closed the portal?'

'No, the portal is still open. I'll leave it a few days before I travel back to find out what is happening. We will need supplies for a little while until we know how to operate the transference machine, and I can get everyone to Terra. We will need food as well until we find what will grow in this planet's soil.'

'The kittens who have travelled through to your 'Rescue Centre', are they being cared for?'

'The kittens will do well, and I expect more to travel to begin new lives there. My mother can't mind speak, but she will take care of them.'

'Will you ever go back, or is this planet to become your home?'

Conrad had been asking himself the same question. So far he hadn't come up with an answer. The safe probability would be for he and Hope to remain until they passed childbearing age. That way the drug companies couldn't use them as breeding stock. 'Truthfully, I don't know, Rufus. I do know we will be here for a long time, probably another of your lifetimes.'

'Do not worry, there will always be someone here for you. You are part of our history now, the great rebuilder. I look forward to seeing you without having to journey to your world.'

'I look forward to seeing you too, Rufus.' Conrad hesitated. 'Rufus, could I bring two of my kittens into town? I would like to look through the cabinets left here by the previous two-legs. I promise not to disturb what you are doing.'

Rufus laid his paw on Conrad's knee. 'I know you won't. I would be pleased to see your kittens. After all, they are also my kittens, aren't they?'

Conrad chuckled to himself. 'Yes, my furry friend, I suppose they are.' He ruffled the fur on his friend's head and received a pleasant trill in return. 'It has been a long time since I heard that sound.'

'It has.' Rufus looked behind him, then back at Conrad. 'I am being called, Conrad. I must leave.'

'I understand. I must go before I am missed too.' Conrad stood, ruffled his friend's fur once more, and walked back to the building. He didn't know why, but sadness built in him as he walked away from the cat. He turned back and looked for him, but Rufus had already trotted out of sight.

Shaking the foreboding darkness from his mind, he slipped inside the building, crawled into the sleeping bag and laid his head down.

A softness touched his nose, and Conrad woke to discover a young kitten's face in front of his. 'You are Conrad-hero?'

'Yes, I am. Who are you?'

'I am named for you. My name is Hero. I am sent to bring you to Catatopia. The Great Rufus needs you.'

The kitten's thoughts portrayed trouble, even sadness. Conrad sat up, squirmed out of his bag, and stood, picking up the kitten with him.

'Where are you going?' Hope asked, her voice sounding in his mind.

'There seems to be a problem with Rufus. I need to go.'

'Be quiet then, and don't wake the others. Do you want me to come?'

'No, stay here. If the others wake before I return, can you keep them inside, or at least close to the building? I'll find out what the problem is, and I'll bring back the cart and trailer.'

'Conrad-hero, we need to leave. The Great Rufus needs you.' The kitten's thoughts indicated urgency.

'I have to go, Hope. Stay safe and keep the group together.'

'Be careful, Conrad. Rufus may be your friend, but other cats may not be, hero or no hero.'

Conrad gave the thumbs up sign, and snuck silently out of the room. Once outside, he tucked the kitten into his shirt and ran.

As Conrad entered the town, he could hear growling and yowls.

'Conrad-hero, the Great Rufus is in the middle of a fight. You must save him.'

Conrad could pick up Rufus's distinctive mind voice. He was defending the two-legs who had arrived, reminding the rest who stood against him of what Conrad-hero had done for them.

He also heard the replies. Before he ran into the middle of the cat fight, he stopped, reached inside his shirt and placed the kitten on the ground. 'Hero, stay here. I don't want you hurt.'

'Please save the Great Rufus. My mother says he has been a fair ruler.'

Conrad smiled. Yes, with what Rufus had seen, he'd lay cards on it that the cat would be a great ruler. He tucked the kitten out the way and rounded the corner. Rufus and Princess were surrounded by a mass of snarling felines. And they were advancing on them as he watched.

Not using his mental voice, Conrad yelled. 'WHAT THE HELL IS HAPPENING?'

The other cats flattened themselves against the roadway and then turned to see what had made the terrible noise. Conrad found himself the object of a snarling group.

'Rufus, Princess, are you okay?' Conrad walked toward them.

'STOP!' ordered Rufus.

Conrad stopped. 'Hero says you need my help, and by the look of what is happening, I can get you out of this.'

'Rufus, please let Conrad-human take us from this. They will hurt us, you know they will.' Conrad could hear Princess pleading.

'Rufus, I'm sorry. I know I said I wouldn't interfere, but I can't let you and your queen be hurt. You are my friend.'

'Maybe I can help.'

Axel's voice sounded behind him. 'Mum thought I might be needed.'

The snarling group in front quietened as Axel moved forward, lowering himself onto all four paws. 'Fellow felines, this is not the way to settle differences. The Great Rufus has been a fair and kind leader, has he not? I sense your displeasure at we two-legs arriving. We are not here to harm you, only to offer help if you need it.'

'No two-legs were supposed to return, so the story says.'

Axel searched for the one who had spoken. 'Do I look like a two-legs to be feared?' he picked up a paw and began washing. 'Am I not like you, only larger?'

While Axel held the attention of the group, Conrad made his way around and scooped up Rufus and Princess. Shielding his thoughts, he stopped Rufus's argumentative ones.

'My son will keep them occupied while I get you out the way.'

Princess trilled in fear at being carried. 'I will not harm you, Princess. Rufus is not afraid. I have carried him often.'

'My friend, I do not wish to be taken "out of the way". This is the way leaders are chosen in Catatopia. This is how I won the battle against the Great Siam.'

'Rufus, they would tear you and Princess apart. I'm sure you don't want her hurt because someone else wants to be leader.'

Conrad placed Rufus down on the ground. 'If you want to get killed, and leave Princess alone and unguarded, then go ahead, go back to the fight. I will keep Princess safe.'

Rufus took a few steps, stopped and washed. 'The large feline who is talking now, is he one of your kittens?'

'Yes, he is one of mine. We adopted him when he and his sister were born. Their mother rejected them. His name is Axel. He was the only one born with paws.'

'He does look like me, doesn't he? Do other females like him?'

Conrad had an idea where this was going. If he were right, Rufus would try to use Axel to secure his own leadership. 'Yes, other females like him, and no Rufus, he can't stay here with you. He is people, but he is also a two-legs. It violates the agreement.'

Rufus stood, and was about to round the corner when Axel appeared. 'I have explained what is going on. The others thought they would be thrown out of their "caves", and we would move in. I have told them that is not the case, and that we will be living far away.'

Rufus looked up at Axel. 'They are happy with that, kitten of Conrad?'

'They are, Rufus, and my name is Axel.'

Conrad smiled at Axel's rebuke of the word "kitten". 'So you have fixed everything, they aren't going to skin Princess and Rufus if we leave?'

'I think they will be okay, but maybe we ought to stay a few minutes, to make sure.'

'I agree.' Conrad's pride in his son shone as he walked around the corner, Rufus and Princess in front of them.

'You did well there, Axel. You soothed the savage beasts.' They were savage too. Conrad had glimpsed the murderous rage some of them had in their minds. They stood back as Rufus addressed the large group.

'You have heard Axel, the son of Conrad-hero, and know he speaks the truth. The two-legs will not be settling here, but will be journeying across this planet to the land of Terra. Is this acceptable to all?'

A chorus of meows sounded, the mental image was one of complete agreement.

'You are also content to keep myself and my queen as rulers, and no longer wish us harm?'

Ashamed of their actions, the meows were lower in vocalisation this time, though the same mental picture communicated to all.

'Good. Then we welcome Conrad-hero and his families to Catatopia, and wish them a good journey to the other side.'

****

Conrad and Axel arrived at the portal building driving the cart and trailer. Hope met them outside the door.

'Is everyone awake and ready to go?' The group had been told they would be making their way to the transmission room the night before.

'Yes, everyone is ready to go, but one person is making a fuss.'

Conrad had no problem in guessing which person wasn't happy. 'Duncan, right?'

Hope nodded and sighed. 'He seems to think we can stay at New Earth. The children and I tried to explain why, but he won't listen. His son even tried, but Duncan is so pig-headed, he won't listen to anyone.'

Conrad swore under his breath. He'd never wished anyone harm, but this guy was becoming a problem. 'Let me deal with him. I'll make him see reason.'

Hope grabbed him by the elbow. 'Don't hit him. We don't need that kind of aggravation in the group.'

'I'll try, but I'm not promising anything.' He stepped toward the door. 'I'll take him for a walk out the back door. Meanwhile, can you and the children get the luggage and food loaded into the cart, ready to go when we return?'

'Sure, we can do that.' Axel stood beside Hope. 'Dad, be diplomatic—if you can.'

'Like I said—I'll try.' Conrad opened the glass door, walked in and made a beeline for the tearoom. 'Duncan, where are you?' he bellowed.

'In here,' came the answer, 'just follow my voice.'

Conrad barrelled in through the door, saw the man, grabbed his shirt collar, dragged him up the hall and out the back door, where he threw him against the wall. 'Now,' Conrad breathed heavily from repressed anger, as well as the adrenaline he'd used, 'I understand you think you are special and should be allowed to live in Catatopia.'

Duncan crossed his arms in front of his chest. 'Yes, I can't see why we have to go any further when there is a perfectly good town here.'

Conrad drew close, his nose virtually touching Duncan's. 'Did you not understand the talk I gave last night to everyone?'

Duncan shrugged his shoulders. 'So there are a few cats to kick out. What's the big deal? After all, they're only animals.'

Conrad screwed up his fists and walked away a few steps. If he stayed near the man, someone's face would resemble jelly, and it wouldn't be his. Under his breath, he counted to ten, then twenty, before turning to once again face the man.

'What you want is not possible, and as to your idea that these "are only animals", you are wrong.' He took a step forward. 'Without the genes from one of these "animals" you wouldn't have a child, and you wouldn't be walking on this planet. So be thankful for what you have.'

Now calm, he grabbed Duncan by the arm, not roughly, but with enough strength to make the man realise it wouldn't be a good idea to struggle. 'We are going to the transmission room, and if you wish, you can go through the transporter first.'

'Sounds good to me. I'll be the first through, and the first of the group to see the new country.'

'If you're sure.' Conrad released the arm he so wanted to twist up the man's back but didn't. 'I suggest you gather what you need, and join the others out the front.'

Duncan moved away inside the complex, and Conrad rested his head against the building. Maybe once they were all in homes on Terra the problems would stop? He hoped so, but troublemakers like Duncan kept pushing until something bad happened. That was in the future, they still had to get to the next station.

'Are you alright?'

Hope stepped out from the corner of the building. 'Duncan joined the group a few minutes ago, strutting, acting so self-important.'

Conrad stood, placed his hands on over his face, and took a deep breath. 'I told him he could be the first to go through the transporter. He jumped at the chance.'

'Conrad, I thought you hadn't worked out how to operate it yet? If you sent someone through, would they make it?'

Conrad smiled and shrugged. 'I suppose we're about to find out, aren't we.'

CHAPTER THIRTY-ONE

The machine hummed, lights appeared on the control board, and everything appeared to be working. The temptation to send Duncan through, "as an experiment", appealed to Conrad, but Hope's disapproving gaze curtailed his desire to be rid of the troublemaker. Instead he, a couple of the fathers, and the children, set their minds to discovering how the machine worked. The instructions helped, but the mathematic calibrations needed to accomplish a perfect transmission proved too hard for the fathers to manage, so the children took over.

What Conrad had surmised might take weeks to accomplish only took a few days. The fact still remained, someone would have to go through first, and return. The possibility that whoever did go first wouldn't be coming back sat in the minds of everyone. Duncan still spouted he would be the first, insisting Conrad keep his word.

Sitting alone inside a vacant room, Conrad only succeeded in giving himself a headache. Could he really send someone through the machine, to what may be their death? A knock sounded at the door.

'Come in.' Conrad didn't need interruptions now.

Enid walked in and sat on a table. 'Are you going to send Duncan through?'

Enid had always been straight with him so he would be straight with her. 'Enid, I know he wants to go, but whoever is first may not reach the other side alive. This transporter is different to the one we used when we arrived here.'

'Yes, I realise that.' She took a breath. 'Conrad, you can never say anything to anyone else, but I want you to send him.'

Conrad sat straighter in the chair. 'You want me to send him, knowing he may be killed?'

Enid's head bobbed.

'Why?'

'Because, if he goes first, but dies, we'll know not to send anyone else, and we'll find another way of getting to where we have to go. Duncan has always been a bully. He's bullied Cyrus, and most people he's come in contact with. For our small colony to survive, we can't have people like him around.'

'But Enid, don't you love him?'

Enid slipped off the desk and straightened her clothes. 'Love, Conrad, has nothing to do with this. Survival does.'

Conrad sat speechless as she walked to the door, opened it, and closed it behind her. If Duncan's own wife could see the problem, why couldn't he?

Conrad shook his head in amazement. Enid had been the deciding factor. Duncan would be the first through the transporter. Conrad's headache ebbed immediately.

He stood. Time to tell Duncan the good news, and instruct him on what he needed to do "when" he got to the other side.

***

Conrad yawned. He'd had a sleepless night, plagued with bad dreams of what would happen today. He sent a silent prayer to Bast everything would go well today, and no one would lose their life. He rose, got dressed and tiptoed from the room he shared with Hope and his children.

Crossing the road, he made his way to the transmission room, fully expecting to be the first there. He found the door open, and puzzled, walked in. Machines buzzed and the "disco floor" was lit.

Duncan stood in the middle of the floor.

'Duncan, what are you doing?' Conrad approached the platform slowly.

'No one was supposed to see me leave, Conrad.' Duncan turned as he spoke. 'Enid told me what she did; how she spoke to you and said to send me.' Duncan's lower lip trembled, and Conrad felt sorry for the man. 'My wife and son don't care for me, Conrad. They don't care if I do die.'

The last thing Conrad needed was to have a depressed, maybe suicidal person, going first to another place on the planet. He couldn't be sure if Duncan would come back, or purposely destroy himself, and maybe the hopes of everyone else.

Time for drastic action. Conrad stepped onto the platform. 'Duncan, do you realise you're a gigantic pain in the bum?' He took another small step. 'The kids and I stayed up late last night so we could teach you what you had to do to be able to get back here. This whole group is depending on you to be the hero you want to be, and this morning all you can do is cry that your wife and kid don't love you.' He grasped the man by his arm, pulled him to the side, and off the platform. 'In the end, the bullies always show themselves to be the cowards they really are.'

Duncan pulled his arm from Conrad's grasp and strode back onto the platform, wiping the tears from his face with a sleeve of his jacket. 'I'm no coward, and never have been. I'll show you, you jumped-up idiot. You're the coward, not me. I should be leader, not you. You let animals dictate terms, and walk all over you.'

Conrad's temper had reached breaking point when he felt a hand gently touch his arm. He spun around to see Enid beside him.

'Leave him be, Conrad. You've done the best you can.' Enid walked to the control panel. 'Are you ready to go, Duncan? Are you ready to make your wife and son proud of you?'

Conrad watched as Enid turned one of the dials a couple of clicks to the left. He looked at the man in the centre of the platform. He hadn't seen the movement.

Conrad took a step forward. 'Enid, are you sure?'

'I know what I'm doing, Conrad, don't worry. Cyrus told me what to do.'

'Just push the button, woman, or do I have to do it myself.' Duncan raged at his wife.

Enid waved her hand in the air. 'No Duncan, you stay where you are. I'm doing what I have to do.' She pushed the button, and Duncan began to dematerialise.

Conrad stood next to Enid and placed his arm around her shoulders. Neither said a word until Duncan had vanished. Conrad glanced at the dials, taking note of which one she had changed. Enid reached across the board and reset it.

'I wonder where he'll end up?'

Enid shrugged. 'Don't know, and don't really care. I had to make sure he would never bother us again.'

'What do we tell the others when they come to see him make the first journey?'

She smiled, and gently patted Conrad's hand. 'We tell them he left a note and went sometime during the night.' Enid rummaged in her pocket and pulled out a note. She laid it on the console, next to the dial she'd changed.

Conrad read it from where he stood and understood why Enid had done what she did. Duncan had intended to maroon them at Catatopia, never allowing them to reach Terra.

'Did you write that, or did he?'

'Do you really want to know, Conrad?' Enid hadn't looked up when she spoke.

Conrad gently patted her on the shoulder. 'No, I don't suppose I do.'

CHAPTER THIRTY-TWO

Terra
The accommodation wasn't much, but each family had their own house to live in. The furniture was basic, but usable. A shed had been found not far from the town, stocked to the roof with provisions. Building material, seeds, farming implements—everything a new town would need to survive.

Conrad hugged Hope to his side as they watched their grown adolescent children larking about. He smiled. His little family, and others like them, wouldn't have to suffer the hate and fear that would have plagued them on Earth.

'Are you going to be okay, not having the stores and modern day conveniences?'

Hope shook her head. 'I wasn't much into shopping trips back on Earth. There may be some things I miss, but as long as the children are safe, that's all that matters to me, and too many of the others.'

Conrad silently agreed with her. He would miss Bill and his mother most of all. 'I suppose we could go back a few times to visit, couldn't we?'

Hope remained silent for a few seconds. 'Maybe.'

****

Charlotte and Dexter sat in the sun, soaking up the rays. Two small kitten children crawled between them.

'Do you think Mum and Dad are okay?'

'Sure they are. Do you still miss them?'

'A little bit. I know they had to go back because grandma and grandpa were getting old, and someone had to look after the cattery, but I wish they'd been able to stay and see the first lot of grandkittens born.' Charlotte leaned over and picked up one of the kittens who struggled against her hold. 'Jasper would have loved her. Mum always loved the kittens when they were small. I remember her carrying us around, and snuggling her face into our fur.'

Charlotte groomed the fur of her kitten, and Jasper quietened, then began a deep purr.

'You still have Enid to talk to.' Dexter prompted.

'I know, but it's hard not having my own mum here.'

'Don't let Enid hear that. She considers herself a mother to all of us.'

'Enid is a wonderful woman, it's just that Mum is … you know … Mum.'

Dexter stood and stretched. 'I realise that, Charlotte, but the transporter has been dismantled, and we're on our own. Pretty soon Enid is going to need looking after; she's getting on in age now.'

He understood how Charlotte felt, but also realised that his parents and the other parents had to go back at some stage. All stayed for the first few years, helping get the food generators operational, and the soil-growing foods established. Relationships between the children had blossomed, and nature took over from there. An understanding that there would be no babies until the colony was properly established had been adhered to.

Frequent trips to Earth were made, to gather further supplies and raw materials. Conrad and Hope had been the last to leave. Chloe and Bill needed care, and the militia were no longer looking for them. They'd been gone six months, and the decision had been made to close down the transporter. They couldn't risk anyone accidently, or on purpose, finding their way to Catatopia.

Rufus passed away soon after Conrad left, and in disregard to the agreement, the cats elected Axel their next leader. He and April split their time between Catatopia and Terra.

Yes, Dexter and the others were relatively happy with their life, and looked forward to improving their part of the world as best they could, for themselves and their kittens.

EPILOGUE

150 years later: Earth

'That's it, Mrs Buckthorn, one big push, I can see the head crowning.'

'Doctor, do you see what I do?'

'If you mean the paws and tabby markings on the baby's head, yes I do, nurse, I'm not blind.'

'What's wrong with my baby, nurse?'

'Nothing is wrong, Mrs Buckthorn. Just give one more push, and your baby will be born.'

The nurse and doctor look aghast at each other, as the mewling baby, complete with fur, whiskers, and tail, lay between its mother's legs.

The End

ABOUT THE AUTHOR

Thanks for reading Catatopia.

This was to be my first novel, but strange things happen in the world of a writer, and five years later I am finally able to give it wings and let it out into the world to be read. I do hope you enjoyed it.

I would love to hear what you thought of the book. You can always leave a review on Goodreads, however you are under no obligation to do so.

I'm J. L. Addicoat and I'm a published Author of three novels. My works are in the genre of Romance, Paranormal and Science Fiction.

A little bit about me.
I live in the small rural country town of Gin Gin in Queensland Australia, with my husband Kevin and two spoilt felines, Ginge and Pookie (Spook).
I have three children, all who have their own families.

Books have always been a love in my life. They bring knowledge, but also an escape into another world where anything is possible.

Visit my Website: https://jladdicoat.wordpress.com/
Friend me on Facebook:
https://www.facebook.com/jladdicoat
Follow me on Twitter: https://twitter.com/JLAddicoat

I have added two samples of my previous novels, Spirit of Love (my debut novel) and Entangled Destinies.

Again, thank you for reading Catatopia.

SPIRIT OF LOVE-CHAPTER ONE

Turning the heavy iron key in the lock, an ominous creak sounded as Julia tried to open the huge, rusting gate. It moved reluctantly. Putting her shoulder to the rusted metal, she pushed hard. "Come on, you ton of junk. Open or you'll end up in a scrap merchant's yard." A loud crack emanated from the protesting metal, and, as if it had heard her, swung open without a problem. She brushed herself down. "See, that wasn't so hard, was it? All I ask is a bit of co-operation."

A tangle of grass and weeds lay ahead. *I have to drive through that?* Julia ground her teeth. "I'm going to have to get a new gardener. This one obviously doesn't know what a lawn mower or grass trimmer is."

The grass moved in front of her. Startled, she jumped back. Something scurried away underneath the tangled mess. She followed its progress with her eyes, until it disappeared into the large, unkempt hedge near the gate.

A sense of foreboding settled in Julia's stomach as she quickly returned to the car. She didn't know what it was about the manor, but each time she visited, the hair stood up on the back of her neck. It felt as if something or someone was watching her.

Starting the car's engine, she drove slowly down the weedy, rutted path, the car bouncing as its wheels sank into the potholes. Julia cringed at the jolts and scraping sounds coming from underneath the vehicle. "I should never have sold the Landcruiser. What was I thinking, bringing the Jag?" She knew what she had been thinking. She was the Mistress of the Manor now, and wanted to show off.

As she bumped along through the avenue of trees, the manor revealed itself. Grey stone blocks of the façade gave a haunting welcome. Julia swallowed a lump in her throat and tears pricked her eyes. It wasn't right. Richard should have been here with her. He'd wanted to restore the old mansion for a while. This was his dream house.

Instead, it had become his burial place.

She'd promised, while she knelt at his graveside, to restore the old manor in his memory. That had been two years ago. The memories of the time still haunted her. Grief and loneliness had held her back. Mentally, she felt stronger now, and able to accept having to carry on alone. "Get a grip on yourself Julia. It's an old house. It's bound to have a few creaks and groans."

Parking the Jag next to the front door, she unpacked, placing the bags in front of the massive wooden doors. The leering gargoyle face on the door knocker sent a shiver through her. Placing a hand over its face so she wouldn't have to look at it, Julia turned the door key in the lock and pushed the door open.

She'd never been inside the manor. Richard had gone

inside, but she had stayed outside in the gardens. Just the look of the grey stone on the outside gave her an eerie feeling. The same feeling assailed her now. She glanced back behind her. The hair on the back of her neck stood up. Something or someone was watching her. She was sure of it.

"Get inside and shut the door. Then they won't be able to see you." Quickly picking up her bags, she kicked a small bag forward with her foot, in an effort to get everything inside and shut the door. After closing it, she turned around and gasped. The entrance opened in front of her. Large marble tiles covered the floor, with the roof looming high above. A hand carved wooden staircase in front of her wound its way to the first floor.

Oh, Richard. If you could only see this as I am now. I can see you running up the stairs. Running your hands over the banisters. Pulling up the carpet to see the wood underneath. I can see the delight in your eyes.

She ran her fingers over a nearby wall. Tracing the raised wallpaper patterns with her fingertips brought a sense of loss, a heaviness to her heart. She could feel the loneliness of the building. To her, it felt neglected, like it hadn't been loved for quite a while. Like her. *Great, now you're associating yourself with a building.* A moldy, musty stench emanated from the old, red, patterned carpet on the stairs, and she wrinkled her nose at the smell.

Once, people had walked up and down the rich, red carpeted stairs. She could imagine children sliding down its curved railing, laughing as they reached the curled end, then running back up the stairs again for another trip. She smiled at the visualization it brought to her mind.

Now, the only footsteps it felt were from the mice chewing holes in its carpet, showing the bare wooden boards underneath. *Yes, this is a very sad house indeed.* As she turned left into what appeared to be the library, she caught a shadowy movement from the corner of her eye. She spun and glanced around, but nothing was there.

"Hello, is anyone there?" Silence was her answer. *Maybe a bird had flown in through a broken window somewhere?* She shook her head, chiding herself for being silly and so jumpy. She laughed to herself. *I'll be seeing ghosts next.* A cold shiver ran through her at the thought.

Turning back, she walked into the library. Stopping just inside the door, Julia closed her eyes and breathed in deeply. She could smell the books. Even if she had been blind, the aroma of the old paper would have told her exactly which room she was in. Bookcases lined the walls from the floor to the ceiling. They were full of dusty tomes, maps and leather clad books. Lifting the dust covers off chairs and furniture as she walked around the room, she couldn't believe so much was still here. With a flick of her hand on a cloth, she uncovered a beautiful walnut sideboard. The glass was intact, as well. It'd look wonderful after she had given it a polish, she thought to herself. Old oil paintings hung in spaces on the walls, created just for them.

She stood in the centre of the room and slowly turned in a circle. It dawned on her how much work was actually needed. Cleaning she could do, but she wouldn't be able to do it all herself. Help would have to be brought in, especially for the wiring and plumbing. Julia lowered herself into one of the chairs, realizing finally, the enormity of the job ahead of her.

How am I to do this by myself? Richard, why did you have to go and leave me?

She felt so small and alone in this big house. Grief welled up within her, remembering how she had felt when Richard had passed away. She had felt helpless then, too. Tears pricked at her eyes. Using the palm of her hands, she rubbed them, wiping the tears away. Angry at her memories and emotions, she drew on the strength inside her. Repeating a mantra to herself, I am strong, I can do this, she stood and crossed the floor to the bookcase in front of her. She loved books. They had been her world when she was younger. In a way, they still were. In them, she was able to escape reality, to lands where magic reigned. It was what had led her to become a writer.

Running her fingertips over the spines, feeling the cracked leather grab at her skin, she could tell many of them needed attention. "Poor babies. I'm going to take care of you. Soon you'll have new bindings and covers." As much as she would have liked to sit and read, there was more of the house to discover.

From the library, she passed through full height wooden doors into the dining room.

"Oh, my."

The room was huge. Old sideboards ran along the outside walls and an enormous table, looking capable of seating twenty people at a time, ran down the middle of the room. The top of it was thick oak, and the legs, hand carved. Skimming her hand over the worn carvings, she thought about the craftsman so many years ago, making them specifically for this table. Hand turned, most probably without any machinery. They would have taken weeks to make.

If she'd needed to buy a table like this, it would've cost thousands of pounds. She wondered how many people had sat around it. Visions of past times flashed through her mind like a silent movie. The clothes they would have worn, the conversations they must have had, the stories the table could tell. Standing up, she noticed a large, covered painting hanging on the wall at the head of the table. Walking over to it, she caught the side of the cloth and gave it a light tug. It fell silently toward her and she stepped back. A cloud of dust engulfed her, making her cough and sneeze.

"Well done, Julia. Give yourself a dose of hay fever as well."

When she looked back up at the painting, a man in period dress stared back down at her.

His face was handsome. Dark hair. Brilliant blue eyes followed her wherever she moved. She giggled to herself, childlike, as she first moved to one side, then quickly to the other.

He stood in a pose typical of many portraits. A small dog lay at his feet, and a feathered hat was tucked under one arm. She read the inscription at the bottom of the frame.

"Richard Pendergast 1645."

"I wonder if he's the man who built this manor? And his name was Richard." *Could it be an omen?*

"Yes, that would be the ol' lord. He did build this 'ere house, a very long time ago."

The voice came from behind her. Julia screamed. Her heart rate would have put a V8 car engine to shame, it was beating so fast. She flattened herself against the wall, looking around for anything to use as a weapon. A very skinny older man and large woman stood in the doorway.

The old man took a few steps toward her.

"No. Stop. Don't. Come. Anywhere. Near. Me." She held out her arms in an effort to ward him off if he got too close. Her heart felt like it was about to leap from her chest. She could see black spots floating in front of her eyes. If she didn't sit down soon, she would be falling down. She worked her way around to lean on the table for support.

"Missus. We be sorry for scaring you…"

"Who the hell are you? Where did you come from?" Her voice screeched at a high note.

She hadn't heard any footsteps behind her. *Who the hell are these people?*

"Missus, please sit down. You'll be all pale, like you are going to fall down." The old man worked his way close, but not too close, and pulled out a seat. "Please sit. We'll be not hurting you."

Julia knew if she didn't sit, she'd faint. Slowly, her back to the table, she edged her way to the seat and sat down. The man walked back slowly to stand beside the plump woman. Both had concerned looks on their faces. The woman walked quickly past her into the next room, returning with a glass of water. She set it down next to her and returned to the man's side.

"Thank you." Julia reached for the water, grateful the woman had thought of it. After draining the glass, she placed it back on the table. "Sorry, you must think me quite strange, but you scared me half to death."

"We be sorry for that, Missus. Me and Jack here saw you walk in, and thought you might be needin' a bit of help to gets your belongings put up. We served the last lord here."

"So you are - servants?" *I never knew there were servants here?*

The woman nodded in answer. "We know you to be the new mistress."

"How do you know I'm the new mistress?" *God, now I'm sounding paranoid.*

"You got the keys, don't you? If you were ameaning to do wrong here, you wouldna have brought your bags with you."

Julia had to admit, the old woman was right.

"Is there a new master to be joining you later?" Her accent was strong, and Julia found it a little hard to understand. *With servants on site, maybe she wouldn't be so alone after all.* Her heart rate began to drop, and she felt less scared than she had been mere minutes before.

"No. There is no *new* master. There has only been one, and he passed away..." The words stuck in her throat. She still found it hard to say he had died.

"Oooo, I am sorry, Missus, we thought we saw someone else walk in here, just after you."

The man's accent was just as strong. Julia accepted she would have to get used to it. *Someone had walked in behind her? Was that the movement she had seen earlier?*

She gasped as the older woman elbowed him in the ribs and hissed at him, "I told you not to say nothin' about that." Turning back, she apologized. "Pardon him, Missus, sometimes he does see things."

Julia tried not to notice as the man rubbed the spot where the woman had elbowed him. She nodded. "I do need a bit of help actually. Can I ask what your names are?"

"My name's Elsie, and this here is Jack. We is husband and wife, and have been with this old house since we was kids. My mam was the governess here once, and his da' worked in the stables. We'd be proud to be serving you, too, if you'd want us?" The woman looked at her with what Julia thought was hope in her eyes.

Feeling uncomfortable sitting while they stood in front of her, she stood up. The spots in front of her eyes had gone, and she felt steadier on her feet.

"I'll have to think about it, but it would be good to have someone who knows their way around here." *I suppose there's nothing wrong with keeping them on for a little bit*, she thought to herself. "Which way is the master bedroom, Elsie?" The manor was so big. She knew she had only seen a small part of it. With Elsie and Jack to help her, she wouldn't be stumbling around, not knowing where she was, and possibly getting lost.

"This way, Missus. Jack can grab your bags for you. We can't have a lady carrying her own. You just follow us, and we'll show you where you need to go." Elsie stepped sideways and indicated the door which led into the library.

Following Elsie out of the room, Julia saw another flash from the corner of her eye, but looking around, couldn't see anything. *Probably a reflection from one of the windows. Nothing to worry about, s*he thought, reassuring herself.

ENTANGLED DESTINIES - CHAPTER ONE

1889

Screams, filled with terror and pain, ripped through the cold English night air. Sarah stood at the window and listened to the sounds the street beneath her. Scared by what she heard and saw, she didn't want to be outside amongst the filth on the streets. Her room provided safety from all that happened below.

She recoiled at the sound, flattening her body against the wall next to the window, fear rippling through her, making her skin crawl. She clutched her thin wrap at her neck with tight fingers as if the action could make her fear disappear.

People ran, shouting in the street below. She could hear a bobby's whistle blowing, but she couldn't tell from which direction it came. Curiosity drew her to the window once more. Leaning out a little, she tried to catch a glimpse through the fog. Being able to catch sight of anything in the murky gloom proved all but impossible. She could see less than twenty feet down the road—not even to the next building. The cold wind that blew through her hair brought with it whiffs of the stench below.

Streetwalkers—poor women who had no other choice than to sell their bodies—ran past. She pitied them. If circumstances were different, she may well be plying her trade with them.

She could only imagine what terrors waited for those poor women, and wondered if they had caught up with one of them. Sarah knew she had a comfortable life compared to what the poor wretches in the street did, but her employer had threatened her with being turned out onto the street before.

The screaming stopped, and no-one passed under the window for a while. Sarah stepped back to close it, shutting the terror outside. As she grasped the damp wooden frame in her hand, a movement caught her attention. She leaned forward, trying to make out who, or what, she'd seen in the darkened doorway of the building across the street.

A man stepped out, and looked up and down the street. Sarah gasped, placing her hand across her mouth too late and stepped back quickly. The man below appeared to have heard her. He looked up. Sarah stepped back from the window. She knew that face and those terrible eyes—Mr Stark. A dark stain on the front of his white shirt looked far too much like blood in the weak moonlight.

****

Hoping he hadn't seen her she quickly closed the window and climbed into her cold lumpy bed. Pulling the sheet and blanket up to her chin she shivered, not with cold, but with fear. Her ears caught the sound of a door opening and closing downstairs. She pulled the bedding higher up her face. Only her eyes remained above the covers. Footsteps sounded outside her door. She cringed, trying to feign sleep in case he should enter. The doorknob rattled. Her heartbeat sounded in her ears. Her mouth grew dry. The door knob grew silent, and she waited.

"Is that you, Edmund?" Mrs Stark called out.

She breathed a sigh of relief but the terror she felt didn't vanish. Every muscle still coiled like a spring, ready to release if he managed to open the door.

"Yes M'dear, it's me. I'll be in soon. I have to wash up first. I was bowled over in the street by some madman running past. Is Sarah with you? She could take these clothes and clean them."

Sarah cringed again. *Please let Mrs Stark say it could wait until morning.* She wished hard, willing her mistress to say it could wait.

"No. Sarah has had enough to do today and has gone to bed. I'm sure she's asleep by now. Just leave them in a pile, and she can take care of them tomorrow."

Sarah breathed a sigh of relief. She wouldn't have to get up, and stand there in front of him. Her taut body slowly relaxed.

He'd seen her, she was sure, but she wouldn't mention a word in the morning.

Her eyelids grew heavy. It had been a long day and night, and she had to be up again early in the morning. She looked at the clock on her side table. Lit by the moonlight coming through the now closed window, she noticed the time; eleven o'clock. She would have to be up again at five. Closing her eyes, she wished hard for pleasant dreams.

****

Edmund snarled, gritting his teeth at his wife's words, as he closed the door, removed his blood-soaked muddy clothes, and washed off the grime of the night. What he would have liked was a long soak in the bathtub, but the stupid girl was meant to be asleep.

He clubbed the side of the tub with a closed fist. Like hell she was asleep. He'd seen her looking at him out of the window. His anger grew within like a fire. He'd heard her gasp and seen the window close. No matter; he would take care of her in the morning. A pleasant chill ran through him at the thought. By the time he got through with her, she wouldn't say a word. He chuckled to himself. He knew she was scared of him. He could smell it whenever he got close to her.

They had attended the theatre tonight. Another boring recitation, but his wife had pleaded with him to take her. Apparently, she was the only one of her circle who hadn't seen it. He *must* take her lest she die from embarrassment.

Personally he wished she would die. The woman was a bore but he'd married her therefore he pretended to succumb to her pleas. The girl had to attend as well, of course, as no self-respecting woman of her stature could ever be seen out in public without her personal servant.

So they had attended the show. Afterward he'd sent them back to the rooms he owned, while he visited the brew house to join with his acquaintances. After being propositioned by a woman while walking home, he decided to slake his needs. She got more than she expected when she took him into an alleyway.

His lust and hunger had only just been sated. He supposed he could continue with his wife, but she tired him; her and all her fripperies. He would be better off without her, although she did have some uses. Her father was very well connected. Through the old man's business contacts, Edmund had been able to increase his holdings quite dramatically. He smiled. The old fool had no idea Edmund was slowly taking over all his businesses and companies.

Through his wife Edmund had gained wealth unimagined by him before. The woman herself was not a beauty, and he never cared what she felt when he was with her. She was barren and of no use to him. Her servant—Sarah—was a good possibility. A pretty young thing, with soft flesh and most definitely fertile. He could smell when her time of month arrived, and he hungered at its metallic tang. She would be a definite comfort. No-one knew the real truth about him, not even his wife. He'd been able to keep his secret hidden quite well. Edmund's memories returned to the day everything had changed.

Picture This!

ART
AGAINST THE WALL

WRITTEN BY LAURA HIRSCHFIELD

The longest painting in the world
is not in a museum.
It's not in a building.
It's not even inside.
Where is it?

The Great Wall uses pictures to tell about the history of California. What can you see in the pictures here?

JEWISH REFUGEES

Some of the artists

The Great Wall is in Los Angeles, California.

It's outside, on a wall.

The painting is over 600 metres long.

That's more than six blocks long!

People call it the "Great Wall".

It took over five years to make.

More than 400 kids helped make it.

A painting on a wall is called a mural.
Murals can be outside or inside.
Not all murals are on walls.
Some people paint murals on ceilings.
Some people paint murals on floors!

Some murals are even made for sitting on!

4

People make murals for many reasons.

Some people make murals to cover ugly walls.

Some people make murals to tell stories.

Some people make murals to surprise you
or to make you laugh.

Outside, murals don't last forever.

Over time, rain washes the colours away.

Paint chips off.

Murals are knocked down
to make room for new buildings.

See how parts of the Great Wall have worn away?

THEN

NOW

A chalk mural

Why would you make a mural that would wash away in the rain?

6

But people still love to make them.
If you could make a mural,
where would you paint it?
What would it show?

The Great Graffiti Debate

What do you think
about graffiti (*gruh FEE tee*)?
Graffiti can be like a mural.
It can be painted
or drawn on a wall.
Some people think
graffiti is good.
They say it is art.
Other people think
graffiti is bad.
They think it
makes a place ugly.

Some people paint graffiti without asking.
But some people ask if they can paint graffiti.
They want to use it to tell stories.
They want to use it to share their feelings.
What do you think?
Do you think graffiti can be art?

What do you think the graffiti artists are trying to say in the pieces below?

Do you think they are legal or illegal graffiti?

Graffiti artists call murals "pieces".

Graffiti artists are also called "writers".

COMIC CREATOR

WRITTEN BY LAURA HIRSCHFIELD

Do you like to draw?

When Ken Penders was a kid,
he loved to draw.
He loved to draw trains.
He still draws today.
It is his full-time job!

what do you think
would be fun about a job
like Ken's?

Ken is a comic book artist.

He is a comic book writer, too.

Ken draws and writes about Sonic the Hedgehog.

Ken draws and writes about Star Trek, too!

It can take a lot of people
to make a comic book.
One person writes the story.
One person draws the pictures in pencil.
One person draws over the pictures in pen,
or uses paint or a computer to colour them in.
One person writes out the words
to fit the pictures.
One person leads the team.

AAAGH!

PICTURES
IN PENCIL

PICTURES
IN INK

Sometimes Ken writes the story.

Sometimes he draws the pictures.

Sometimes he gets to do both.

Sometimes Ken uses his computer for colouring.

First, he makes a drawing in pencil.

Then, he scans his drawing
into the computer.

Finally, he uses a computer program
to colour in his picture.

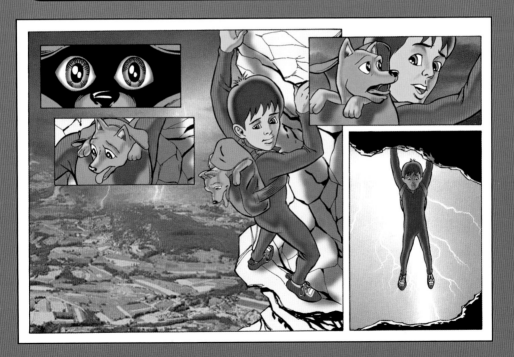

PICTURES COLOURED BY COMPUTER

13

Sometimes Ken has a hard time
thinking of new ideas for comic books.
When that happens,
he changes what he is doing.
He might go from writing a story
to drawing a picture.
Sometimes he just
isn't ready to work.
He says,
"I'll read newspapers or a good book.
Or I'll see a movie and rest
until I'm ready."

KEN ALSO RESTS
BY SPENDING
TIME WITH HIS
SON, STEPHEN.
THEY ARE BOTH
BIG STAR TREK
FANS!

EEYARG!!

You can be a comic book artist one day, too.
Ken has some good advice.
He says to "study everything,
write about anything,
and draw anything."
He also says to try things
that you think you don't like.
"If you only write
or draw things you like,
you will never get better.
When you do the things you don't like to do,
you can get better at all kinds of things."

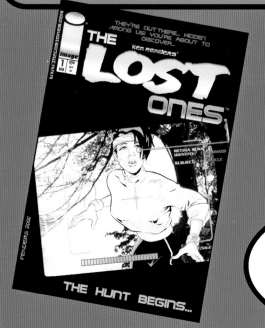

If you were a comic book artist, what kind of characters would you draw?

Old Sam's Secret

Written by Barbara Diamond

Illustrated by Christen Stewart

It was Saturday morning.
Mike was the first one at the empty section,
and he wasn't happy.
He was there to help Old Sam.

It was all Ben's dad's idea.
Old Sam had said he would pay Mike and Ben.
They had to help Old Sam pick up
old broken things from the rubbish in the section.
No one knew what Old Sam did
with all the rubbish.
Old Sam kept that a secret.

Mike was a little afraid of Old Sam.

Some people said he was mean.

They said he was crazy.

Old Sam was coming now!

Where was Ben?

Why do you think Old Sam picks up rubbish?

Old Sam did not say a word to Mike.

He gave Mike a rubbish bag.

Mike and Old Sam began to fill their bags.

They worked side by side.

Old Sam is quiet, thought Mike.

But he doesn't look so mean up close.

I wonder what his secret is?

"Are you cleaning up this whole section?" asked Mike.

"No, not that," said Old Sam.

"Then what?" asked Mike.

Old Sam smiled.
"No one has ever asked me.
After we fill these bags, I will show you," he said.

Just then, Ben showed up.

"Hurry up," said Mike.
"Old Sam will show us what he does
with all this junk after we fill these bags."

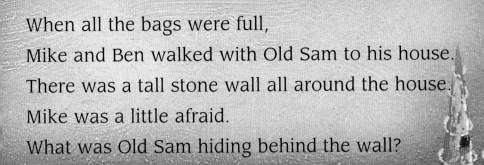

When all the bags were full,

Mike and Ben walked with Old Sam to his house.

There was a tall stone wall all around the house.

Mike was a little afraid.

What was Old Sam hiding behind the wall?

21

Old Sam opened the gate.
Mike and Ben stared and stared.
Inside, everything glittered.

"Wow!" said Ben.

"How do you do this?" asked Mike.

"I make shapes out of steel pipes and rods.
I wrap them with wire mesh,
then I coat everything with sticky mortar.
After that, I stick on bits of glass
and old broken things."

Now Mike knew Old Sam's secret.
And he knew Old Sam wasn't crazy,
unless it was crazy to build
the most beautiful place he had ever seen!

This story is based on a real place in Los Angeles, California. It was made by Simon Rodia. (Some people called him Sam.) His creation is called Watts Towers.

23

Self-Portrait in Front of the Easel, 1888

Portrait
of a Painter

Vincent van Gogh, 1853–1890

Written by
Linda Johns

Not long ago, the painting below
sold for more than 80 million U.S. dollars.
The artist who painted it
has been dead for over 100 years.

Dr. Paul Gachet, 1890

This painting was
the most expensive
painting in the world
when it sold in 1990.

How do you think van Gogh would feel if he knew how much someone paid for his painting?

The artist was
Vincent van Gogh.
He painted 800 pictures.
But he sold only one painting
in his lifetime.

Vincent van Gogh was born in Holland.
He never had much money.
He had a hard life.
But he loved to draw.
He loved to paint.
Sometimes art
was the only thing
that made him happy.

Vincent van Gogh
drew this when
he was just
nine years old.

Vincent

Thatched Cottages at Cordeville, 1890

Van Gogh made art all his life.
He liked to paint things
that he saw.
He painted pictures
of the people he met.
He painted pictures
of the places he went.

Peasant Woman Gleaning, 1888

Self-Portrait, 1887

This is a picture van Gogh painted of himself. What do you think this painting shows?

He used bright, bold colours.
He used fast brush strokes.
He used lots of paint.

Van Gogh painted what he saw.
But he also painted what he felt.
His paintings showed his feelings.

Near the end of his life,
Vincent van Gogh lived
in the country.
He lived in a yellow house.
He put yellow in many
of his paintings.
He loved yellow sunflowers.

Can you see how textured his paintings are?

Sunflowers, 1888

This is one of van Gogh's most well-known paintings.

29

But Vincent van Gogh was not well.

He felt sad and angry
a lot of the time.

He got very sick.

One night he cut off part of his ear.

He had to go to a mental hospital.

But he still painted.

Self-Portrait with Bandaged Ear, 1889

Starry Night Over the Rhône, 1888

Vincent van Gogh
died in 1890.
He is now very famous.
His life was short,
but his work has made
a big difference to people
all over the world.

31

Index